THE SEA'S REVENGE

& OTHER STORIES

To my children (again):
Conall, Ríona and Tarlach

Scríbhinní Mháire

THE SEA'S REVENGE

& OTHER STORIES

Séamus Ó Grianna

edited by Nollaig Mac Congáil

The publishers gratefully acknowledge the financial assistance of
the Arts Council/An Chomhairle Ealaíon

First published in 2003 by Mercier Press
Douglas Village, Cork
Email: books@mercierpress.ie
Website: www.mercierpress.ie

Trade enquiries to CMD Distribution
55A Spruce Avenue
Stillorgan Industrial Park
Blackrock, County Dublin
Tel: (01) 294 2560; Fax: (01) 294 2564
E-mail: cmd@columba.ie

© Estate of Séamus Ó Grianna 2003
Selection © Nollaig Mac Congáil
ISBN 1 85635 413 X
10 9 8 7 6 5 4 3 2 1

A CIP record for this title is available
from the British Library

Cover design by mercier vision

Printed in Ireland by ColourBooks, Baldoyle
Industrial Estate, Dublin 13

This book is sold subject to the
condition that it shall not, by way of
trade or otherwise, be lent, resold,
hired out or otherwise circulated
without the publisher's prior consent
in any form of binding or cover other
than that in which it is published and
without a similar condition including
this condition being imposed on the
subsequent purchaser.

No part of this publication may be
reproduced or transmitted in any
form or by any means, electronic or
mechanical, including photocopying,
recording or any information or
retrieval system, without the prior
permission of the publisher in writing.

Contents

Acknowledgements	6
Foreword	7
Séamus Ó Grianna: The Voice of the Gaeltacht	10
Introduction	19
God Rest Mickey	25
Denis the Dreamer	40
Manus Mac Award, Smoker and Storyteller	52
Home Rule	65
The Sea's Revenge	75
Blagadán	86
Single Combat	95
At Sunset	102
Mayday Magic	113
A Dog's Life	125
The Best Laid Schemes	135
Fair-Haired Mary	148
The Woman Spy	165
The Fruits of Education	178
Edward Devanny	194
Appendix 1: Autobiographical Note	209
Appendix 2: From the Gaelic of Máire	211
Notes	215
Glossary	217

Acknowledgements

I would like to thank the publishers An Gúm and Mercier Press for permission to print these translations or versions of stories which they published in the original Irish.

I am obliged to *Éire-Ireland* for permission to reproduce a version of my introduction which they originally published.

I am also grateful to Séamus Ó Grianna's son, Feilimí, for allowing me to reproduce these stories here and for generously donating the manuscripts to the James Hardiman Library, National University of Ireland, Galway.

Tá mé buíoch d'fhoireann Leabharlann James Hardiman, OÉ, Gaillimh, as a gcabhair agus as a gcuidiú agus mé i mbun mo chuid taighde.

Finally, a special word of thanks to my friend Dr Andrew Moriarty for his encouragement and assistance with this and other works.

Foreword

It is among the many ironies of the Gaelic revival, that the work of the most prolific writer of Irish in the early decades of the independent state is known, if at all, to the general Irish reader almost entirely at several removes through the brilliant parody of it in Myles na gCopaleen's *An Béal Bocht* (1941) or its English translation *The Poor Mouth*. Only Tomás Ó Criomhthain's *An tOileánach* (*The Islandman*) provided more grist for Myles' satiric mill than did the early novels and stories of Séamus Ó Grianna (Máire), the butt of most of the humour in the sections of the novel set in the Rosses of Donegal. But then it seems to have been Ó Grianna's fate to be pummelled by heavyweights, as when Máirtín Ó Cadhain lampooned his style in a 1948 piece entitled 'An Fhiannaíocht' ('Fenian lore') in the journal *Ar Aghaidh*, and more recently the novelist and critic Alan Titley had a go at him in *Irisleabhar Mhá Nuad* in 1983. On the other hand, the man himself conspired at his future anonymity; for example, he wanted none of his work published or reprinted in the standardised orthography introduced in 1948. Ó Grianna may even have found his current anonymity a perverse vindication of his contempt for what he saw as the hypocrisy of state and citizen toward independent Ireland's putative first official language. It would, however, have been difficult for any of his contemporaries to see Ó Grianna as a hapless victim of the cleverness and linguistic dexterity of others. In his heyday, he was the one who inflicted the punishment, lashing out at enemies, real and imagined, in any forums available to him. He was particularly virulent in the official Gaelic League journal *Fáinne an Lae*, from whose editorial chair he was finally evicted for his scurrilous attacks on those he saw betraying the Irish language and its cultural traditions as spoken and lived by native speakers, especially those of his native Donegal.

The problem was that Ó Grianna was one of the great Irish satirists in either of the nation's languages. Genuinely and savagely indignant, vicious, unjust, petty and often hilarious, he would never find the worthy adversaries against whom to test, hone and polish his art. English-speaking Ireland was largely oblivious, while many of those Irish-speaking writers and activists who knew his verbal skills, some of them all too well and intimately, were content to mute his influence by marginalising him within a movement that was itself slipping steadily from the Irish mainstream in the 1930s and after. The question of what might have been had he been publicly challenged in his prime by the likes of Liam O'Flaherty or his own brother Seosamh Mac Grianna (with whom he could not even agree on the Gaelic form of the family name) must remain intriguingly unanswered.

In the end, as a satirist he probably did more harm than good, although it is hard to fault him for the inadequacy of his targets.

One leading Gaelic intellectual did, however, stand up to Ó Grianna, in the process provoking him to develop and express his ideas on issues of direct relevance to this collection. In 1920, novelist, playwright, and critic Piaras Béaslaí, himself a learner of the language, took pointed exception to a series of essays by Ó Grianna in which he lambasted '*Gaeilig na Leabharthach*' ('book Irish') in favour of the living speech of the Gaeltacht native, and posited the idea that there was a distinctive *Art Gaelach* that should be the critical standard for all writing in the language. Above all, Béaslaí challenged Ó Grianna to define the nature of this elusive indigenous aesthetic. Béaslaí's intervention was signficant here because it was Ó Grianna's understanding of the thematic and formal demands of *Art Gaelach* that shaped his own voluminous fiction throughout his lengthy literary career, albeit jostling uneasily with the eclectic influences of Republican orthodoxy, popular romantic fiction, the French *conte*, and that ever-present bane of Irish fiction in the 1920s and 1930s, O. Henry.

Indeed in this term *Art Gaelach* we find encapsulated the two aspects of his work a modern reader finds most compelling. First, there have been very few writers since the revival with so inalienable a right to the title 'Gaelic'. A native speaker from a virtually monoglot Irish-speaking community in the Donegal Gaeltacht, Ó Grianna grew up in a family immersed in Gaelic tradition, a family that became legendary for the linguistic and cultural accomplishments of its members. And while subsequent education and reading could at times work at cross purposes with this native heritage, Ó Grianna stands pre-eminent in his time as the authentic voice of the Gaeltacht, recreating from a profound understanding of the native mindset and an unparalleled command of his linguistic medium a world vanishing every bit as quickly and irrevocably as was that of Tomás Ó Criomhthain and the other Blasket writers. And while, unlike those writers, Ó Grianna fashioned most of his work as fiction, the vision behind that fiction was totally and unapologetically his own, unmediated by the revivalist concerns of those like Brian Ó Ceallaigh, Pádraig Ó Siochfhradha, George Thomson, or Máire Ní Chinnéide, who stand between the readers and authors of the Blasket autobiographies.

There can, then, be no doubt about Ó Grianna's claim to be 'Gaelic'. But was what he produced 'art'? As time went on, he himself came to doubt it. Even as early as 1927 he could tell Muiris Ó Droighneáin that he had never felt he had it in him to create real literature. By 1969, the year of his death, he was ready, in the voice of the embittered, unheard and unheeded moralist, to pronounce his whole literary career a mistake.

As readers, we must ponder for ourselves what Ó Grianna meant by *Art Gaelach* and how well he met its aesthetic criteria in his own work. That he thought a good deal about the question should be obvious from the stories in this collection, in several of which storytellers are central figures. One thinks in particular of 'Manus Mac Award, Smoker and Storyteller', although one must wonder just how Ó Grianna squared his own practice with the principle evoked here: 'A good story must not have one word that is not necessary. It must point towards the end from the very beginning. It must stop in a way that will make you remember it and have no loose strings hanging out if it.' There is no shortage of strings in any of Ó Grianna's plots, but how many of them are loose? That depends, of course, on how tight they are supposed to be.

What may now be most suggestive about Ó Grianna's fiction is not that it embodies the obscure or forgotten essence of *Art Gaelach*, but rather that it provides an important example from the Gaelic side of what may be a distinctive *Art Éireannach* in Irish fiction: a morphing of various traditional genres, folktale, yarn, reminiscence, short story, novella, found also in other Irish writers as diverse as James Stephens, Séamus O'Kelly, Máirtín Ó Cadhain and Pádraig Ua Maoileoin, to name a few. Moreover, this issue of generic hybridity seems far more obvious when one reads Ó Grianna's work in English, in the process removing it from the standard Gaelic dichotomy that asks whether most of his stories should be seen primarily as dressed-up *scéalta gearra* (folk stories that happen to be short) or as botched *gearrscéalta* (literary short stories). We should not, however, approach these stories primarily for what they tell us about the social history and customs of the Gaeltacht in which Ó Grianna grew up (although they tell us more on these subjects than does the work of any other single writer in either Irish or English) or for the new insight they offer on the instability of traditional genres in Irish literature. Above all, they are a good and satisfying read. Ó Grianna himself probably saw stories he wrote in, or translated to, English as his personal concession that the entire revival project had failed. But it is a good thing we have them, and Nollaig Mac Congáil deserves our thanks for restoring to us, in a new linguistic medium, one of twentieth century Ireland's most distinctive voices.

PHILIP O'LEARY, BOSTON COLLEGE

Séamus Ó Grianna: The Voice of the Gaeltacht[1]

Séamus Ó Grianna was born in Rannafast in Donegal in November, 1889. At that time, Rannafast was virtually unheard of since it was situated in an inaccessible, bleak spot in the north-western corner of Donegal. In material terms, the area could not support the large population which inhabited it. While subsistence farming was the order of the day, a living could not be eked from the small holdings on their own or from the offshore fishing in small crafts. In order to supplement the family income, children were hired out to the Lagan farmers and, after several seasons of hard, physical work, they graduated to become migrant, seasonal workers in Scotland and North England. However, if Rannafast was greatly lacking in material wealth, there was one commodity of which it had an abundance: its oral tradition. Were one to compare all the Gaeltacht areas of Ireland in the twentieth century in this regard, one would be hard pressed to find an area as rich in song, story and other lore as Rannafast. Its reputation as *an ceantar is Gaelaí in Éirinn* ('the most Gaelic locality in Ireland') induced an tAthair Lorcán Ó Muirí to found Coláiste Bhríde there, one of the most famous of the *coláistí samhraidh* ('summer Gaelic colleges'). Thousands of students came to Rannafast to study Irish from the college's foundation in 1926. They came to study the rich, musical, idiomatic language spoken there among a people who always prided themselves on their oral heritage.

That was the life into which Séamus Ó Grianna was born. He was directly descended on his mother's side from the *Dálaigh*, the O'Donnells of Rannafast, who boasted many poets in former generations. Also among his relations were many noted storytellers, not least his own father. It is not surprising, therefore, that Séamus was imbued with this wealth of oral lore from his earliest years. There was no escaping it, either in his own home or in the neighbouring houses which he would visit at night. It was to remain with him for the rest of his life and considerably influence his outlook and philosophy on Irish literature and language. Oral learning was the first form of learning with which Séamus became acquainted and the one for which he had most regard as is evident, for instance, from the chapter '*Scéalaíocht agus Tairngreacht*' in *Caisleáin Óir* (1924).[2]

When he went to national school at the age of four, without a word of English, he was introduced to a formal, English learning, which was foreign to him in language, content and administration. He attended school for ten years. His parents were keen that he should continue his education into secondary school for various reasons, not least economic ones. He failed the examination, however, and this put paid to any chances he might have had of continuing his formal education.

In 1903, at the age of fourteen, Séamus packed his bundle and headed off for the hiring fair in the Lagan. He was hired to a farmer near Gortin, County Tyrone. This was his first experience of life away from home and, since he had been mollycoddled by his parents, his new station was not to his liking and he headed home after a few days. The following year he stayed a week. There was no point in sending him off on his own again.

When he was sixteen, he went to work in Scotland along with his father and neighbours. While he spent several seasons over in Scotland working at various jobs such as thinning turnips, picking fruit, tatie-hoking and navvying, his constitution was not suited to such tough physical work. While over in Scotland, Séamus' interest in learning was rekindled by two independent-minded, well-educated men from his native west Donegal. Frainc 'Ac Gairbheá and Master Mac Comhaill convinced him that he was not a failure just because he had failed an examination several years previously. They introduced him to a whole new world of writers and poets from Ireland, Scotland and even England that would never be included in the national school curriculum back home. His eyes were opened for the first time to what constitutes literature and learning:

> Fuair mé ar ndóigh an t-oideas ab fhearr a bhí in Éirinn ins an bhaile. Agus chan ó mháistrí scoile a fuair mé é ach ó sheanfhondairí Rann na Feirste. Uathusan a fuair mé meáchan mo chuiol foghlama. Uathusan a fuair mé eolas ar litríocht na Craobhruaidhe is na Féinne, ar Chearbhallán, ar an Dall Mhac Chuarta agus ar Chathal Bhuí. Ach bhí eagla ar fad orm nach raibh maith san oideas sin. Bhí eagla orm gur díobháil agra chinn a d'fhág *Lycidas* dothuigthe agam nuair a bhí mé 'mo ghasúr. Bhí Milton mar a bheadh néal dubh crochta os mo chionn, riamh nó gur nocht Burns mar a bheadh grian gheal loinnireach shamhraidh ann agus gur scab sé an ceo síos siar.³

Under the direction of Master Ó Baoill, who was then the teacher in Rannafast, Séamus started his studies again at home. In the year 1910 he attended Coláiste Uladh, in Gortahork, one of the early Gaelic League summer colleges. These colleges were set up to train teachers for Gaelic League classes, to instruct teachers in language teaching methods, and to teach Irish language and culture generally. This was a very important period in Séamus' career. It represented his introduction to formal Irish learning and to those people closely involved with the Gaelic League movement. Séamus did not find the course at Coláiste Uladh particularly appealing. However, it launched him upon a new life as a travelling teacher for the Gaelic League in the north-west of the country for two years and it helped him to make the acquaintance of fine Donegal Irish scholars like Séamus Ó Searcaigh, who was to stimulate him and encourage him to write.

In 1912, Séamus went on to St Patrick's Teacher Training College in Drumcondra, Dublin, where he studied for two years. He qualified as a teacher in 1914, achieving distinctions in all his subjects except music. For the next six years he was to teach in various locations. His first post was in Cill Scíre, County Tyrone, in the parish of Fr Maitiú Mag Uidhir, the President of Dáil Uladh (Ulster Gaelic Assembly of the Gaelic League) at the time, with whom Séamus had become acquainted in Gortahork. Young, enthusiastic and full of a sense of purpose, he wrote his first novel *Castar na Daoine ar a Chéile is ní Chastar na Cnuic ná na Sléibhte* during his stay in Cill Scíre. It was published seriatim in *The Irish Weekly* and *Ulster Examiner* from 24 July 1915, to 18 December 1915. According to the publicity note heralding the first instalment, Séamus' aim in writing this novel was to make the Irish language both contemporary and popular:

> In looking through the different Irish books recently published, it occurred to me that little attempt was being made to describe modern life in Irish – that the language was solely devoted to describing Finn Mac Cool and other myths, who had very little interest for the ordinary Irish reader, and that if Irish is to become a popular language it must become a vehicle of modern thought.[4]

Unfortunately, *Castar na Daoine* was a complete failure and never published in book form.[5] The plot verged on the incredible, characterisation was weak, and the whole failed to capture the attention of the reader.

In 1915 Séamus took up a teaching post on Inis Fraoich, an island off the north-west Donegal coast. His lifelong friend Peadar O'Donnell, the novelist and active socialist, had previously held this post. During his stay on Inis Fraoich, Séamus started to write to the newspapers about the Irish language and the language revival generally. He also wrote a few stories in English, thinking, as he later admitted, that he was going to follow in the footsteps of his contemporary, the Donegal writer Patrick MacGill. At this stage of his career, Séamus was still overawed by English literature and the English language. He was later to renounce both:

> Ba ghairid gur stad mé de scríobh i mBéarla. Fuair mé taisbeánadh a d'fhoscail mo shúile domh. Chuala mé glór mar a thiocfadh sé amach as

na néalta ... Ireland as we would surely have her. Not free merely but Gaelic as well. Agus ansin chonaictheas domh go bhfaca mé bladhaire tineadh ag éirí ó Chnoc Teamhrach agus go dtearnadh m'athbhaisteadh i gcreideamh na Féinne. Sin an rud a thug orm toiseacht a scríobh i nGaeilige?[26]

The spring of 1916 saw Séamus back on the mainland, this time as principal of Mín na Manrach school in his native Rosses, a job he held for four years. Ó Grianna's career as a teacher was neither long nor distinguished. He disagreed with the curriculum laid down by the National Board of Education and also with the teaching methods prescribed. Inspectors descended on him like midges and castigated his efforts, not to mention his manner, hygiene and general conduct. He ended his teaching career in 1920. During this period Séamus, or 'Máire' as he now called himself, began to publish numerous articles in Irish in the official Gaelic League publication. He dealt with those aspects of the language revival which were to keep him in copy for years to come: 'book Irish' and the Irish of the Gaeltacht, the Irish colleges, methods of teaching, Irish in the Gaeltacht, Irish literature, etc.

In the summer of 1920, Máire was closely involved with the establishment of a new summer college, Ollscoil Uladh, in Dungloe. It represented all that Máire considered should be found in an Irish college and it is to be regretted that, owing to political circumstances, this college was short-lived:

> Caint uilig atá ins an choláiste seo. Amhráin, scéalaíocht, fiannaíocht, díospóireacht, seanfhocla, cora cainte agus gach rud dá bhfuil le cluinstin as béal an chainteoir dúchais. Níl am ar bith dá chur amú a' méaradrú ar an charbad chruaidh nó ar an teangaidh bhig. Gaeilig atá ag cur bhuartha ar na hoidí agus ar na mic léinn. Agus Gaeilig an lae inniu fosta – beo bíoga mar tá sí dá canstan ag na cainteoirí dúchais. Ní ligeann siad orthu féin go bhfuil díochlaonadh nó rud ar bith den chineál sin ar an tsaol.[7]

In 1920, Máire got a job with the Ministry of Education of the Provisional Government in Dublin. His brief was to attend to matters relating to Irish, initially in his native county. In this he was not very successful. Teachers considered him a black sheep in their profession. The clergy were not supportive as, years earlier, they had severed their links with the revival movement. Even Sinn Féin was less than enthusiastic about Irish. Máire experienced the same lack of interest in Irish no matter what part of Ireland he visited. In 1920 he wrote *Mo Dhá Róisín* (his first novel to be published in book form). The plot revolved around Gaeltacht life, the Irish summer college, the Irish revival movement, the fight for independence and the inevitable love story. Máire stated his motive for writing this partly autobiographical novel as follows: 'Ba é mo bharúil gur mithid dúinn iarraidh a thabhairt scéaltaí a scríobh a léifí mar mhaithe le scéaltaí agus gan a bheith choíche ag smaoiteamh ar ghramadach, ar chora cainte agus ar dhántaí nach raibh iontu ach fuaimeannaí.'[8] Another reason Máire had for writing Mo Dhá Róisín was: 'Nuair a chonaic mé an cineál Gaeilge a bhí dá scríobh, cuid de ag daoine nár mhó ná go raibh an chéad leabhar foghlamtha acu, dar liom go dtaispeánainn an difear a bhí idir Gaeilig agus Gaeilig.'[9] A great success, the novel sold over 10,000 copies. The strong theme of nationalism developed in it helped sales of the book considerably. Although Máire was unhappy with the book and let it go out of print, Mo Dhá Róisín marks the start in earnest of his creative writing.

The early 1920s were years of turmoil in Ireland. It was impossible to remain detached from all that was happening. When the Civil War came, Máire sided with the Republicans. He was arrested in 1922 and imprisoned with three of his brothers for about a year and a half. One would expect that his creativity would have increased in prison, but not so. He spent his time in prison smoking and conversing with other prisoners. He was released at the end of 1923. The following spring he was made secretary of the Irish language organisation An Fáinne, a post he held until the end of 1929. He now had to settle down in Dublin where he lived for the rest of his life, except for six months in late 1926 and early 1927 when he went to the south of France for health reasons.

From 1924 until the 1930s Máire was completely involved in the language movement. He was on the executive committee of Conradh na Gaeilge, he was appointed editor of Iris an Fháinne in November 1924; he lectured in many different venues; he participated in talks, seminars and lectures; he conducted Irish classes; he was heavily involved with such Irish-language organisations as Comhaltas Uladh and Cumann Cosanta na Gaeltachta; and he wrote numerous articles for papers and journals. By this stage, those involved in the revival movement were well acquainted with Máire, for he had achieved a certain notoriety for his views. As often as not, the following remark would be made about Máire's contribution to any discussion: '[Máire] atá tugtha don bhfírinne a bhíonn searbh agus is gnáth treasnaíl agus géaraighneas mar a mbíonn sé ag cur de.'[10] This criticism reveals that Máire had declared war on behalf of the Gaeltacht, of the material needs of its people, and of the Irish language which they alone had cherished and retained in its natural form. He proved to be no mean champion.

The 1920s and 1930s were prolific years for Máire, mostly in the realm of journalism rather than creative, literary output. This is not surprising, given his complete involvement with the Gaelic movement.

However, in the 1920s, Máire wrote two works – arguably his best – which were to act as a model for the rest of his prestigious literary output in years to come. The works in question are the novel *Caisleáin Óir* (1924) and a collection of stories *Cioth is Dealán* (1926). Both reflect the old Gaeltacht world, the world of storytelling and superstitions, of material hardship, of forced emigration and inevitably – in all of Máire's works – of arranged matches and unrequited love. This is Máire at his best, depicting the life he knew and understood, the life which lent itself to full expression in his idiomatic, mellifluous Irish. The idyllic and romantic portrayal of traditional Gaeltacht life in these works has enchanted readers ever since. Remember that Máire never aspired to be one of Ireland's modern, analytical, psychological writers. His aim in writing was rather after the manner of the *seanchaithe* (traditional storytellers) of old: to entertain pleasantly and not dwell on the harsher realities of life. Since these two works were so well received, Máire continued in this vein in the rest of his creative works. He concentrated particularly on the short story, as he felt that he could best express himself in that genre.

With the exception of *Micheál Ruadh* (1925), which is undiluted *seanchas* ('lore') about a Rannafast hero of yesteryear, the only other books published by Máire in the 1920s and 1930s were directed primarily at learners of Irish. Amongst these were several volumes of *Sraith na Craobhruaidhe* and *Feara Fáil*, a collection of short, biographical sketches of a range of Irish heroes. It is evident from such works that Máire was, in a practical way, trying to provide Irish reading material of various kinds for the new generation of Irish schoolgoers and people generally.

Máire was made editor of *Fáinne an Lae*, the official organ of the Gaelic League, in 1927, a post he held for some two years, on and off. The bulk of his journalism appeared in it during this period. Sometimes he himself would supply all the copy for an issue. In the columns of *Fáinne an Lae*, Máire gave free rein to his thoughts and robustly expressed his views on any topic which related, however tenuously, to Irish. He attacked on all sides, showing no mercy. He castigated, he named names, he pointed the finger at the offending parties.

There are several possible reasons for Máire's vehemence. Máire was reared in a life which lacked many material comforts. The strong, oral tradition of the locality was one of the few luxuries enjoyed by the people. Máire and others firmly believed that when Ireland achieved her freedom, the picture would be completely altered. The people of the Gaeltacht would prosper, the inhumane hiring fairs and seasonal migration to Scotland would cease, and the Irish language and Irish culture would return to their rightful place. For such aims was the fight for independence carried out. However, Ireland did not achieve her freedom.

Six counties were left under the jurisdiction of England, an agreement which was totally unacceptable to Máire and to other Republicans, and which caused the Civil War. Máire had an undying hatred of the new Free State Government on political grounds, for it had betrayed Irish ideals of freedom. The Free State committed as many barbarities on the Republicans as the Black and Tans ever did, or so he contended.

It is important to be aware of Máire's hatred of the Free State Government – a hatred, incidentally, which he transferred to all Irish governments in later years – in order to understand some of his other criticism. After the founding of the Free State, the Gaelicisation of Ireland depended almost entirely on the will and good offices of the state. Since Máire believed that the state had already destroyed nationalist aspirations, he did not hold out much hope for the Irish language. It was, of course, quite right at the time to remind the new state of its linguistic and cultural obligations, and Máire certainly did not let its failings go unnoticed:

> Tá an Rialtas sin i dtreis le seacht mbliana agus cad é tá déanta acu don Ghaeilig? Feiceam. Coimisiún na Gaeltachta? Chuir sin an scéal ó dhoras ar feadh chupla bliain. Thug sé gléas don lucht ceannais gealltanais a thabhairt uathu agus iad ag iarraidh vótaí. An Ghaeilig ins na scoltacha? Tá sé le feiceáil ag duine ar bith a bhfuil a shúil ina cheann nach fiú biorán an méid atáthar a dhéanamh ins an chuid is mó de na scoltacha. An Ghaeilig i gcúrsaí seirbhís an stáit? 'A chara' ag tús gach litre agus 'mise le meas' ar deireadh rud a d'fhéadfaí a dhéanamh le cupla míle de stampaí rubair. Le scéal fada a dhéanamh gairid, ní thearnadh na gealltanais a tugadh a chomhlíonadh.[11]

The new government – in the form of the Department of Education – was responsible for the teaching of Irish. Máire questioned how one could possibly expect effective teaching of Irish if the teachers themselves knew next to no Irish. Furthermore, there were inspectors of Irish running loose in school corridors who were '*chomh gann i nGaeilig leis na hoidí féin*' ('as linguistically challenged as the teachers themselves'). In third level institutions, Máire saw only 'congenital idiocy in university robes mumbling inanities about Gaelic literature and Gaelic scholarship'.[12]

In Máire's view, the real and only custodians of the language were being ignored, or worse, in the plans afoot for making Ireland Irish-speaking. The native speakers did not appear in these plans. It was the government's intention to bring the Irish language into the twentieth century, to rid it of its idiomatic characteristics, to make it a vehicle of efficient bureaucracy. The government simplified the spelling, changed the alphabet, and committed what Máire considered other atrocities on the language. There were two forms of Irish in use: *Gaeilig na Gaeltachta* and *Gaeilge an Rialtais*, or *an Ghaeilig Oifigiúil*, or *an Standard*, or *Gaeilig na Leabharthach*, as Máire variously called it. The former embodied all the *dúchas* of his native Rannafast, the latter was a hideous changeling. He attacked this effrontery wherever it appeared. Not only was he at loggerheads with the government and its areas of influence, such was his disillusionment that he fell out with the Gaelic League and the whole language movement generally, since he felt that both were going the way of the government in matters of Irish. One could say that, from the 1930s onwards, Máire carried the Gaeltacht speech and life that he knew and revered, in his own head and released them into his creative works.

Prompted by necessity, Máire started translation work for *An Gúm* in November 1930. He spent a year and a half at this work which was nearly as hard on the body as it was on the brain. *An Gúm* had been established to handle and encourage publication of Irish material. The translation of often inferior works into Irish was one of its activities. Máire parted company with *An Gúm* at the earliest opportunity. In 1931, he married Connie Mac Donnell, who had been his nurse once when he was ill. In the following years, they had a family of eight. Máire got a clerical job in the Custom House. He subsequently worked on De Bhaldraithe's English-Irish dictionary and, towards the end of his life, on Ó Dónaill's Irish-English dictionary.

Only in the 1940s did Máire's creative writing start to appear again in book form, after an absence of over a decade. It wasn't that he had stopped writing, simply that it was very difficult to get a publisher for an Irish book that would not be used as a prescribed text in the schools. Up until his death in 1969, Máire wrote over twenty books, published between 1940 and 1968, most of which were collections of short stories. He also wrote two volumes of his autobiography: *Nuair a Bhí Mé Óg* (1942) and *Saol Corrach* (1945). Anyone seriously interested in studying the background to Máire's life and philosophy, should read his *Rann na Feirste* (1942), where he recounts the history, lore and tradition of singing and storytelling in his beloved Rannafast. This is his labour of love.

Máire was one of the most prolific of modern writers in Irish. He was among the most successful of all the Gaeltacht writers and he not only inspired many other Gaeltacht writers to start writing, he was also the means whereby thousands of other Irish people learned Irish and were introduced to Gaeltacht life and culture. More than any other Gaeltacht writer, Máire tried to usher the traditional oral literature into a written mould, not forgetting its roots in the process. His inspiration was the Gaeltacht – its people, their lore, their versatile speech. In spite of the fact that he spent much of his life in Dublin, he maintained that he could not write in Irish about Dublin life, nor could he write about Rannafast life in English.

Máire always anticipated that his works would be read by, or to, his old neighbours in Rannafast, as they actually were. These were not modern, discriminating, literary people, but people reared on story and song. Máire presents to them a world with which they are familiar: the mountains, lakes and shores, very seldom disguised. He introduces characters with whom they are very familiar – members of his own family and local people, dead or alive, renowned for such various attributes as fighting, rowing, intelligence, dancing, singing, cutting turf – all of which were greatly prized in traditional Irish life. Their ordinary, everyday lives and that of their forebears are recalled time and time again: matchmaking, *poitín*-making, taking cattle up to summer pastures, knitting, taboos, superstitions, reciting poems, prophecies and stories. The world created by Máire in his writings is not necessarily the real Gaeltacht world, but it has most of the essential physical elements of it. It is also infused with his melancholic, romantic, cynical, mischievous, star-struck view of life and love. His fictional world is a far step from his controversial involvement with the Irish Revival Movement which culminated, towards the end of this life, in his defiant endorsement of the Language Freedom Movement – a movement which sought to oust the Irish language from its official position in the state.[13]

Nollaig Mac Congáil

INTRODUCTION

Máire's English Short Stories
Máire, a prolific writer in most of the different literary genres, excelled particularly in the short story. During his lifetime he had thirteen collections of short stories published and the number of stories in each collection ranged from seven to twenty-nine.[1] His first and most celebrated collection *Cioth is Dealán* appeared in 1926 and his final collection, *Oidhche Shamhraidh agus Scéalta Eile*, was published in 1968, the year prior to his death. It is of interest to note, however, that Máire's earliest stories were written in English in 1916[2] and, some years prior to his death, he translated/reworked some of his Irish stories and wrote some original stories in English.[3]

When Máire started primary school at the age of four, he knew no English. The medium of instruction in the school was English and no allowances were made for monoglot, Irish-speaking pupils:

> I remember myself when a little boy at school, I used to hate Irish because the teacher would slap me almost daily for not knowing English. And a number of years under such a system was enough to make me often curse my early environment and look with envy on the more fortunate children of neighbouring townlands who had daily opportunities of learning English, having in their midst a public house, a post office, a few shops, a police barracks and other outposts of civilisation.[4]

Máire stayed at school until he was fourteen years of age. He failed, however, to progress to the secondary tier of education. Although he could rhyme off popular songs like 'Brennan on the Moor', 'Moorlough Mary' and 'The Ould Orange Flute', John Milton's *Lycidas* at the other formal end of the academic register put an end to his scholastic ambitions for the time being.

In the course of time, however, he returned to education as a mature student and qualified as a teacher by a circuitous route in 1914. He had developed, in the interim, a strong interest in English literature, particularly of Shakespeare. His lack of competence in English had put paid to his earlier academic aspirations, however, and he was still smarting from the hurt it had caused him.

Two of his early attempts at creative writing were in English and they appeared in a local newspaper:

> I started writing thirty years ago. I started in English. I wrote some insignificant stories for *The Derry Journal*. And, God, how proud I was when

I saw my name in print for the first time! And the hope I had I would be famous throughout the world. I'd be as good as Patrick MacGill.[5]

The first tale, 'Destiny', a romantic love story set during the First World War, was strong on language, style, sentiment and ideology, but full of irrelevant digressions, weak on plot, characterisation and story-craft:[6]

> Torlough O'Brien was the only son of his widowed mother. His father had been a soldier, had fought under Buller at Spion Kop and returned home minus a natural leg and plus a wooden one, which exchange went a long way towards silencing anyone who ventured to doubt that the old soldier had been face to face with the actualities of war. To compensate for the deficiency sustained in the substitution of timber for flesh and bone, he was kindly presented by a neighbour with a walking-stick – an old blackthorn which was indeed worthy of a soldier. Now this same stick served a double purpose for its new owner. It helped to preserve his bodily equilibrium and also to illustrate a movement in rifle-firing or a thrust in a bayonet charge.
> ... for the two sentinel peaks which guard the pass leading to Letterkenny keep all Anglicising influences without the pale of the Lough Bearra districts. The stalwart sentries regard the old Gaelic customs and manners as the password which gains admission into the glen which they protect. And for such things as honeymoon, sixpenny hats, complexion powders and false teeth, the sentries have but one answer, viz. 'This far you shall go and no farther.'
> 'Aileen, darling, in return for my love, may I ask to be admitted into your circle of friends? May I ask if you will keep a little corner in your heart for me?'
> And she answered, 'Always, Torlough, always!'...

The second story was 'Two Days a Teacher' which is, in large part, autobiographical and relates the experiences of a newly-qualified teacher, sent on his first posting to an island where he tries without success to implement all the theory he has learned while training as a teacher. This is a more readable effort because it falls within the world and the personal experience of Máire:[7]

> 'It is,' said I, 'I am affher bein' down in the school and guess what they are at! Instead of learnin' to read and write and work with figures as we used to do, it's what some of them had blocks of wood and thim buildin' wee houses. Some more war on their knees on the flure makin' pictures on sand, others war makin' some kind of fixtie foxties on their copies. The masther himself was mixin' some salt and wather, whatever kind of mixtie maxtie he was at. "Objeck lissen" I think he called it. He was another while tellin' them about the hight of some mountains away in

America. Then he joined to talk about a big bald-headed man who came to England before the time of Our Lord. Julius something he called him. Wal, he tould them that the sun does not move – as if he would take our eyesight off us, and what was he not talking about! He even tuk out the children and put them to jump over ropes outside. Now, I said that and as much more to Johnny and he couldn't put against me. I said it to him over there at the Cloghan.' And he looked through the window in the direction of the said Cloghan, as if attaching some importance to it, as being the scene of an educational debate between himself and his honest neighbour. 'I say it again to you,' he resumed, 'just as I said to him, there's just far too much didoes and nonsense in school nowadays and no real, solid learnin' goin' like there was in the ould times.'

Apart from a poem *à la* Burns, that ended Máire's literary efforts in the English language for decades.

He puts forward the following reason for his rejection of English as his literary medium henceforth:

> But I soon stopped writing in English. I experienced a revelation which opened my eyes for me. I heard a voice as if coming out of the clouds ... 'Ireland as we would surely have her. Not free merely but Gaelic as well.' And, I thought I saw a flame of light rising from the Hill of Tara and I was rebaptised in the Creed of the Fianna. That is what made me start writing in Irish.[8]

Máire started writing short stories in Irish in the 1920s and concentrated on that genre for decades afterwards. He had made a conscious study of the short story, particularly of the nineteenth century French short story writers, before engaging this genre. It proved to be his forte for the rest of his writing career. However, despite the fact that he wrote hundreds of stories and that he himself had a great command of the English language and that he lived for more than half of his life in English-speaking Dublin, no English versions of his stories by himself or anyone else[9] were ever published, thus depriving generations of Irish people, not to mention non-Irish speakers throughout the world, of the pleasure of savouring his works.

Máire had indicated that the reasons for turning his back on writing creatively in English were ideological and nationalist. This was certainly a factor and these were to change later on in his life. There were other and, one would think, more practical reasons, however:

> I could not write in Irish about Dublin life, even if I tried it. And the reason is because there is no life in Dublin of which Irish is the expression. For the same reason I could not write in English about my

>   native Rann na Feirste. I might give awkward translations of Eoin Roe and Condy Eamainn, but their own mothers wouldn't recognise them in the new garb ... I wrote in Irish because it was the only language that could adequately describe the life and the people I knew ... [10]
>
>   If wouldn't matter if I knew all the English of the world, I couldn't write in English about Rannafast people. How could I express the conversation of Eoin Roe or Owen O'Boyle in English? I couldn't make the slightest attempt at it even if I were to live five hundred years ... The sort of English I have is, for the most part, dull and insipid and I picked it up from books and papers.[11]
>
>   The few who chose Irish as their literary medium did so for the best reason possible – because it was their native language and the only language that could express the life they knew and could write about.[12]
>
>   I am a very fluent speaker of Irish ... The language comes to me with the same ease and spontaneity as the drawing of my breath. It comes to me the way I want it – in gushes, in torrents, in squalls, according to the theme I am speaking on ... I would want to talk about the people of my native Rannafast and of the way they lived when I was young. Then I would describe the characters I knew, the things they did and the things they said, their songs and their stories ... [13]

In short, throughout his creative life, Máire only wrote about the life of his native Rannafast in the late nineteenth and early twentieth centuries; the language of that community-based life was Irish and Máire considered that his only writing abilities lay in the Irish language. Despite that strongly-held conviction and the other nationalist and ideological one mentioned earlier, during the 1960s, Máire translated and sometimes reworked considerably some of his stories and even wrote some original stories in English. Why the change of view, especially in light of all he said on the matter throughout his life?

In those latter years of his life, Máire had long since stopped his creative writing in Irish.[14] He had given up all hope of the salvation of the Gaeltacht and the revival of Irish. He hated all political parties, Irish language organisations, the Department of Education, in short, everyone and everybody responsible for and involved in the language revival since the foundation of the state. He preferred to see the Irish language die completely with dignity than preside over a lingering, emaciated, terminally-ill patient. In 1966 he became a patron of the Language Freedom Movement whose raison d'être was, basically, to put an end to the privileged position of Irish within the state:[15]

>   But Irish can never replace English as the vernacular of the Irish people. And why not if English could be replaced by any one of the other lan-

guages I have mentioned? Because these other languages are fully flowered. Irish is an old language whose growth was arrested centuries ago. It was a beautiful language; even what remains of it is beautiful. For that reason, every assistance and encouragement should be given to anyone who wants to study it. But there is a world of difference between fostering a love of Irish and the attempt to make it, by brutal compulsion, the one and only language of the nation.[16]

Out of that disillusionment, out of the realisation that Ireland was Anglicised by then, out of the wish to make his writings accessible to his grandchildren and great-grandchildren, to future generations of once Gaeltacht people who would not have linguistic access to his depiction of their traditional way of life, perhaps all these reasons inspired him to present these stories in English. We cannot even know whether he intended them for public consumption.

The stories are presented here as they are written. The readers will make up their own minds about them. They represent, by any standards, a unique collection of Irish writing. It will be interesting to see how they will be received by a completely different readership from that at which they were originally directed, in a different medium and in a completely different Ireland.[17]

NOLLAIG MAC CONGÁIL

God Rest Mickey

It was marrying-time in the Rosses. That is to say, the time between Twelfth Day and Lent.
Conall Ferry wanted to get married. It would not be easy for him for he was a shy, backward creature. He never went to dances or to any social gathering where a young man would meet girls and get to know them.
He went to Mass only once a year and that was on St Patrick's Day. But it was not want of faith that kept him from going to Mass. No, it was want of clothes. He had nothing but little rags of things that his mother used to buy for him at the local fair. But for a long time he did not seem to mind. In fact, the neighbours were of the opinion that he preferred the rags, so that, when he took the notion, he could stretch himself on the earthen floor in front of the fire.
That was all right until he took it into his head to get married. Then he had to take stock of himself and of his situation. It did not take him long to come to the conclusion that to get married he must find a woman and a decent pair of trousers. His one and only pair was a thing of shreds and patches.
He told his mother of his intention to get married. She immediately agreed. She said it was time for him and she asked God's blessing and guidance for him. That was all she said. Conall stood and looked at her. Was it possible she did not understand that he must buy a pair of trousers? Nor did she. She had her own solution to the problem.
'Mother,' said Conall at last, 'could you give me the price of a pair of trousers?'
'I could not, son,' replied the mother. 'There isn't a red copper in the house except the rates money and that must be paid tomorrow. But tell me this, have you got the woman? If you have, it ought to be easy for you to get the trousers. You could borrow a pair.'
'I'd be ashamed to ask for the loan of a pair of trousers to get married in,' said Conall.
'Ashamed!' said the mother. 'Have you never heard the old saying:

be ashamed to ask and go empty-handed? You won't be the first man that got married in borrowed clothes. But let us take first things first. I asked you if you have got the woman. If you have, go down to Manus Roe O'Donnell and ask him for the loan of a pair of trousers. Manus and I are related. And if the blood of the Red O'Donnells has not gone pale, Manus Roe won't see my son stuck for a pair of trousers to get married in.'

'Since I must go a-borrowing,' said Conall, 'wouldn't it be better for me to get the trousers first? Wouldn't I be in a nice fix if I asked a girl to marry me and she consented, and then if I were left sitting high and dry for want of a pair of trousers?'

'Wouldn't it be just as awkward,' said the mother, 'if you got the loan of a pair of trousers to get married in, and then to be left sitting high and dry for want of a bride? But I suppose you know your own business best.'

Manus Roe O'Donnell was a thrifty, hard-working man and he had what no other man in the parish had – three pairs of trousers. He had a Sunday pair, an everyday pair and an in-between pair that could not be said to be either new or old. Manus was a kind-hearted man, especially to his own kith and kin (for the blood of the Red O'Donnells had not gone pale).

'Certainly,' he said to Conall. 'I have a good serviceable pair of trousers that will do you grand ... Here they are ... Into that room with you and put them on ... A bit on the long side. But we'll remedy that. Turn up the ends of the legs ... Another few inches ... There. A grand fit. And now I wish you the best of luck.'

'I have the trousers,' said Conall to himself. 'All I want now is the woman.'

There was a girl in the townland – Sawa Gallagher – and Conall had her in his eye. He had often talked to her. She was a very nice girl, he thought. She had bewitching eyes and a bewitching way of saying things.

Of course, Conall had never mentioned marriage to her. He was too shy for that. But it would not be necessary for him to propose to her in person. He could get someone to take his message to her. That is how it was done in the Rosses at the time.

Conall approached a young man from the neighbourhood – Mickey Sweeney. Mickey was a fine, jolly fellow and was always ready to do a neighbour a good turn. It was also said of him that he was something of an advocate, and that at least three men had been accepted as husbands who might have been refused if any other man but Mickey had been entrusted with their message.

'Mickey,' said Conall, 'I am thinking of getting married.'

'Well done yourself,' said Mickey.

'Mickey, I want you to ask the woman for me.'

'That I will, and welcome. I'll fix you up, my boy. And we'll have a night at your wedding that there wasn't anything like it in the Rosses within living memory. Who is the lucky one, by the way?'

'I have a nice, wee girl in my eye for a long time,' said Conall. 'Sawa Gallagher.'

'Sawa Gallagher!' said Mickey in a trembling voice. Sawa Gallagher! The very girl that Mickey himself had a notion of. The girl that he meant to ask in marriage when the time came. Wouldn't he be nicely tricked if his darling were to marry another man? Mickey did not want to marry for a few years. He was afraid that if he did his father would not give him a fair share of the land. He was in a fix. What if Sawa were to prefer the bird in the hand to the two in the bush? It was a sort of worldly wisdom that women were supposed to have had from the beginning of time!

'I'd advise you to try some other girl,' said Mickey when he had recovered from the shock. 'I am told that Sawa Gallagher is all but promised to Big Jack McGee from Milltown. And if you were to get a refusal, it would be against you. That is the worst thing that could happen a man. A girl might be quite willing to marry you today but let her hear that you have been refused by another and tomorrow she won't look at you. That, of course, applies to every man as well as to you. Women are strange creatures. Most of them would spend seven lives single rather than take 'another woman's leavings' as they say. I'd advise you then not to run the risk of a refusal by asking Sawa Gallagher. What about Madge McCarron?'

'I don't like her,' said Conall.

'Sheela Rodgers, then?' said Mickey.

'If you are not willing to take my message to Sawa Gallagher,' said Conall, 'say so. I'll look for some other person to go on the errand for me.'

'Have sense, man,' said Mickey, pulling himself together. 'I'll be your messenger. Why wouldn't I? I was only telling you, for your own sake. That's all.'

'All right,' said Conall. 'That's that settled. I'll go now and get a drop of poteen. And tomorrow night, you'll take my message to Sawa Gallagher.'

The following night Mickey set out on his errand. He had to go. If he didn't, Conall could easily get another man to go in his stead. But, in the meantime, Mickey's brain had not been idle. He had done some hard thinking. He had come to the conclusion that there was only one way left to him to play the game. And it was this: he would deliver Conall's message. And, if Sawa showed any inclination to consent, Mickey would propose himself – let his father do what he would with the land.

Mickey arrived at Sawa's home. There was a welcome for him, as usual.

'Any news?' asked the woman of the house.

'I have strange news,' said Mickey. 'You'll hardly believe me when I tell you, but it is the truth. I am here tonight on a funny errand. I have been sent with a proposal of marriage to Sawa.'

Sawa busied herself putting turf on the fire.

'Any harm in asking you who sent you?' said the old woman.

'I suppose it must be told,' said Mickey. 'But let nobody put the blame on me. I am only delivering my message. I couldn't refuse any man that request. Of course, I advised him to have sense and come down to his own level. But it was no use.'

'But, in Heaven's name, who is he?' asked the old woman of the house.

'You wouldn't guess in a thousand years,' said Mickey. 'Conall Ferry.'

'He should be thrifty if he is anything to his father and mother,' said the old woman.

'Well now, I shouldn't say it,' said Mickey, 'but at a time like this one must tell the truth at all costs. He is very lazy. Some of his potatoes have yet to be dug. Rotting in the ground, they are. And he is the very devil for drink. Last fair day he sold a calf and drank the price of it to the last penny along with a gang of tinkers. He was stretched and dead drunk in Murriseen's yard in the evening.'

'He must have the gift of sobering quickly,' said Sawa. 'I met him on his way home and he was as sober as you are now.'

'I'm only telling what I heard,' said Mickey. 'I wasn't at the fair. I never go except I have some business there – a beast to buy or a beast to sell. But, whatever about the drink, he is lazy. That is no hearsay. I know for certain that he never takes a spade in his hand any year before the beginning of April.'

'And when did he dig the lea field beside the house?' asked Sawa. 'Was it last April?'

This was something that Mickey had not been expecting. Sawa was standing up for Conall. She was defending him at every stage ... Then it occurred to Mickey that perhaps he had played the wrong card, that it might have been better if he had pretended that he did not mind whether Sawa would accept Conall or refuse him.

'What is your opinion?' he asked the old pair.

'We'll leave it to herself,' said the father. 'She must decide. It's her lot in life that is being settled, not ours.'

Mickey realised that he had lost the game. He must act quickly. He could not give Sawa time to decide. He was seized with a sudden fear that she might accept the offer. And then all was lost.

'Well,' said he, trying to smile, 'I had better give over my nonsense.

Poor Conall Ferry! I hope you will all understand that I didn't mean a word of what I said about him. But sure there is no harm in a wee joke. It is my own marriage I am trying to arrange. And I am my own messenger. I've come to ask Sawa if she will marry me.'

No one replied. Sawa was carding wool. She seemed all absorbed in her work as if Mickey's proposal had nothing to do with her.

At last the old woman broke the embarrassing silence. 'I didn't think you had any intention of getting married for another year or two,' she said.

Sawa went on carding.

'I kept my intention to myself till I was ready to say the word,' said Mickey.

'Well,' said the old man, 'as I said when I took you to be another man's messenger – and pardon me for failing to understand your joking – we won't stand between our daughter and her choice. It is a matter for herself. What do you say, Sawa?'

'I am not in the humour for saying anything tonight,' said Sawa. 'I am too vexed. For if there is one thing in the world I detest in my heart and soul, it is slandering and backbiting. Conall Ferry is not lazy. He is not a drunkard. He minds his own business. No one ever heard him say a hard word against a neighbour. It would be a good thing if some of us took example by him.'

'Come,' said the mother, 'give over the preaching and say one thing or the other to the offer that is made to you.'

'I had no intention of getting married this winter,' said Sawa. And she went on with her work as if she wished to let Mickey see that, although she was going to marry him, she was still vexed with him over what he had said about a decent, kindly neighbour.

That was that. The following morning the news spread like wildfire through the parish. And the women, young and old, had something to talk about. Great news entirely! Conall Ferry sent a messenger with an offer of marriage to a girl. And the messenger made the match for himself.

The following week Mickey and Sawa were married. Conall Ferry went to the nearest still-house and spent the whole day drinking. At dusk he staggered home. Later on he went to the wedding-house – without, of course, any invitation. He came in and slumped down on a seat inside the door. After a little while he got to his feet. There was a crazy look in his eyes. He staggered along the floor to the fire and began his drunken babble. He would have to see Sawa, he said. He had a question to ask her. Why had she played such a dirty trick on him? And he had a few words to say to Mickey, he said.

Sawa pushed Mickey into a room off the kitchen. The man of the house tried to calm Conall, but it was no use.

'I am as good as that mangy son of a mangy cobbler any day,' said Conall.

'For two pins I'd go down and break his neck across the doorstep,' said Mickey to Sawa.

'Oh, Mickey,' said Sawa, putting her two arms around him to hold him back from the fray. 'Surely to Heaven you wouldn't beat that poor creature. You would be disgraced forever if you were to lay a finger on him. The poor thing is not worth beating.'

'Only he's drunk,' said Mickey, 'I would give him something that would make him rub his ear.'

'Drunk or sober, he is not worth noticing,' said the bride. 'Sure, if the poor creature had the faintest glimmer of understanding, he wouldn't imagine that I would marry him.'

'But you stood up for him that night,' said Mickey.

'I did stand up for him,' said Sawa. 'I was so raging mad with you for having come on his errand that I would contradict you no matter what you said. It makes me angry every time I think of it. How could you, how could anyone, imagine that I would marry that poor, snivelling idiot? Not if he was the only man on the ridge of the world. I was furious with you, so I was.'

'Well, darling, all that is past and done with,' said Mickey.

II

Five years and some months after that Mickey Sweeney lay dying. Sawa was at the bedside, a picture of sorrow. Kindly neighbours were coming in to sympathise and to give any help that they could give. My father came in with a creel of turf and put it down in a corner of the kitchen. Sawa did not speak to him. Later on my mother came in with a bottle of milk. She put the bottle on the ledge of the dresser and came up to the fire. 'How did he get over the night?' she asked Sawa.

'Poorly,' said Sawa. It was all she said.

Conall Ferry came in. 'How is he since?' he asked Sawa.

'Oh, Conall, Conall, I am afraid he is dying,' said Sawa. 'He is sinking fast ... Isn't it the cruel blow, Conall?'

He was sinking fast and no doubt. The following morning, about an hour before daybreak, he died.

The neighbours gathered in. Conall Ferry foddered the cow and brought in turf. Messengers were sent to the shop for clay pipes and tobacco. And the house was made ready for the wake.

Night came. The house was full of people, from the fire to the door. 'Conall,' said the widow to Conall Ferry, 'let you give out the tobacco and give it out in plenty. Give them their fill to smoke. It is what he'd wish himself for he had a big heart.'

A crippled, grey-haired old woman went up to the bed where the corpse was laid out and began to keen. Mickey's mother it was. No one seemed touched by her lamentations. Her voice was weak and husky. She had only a few words and she kept repeating them. 'Ochone and ochone, my child, my own dear child!'

After some minutes, Sawa got up and joined the old woman ... A dead silence fell on the house. Before long, all the women were in tears and many of the men. They did not seem in the least touched by the old woman's grief but Sawa's keening wrung their hearts.

'Oh, Mickey, Mickey! You couldn't sleep last night but you are in a heavy sleep tonight. A sleep that you will never waken from. Last night was the long and cruel night for you, Mickey. You thought it was the darkness that was crushing the life out of you and that you would get your breath if only you could see the light of day. Many a time you asked me to go outside to see if the streaks of dawn were appearing in the sky. Oh, Mickey, Mickey, you had to go before the dawn came. It was the black dawn for me – the dawn that I can never forget ... This time last night you asked for a drink but there is no thirst on you tonight. Why did you leave us, Mickey? Why did you die? Why did you leave your wife and child alone in this bitter world? Oh, Mickey, your child, your child! He thinks you are only asleep and he is asking me when you will waken. But he will have a long and weary wait for you to open your eyes ... Oh, the cruel fate that spared me to see you close your eyes in death and go from us forever!'

Conall Ferry handed out the tobacco in plenty the two nights of the wake. He looked after the cow. He brought in turf and kept the fires going. He did everything that a man could do about the house.

'Conall Ferry is a good-natured soul,' said my father to my mother. 'And he is a harmless, poor creature. Many a man in his place wouldn't come next, nigh or near the house. But he did the right thing. It is grand to see such Christian charity.'

'Christian charity, my eye,' said my mother. 'Conall Ferry still has a wee notion of Sawa. You might see them married before this day two years.'

'That is not a nice thing to say.'

'It may not be very nice but it could be the truth. The day before poor Mickey died several people came in, yourself among them. Sawa spoke to nobody but to Conall. And somehow I thought there was a note of friendliness in her voice.'

'You are full of malice, woman,' said my father.

'Time will tell,' said my mother.

The day of the funeral came. The corpse was brought to the churchyard and buried. Conall helped to fill the grave. He put green scraws over it and beat them smooth with the back of the spade. Sawa keened until she was tired. At last the neighbours persuaded her to come home.

Sawa was forever talking about her dead husband. She recalled the places where they had been together. She remembered a hundred little things that he had said to her. Sometimes she would stand on the height above the house and keen at the top of her voice. Some of the neighbours tried to reason with her. 'It is not right for you, Sawa, to be crying like that,' said Shoogey Brennan to her one day. 'You should try to count your blessings as my poor mother, God rest her, used to say to my father when wee Hughie died. Remember that things could be much worse with you. You are young and strong. And your only care is that one little boy, God bless him. Many a poor widow was left with a houseful of small children.'

'Isn't it small consolation for me to cry my fill,' said Sawa. 'Sure I don't care now what happens. I don't care whether I live or die. I had the best man that ever a woman had and Death took him from me.'

Shoogey's next visit was to Mickey's parents. The poor old pair were sitting over a dying fire, looking sad and sorrowful.

'I've just come down from Sawa's,' said Shoogey. 'The poor creature is heart-broken with grief.'

'The grief is far from the heart,' said the old woman. 'Alas for my poor boy that killed himself trying to give her an idle life. If he had minded himself, he wouldn't be under the sod today. But he didn't. She wouldn't let him. Now she is keening. But there is too much poetry in her keening. I know her only too well. I know the seed and breed of her. The tribe of the tuneful wail and the dry eyes. 'Tis we have the cause of grief. Our darling son gone before us to the grave.'

III

A week or so after the funeral Conall Ferry paid a visit to the widow. 'I thought you might be lonely,' said he. 'That's why I've come.'

Sawa burst out crying. 'Oh, Conall, Conall!' she sobbed. 'If Mickey were alive it's right glad he'd be to see you. For he was often talking about you.'

'I know that,' said Conall. 'I'll miss him very much. But we must take things as they come in this weary world.'

'It is easy to talk like that, Conall,' said Sawa, 'but if you could only feel the pangs of sorrow that are piercing my poor heart,' and she looked the picture of misery.

'Do you know,' said Conall, 'what Big Father O'Donnell said to my mother when my poor father died – Lord have mercy on the dead! He told her to stop crying. He said it was flying in the face of Heaven and it might keep the departed soul in Purgatory.'

'I didn't know that,' said Sawa. 'I would not for the world do anything that would keep my dear darling one minute from his eternal happiness,' said Sawa. And she stopped crying.

'Pray for him,' said Conall. 'It is the best thing you can do. The best thing for him and for you.'

'If I had money, I'd put a tombstone over his grave,' said Sawa.

'He is buried in a nice spot,' said Conall.

'If the grave were touched up a bit. Do you know what I'd like to do when the summer comes since I cannot afford a tombstone. I'd like to get shell-sand and beach stones from Dunmore and put them on the grave.'

'I'll do that for you any time,' said Conall. 'It is the least a man can do for a friend. We'll get the sand in Dunmore but we must go to Illanala for the stones.'

It was a nice morning in summer. The Kindoorin boats were going to fish. A nice sailing breeze was blowing from the south-east and the tide had just turned. A boat sailed down from the mouth of the creek with two people in it – Conall and Sawa on their way to the islands to fetch materials for ornamenting Mickey's grave. Long Jimmy Ward's boat came down after them. Jimmy's boat carried two sails and a jib and would soon overtake Conall's.

'I wonder what boat is that in front of us?' said Long Jimmy.

'It looks like Conall Ferry's boat,' said Frank Harley. 'It's her all right. That is Conall at the helm.'

'But who is the woman?'

'The widow Sawa.'

As they approached Conall's boat, they stopped talking. When they drew alongside, Long Jimmy spoke. 'It's a fine morning,' said he.

'It is that,' said Conall, without looking round.

'A beautiful morning,' said Sawa, 'thanks be to the Eternal Father for all His gifts and graces.'

Long Jimmy's boat swept past. The crew began talking again. 'Sawa is getting the widow's courage already,' said one man.

'Bedad, she is,' said another.

'Going to the islands they are,' said Big Donagh McGrenna, 'to get shell-sand and little, round stones to put on Mickey's grave.'

'Upon my soul but you might see a funny ending to the decorating of Mickey's grave,' said Black Hughdie O'Donnell. 'It is a queer world, so it is. Let nobody die as long as he can remain alive.'

'Have a heart, Hughdie,' said Long Jimmy Ward.

'It's the truth I'm saying,' said Hughdie.

'Could it be possible after all her sad lamentations when Mickey died?'

'It didn't come from the heart. May God forgive me.'

'But she drew floods of tears from your eyes the night of the wake. I saw them streaming down your cheeks. How could that happen if you thought her grief wasn't real?'

'I'll tell you,' said Black Hughdie. 'Maybe I am a queer fellow. People often told me I was. But it was the old woman that drew my tears. She was sobbin' and ochonin'. It was all she could do. But when Sawa started I thought she put words and music to the sorrow that was tearing the old woman's heart.'

Conall and Sawa went to the islands and took in a cargo of shell-sand and beach stones. When they came as far as Illanbo on their way back, Conall moored the boat and the two went ashore. They were hungry and they wanted to eat. Besides, they had to wait for the flood-tide before continuing their voyage home.

Conall made a fire. He fetched a canful of water from a running stream. Sawa made the tea. And they sat down to eat. It was a most beautiful evening. The sea was one flood of molten gold from the White Strand to the Stags. The mountains away back on the mainland shone in varying tints, pale blue, amber, purple and pink by turns.

'Isn't it a beautiful evening?' said Conall.

'Thanks to the Almighty Father,' said Sawa. 'Do you know what struck me just now – that this little island would be a nice place to live on.'

'It would, if it were summer the year round,' said Conall.

Just as the sun was setting they came up to Kindoorin with the flood-tide.

'We'll moor her here in the creek for the night,' said Conall. 'And, please God, we'll go up to Moorloch with tomorrow morning's tide.'

The next day they went to the graveyard. Conall put the sand on Mickey's grave. He put the small white stones round the edges. And, in the centre, he made a cross of little sea-shells.

'May God reward you and give you health and strength,' said Sawa. 'That is a grand job you've done. I am very pleased with it. I never like to see a neglected grave. It looks like forgotten memories. And it will be many a day before I forget poor Mickey. As my granny used to say in the song, the waves of the sea will be red and the mountains will rock in the wind before I can forget.'

Conall was silent. Standing like an artist contemplating his masterpiece.

'You have a great pair of hands and a great head,' said Sawa. 'Only yourself could do it. And the cross in the centre puts the finishing touches on it.'

'It is the nicest grave in the churchyard,' said the artist with a feeling of pride. 'But I must come up and look at it from time to time. The winter wind will blow away some of the sand but I will keep my eye on it.'

'Come in till I make a drop of tea for you,' said Sawa when they came as far as her house on their way back.

'Don't bother,' said Conall.

'Come in, man,' said Sawa. 'You must be tired in body and mind after all that work. A wee mouthful of tea will freshen you up.'

They went inside. When they had finished the tea Conall put his hand in his pocket to get his pipe. It was broken in two pieces.

'I must go home,' said he.

'What hurry is on you?'

'I must have a smoke,' said he. 'It is a bad habit, they say. But there you are. As soon as I eat, I must smoke. And my pipe is broken. See! Nipped right in beside the bowl. It must have happened when I put my shoulder to the boat to push her out.'

Sawa put her hand into a little hole in the wall beside the fireplace and took out a pipe. 'This is a pipe that poor Mickey had, God rest his soul,' she said. 'You can have it. If he were alive, he'd be glad to see you smoke it ... Just a bit of a clay pipe. How true the old saying is, the least little thing we possess often outlives us.'

The winter came and with it the herring-fishing. 'If I had a net, I'd go fishing,' said Conall one evening to the widow. 'I am promised a place on Long Jimmy Ward's boat. But my net is useless. It was piled up in the barn last winter. The roof was leaking and the rain got at it and rotted it.'

'You could take Mickey's net, God rest Mickey,' said Sawa. 'Indeed, I thought one time that I'd never let another man dip it. But the times are getting hard. And what can a poor widow do? Oh, cruel death!'

'It would be useless to let a good net go to loss,' said Conall. 'I'll spread it out tomorrow and, if there are any broken meshes, I'll mend them.'

The following day Conall spread out the net. He mended the broken meshes and he stitched it on to the back rope in a few places where it had come loose. Later on he went off to Inishfree to the herring-fishing as one of Long Jimmy Ward's crew.

After a week's fishing he had two pounds saved. One pound was due to Sawa – the net's share. On Saturday night Conall came to her house. He sat in the corner beside the fire.

'I am sure you are hungry,' said Sawa, hanging on the kettle.

After tea, Conall took the clay pipe from his pocket and lit it. He smoked for a while in silence. Then he took a purse from his pocket and opened it. 'This is your share,' said he, and he handed Sawa a pound note.

'May the Almighty Father save you from the dangers of the sea,' said Sawa. 'That is a fine week's earnings.'

'Indeed it is not,' said Conall. 'They did not come in near the coast this time. The main shoals kept far out to sea. The big boats from the islands took heavy catches. But small boats like ours had to keep near shore.'

'Perhaps they will come closer to the coast next week,' said Sawa.

'I am afraid not,' said Conall. 'Bob Delap tells me – and Bob is a man of knowledge – he tells me that when the first shoal passes far out to sea, the rest will follow the same course.'

'Welcome be the will of God,' said Sawa. 'Sure, it is good to have even this much.'

Conall looked into the open purse which he held in his hand. 'Poor enough for a week's fishing,' he said. 'Only two pounds. It is hardly worth dividing. Perhaps I should give you the whole lot this week. I can wait.'

'You'll do no such thing,' said Sawa. 'You must keep your own share for you have earned it hard. Many a time during the week I thought of you. Often, in bed at night, when I'd hear the wind moaning outside the window, I used to think of you. I used to imagine you tossed on the waves from the Needle of the Foreland to the Stags of Aran. Many a prayer I said for you … Keep your money. Sure, if I'm hard pressed, I can ask you for the loan of a shilling or two. And keep your courage up. The darkest hour is the hour before the dawn. Maybe next week the herrings would be piled up to the heads of the creeks – no matter what Bob Delap says.'

IV

Marrying-time came round again. One evening, Conall was in the widow's house, sitting by the fire. There was nobody there but the two of themselves and Sawa's little boy.

'Conall, give me a penny,' said the boy. 'I want to buy sweets.'

'Sit down and have manners, Shaneen,' said the mother ... 'Sit down, I say. Where did I put the rod I had? ... Conall, don't give him any pennies to buy sweets. He has his teeth destroyed already eating sweets. The other night he kept me awake for hours crying with toothache.'

'Conall, give me a match. I want to make a blue light in the darkness behind the dresser.'

'Shaneen, did I speak to you? If I have to get up to you, I'll tan your bottom for you, so I will. And then I'll make you go to bed. You must learn to behave yourself.'

'Conall, are you related to mammy?'

'Shaneen, come up to me. Strip off now and into bed with you. I'll teach you to have manners. Strip off at once!'

The boy was soon fast asleep. 'The poor fellow is as tired as a man would be after a day's turf-cutting,' said Sawa, looking in the direction of the bed. 'And no wonder. He is on the go all day long.'

'He is a likeable little lad, God bless him,' said Conall.

'But he is full of mischief,' said the mother.

'But sure if he wasn't full of mischief, he wouldn't be a boy at all,' said Conall. 'He is a grand little fellow, so he is. I am very fond of him.'

'And he is very fond of you,' said Sawa. 'You should see the gladness in his face when he hears your footsteps coming to the door. And any evening that you don't come, he's never done asking me: "Mammy, what happened to Conall tonight?"'

'Will we have any marriages at all this year?' said Sawa. 'Not a sign of a stir anywhere.'

'They are time enough,' said Conall, meaning that it was only the beginning of the season.

'Indeed, that is true,' said Sawa. 'Time enough in every way. Marriage brings its troubles and its sorrows – at least to some people.'

'Even so,' said Conall, 'it must be faced sooner or later, I suppose. It is a poor thing to be all alone when old age comes.'

'There should be quite a crowd ready for the road this winter,' said Sawa, and she mentioned the names of five or six young men.

'Sawa,' said Conall, 'I was thinking myself of getting married this year.'

'You don't tell me,' said Sawa. 'Lots of people thought you'd never marry. I thought it myself. Why, I don't know. A silly notion that got into my head. A silly notion, that is all. Why shouldn't you get married if you want to? Any harm in asking who the woman is?'

'I find it hard to make up my mind,' said Conall. 'It's like this. The woman that would marry me, maybe I don't care for her. The woman that I want, maybe she wouldn't have me.'

'You must put that to the test,' said Sawa. 'That's all there is to it.'

'You wouldn't ...' said Conall, and then he stopped. 'Ah, no, it wouldn't be fair to ask you.'

'What wouldn't be fair?' said Sawa. 'Come on. Out with it. What were you going to say?'

'I know it is not fair to ask you and all the trouble and sorrow that you've had,' said Conall. 'But I was wondering if you could advise me. If you know of a good girl that might have me.'

It did not take Sawa long to reply. Out came her answer like a shot. 'What about Hannah McGee?' she asked. 'She is not too young, I know – two years older than I am. But then, you are not too young yourself. She is a good, thrifty girl and she has a bit of money. Of that I am certain. If you like, I'll be your messenger, any day or night you say.'

Conall got red in the face. He felt his mouth going dry. Hannah McGee! The very girl that he had asked two years before that and she refused him. 'No,' said he in a shaky voice. 'I don't like her.'

'Well, then, some other woman,' said Sawa. 'There's plenty of them in the world, thank God for His abundance. But you must keep your courage up. And I'll give you a tip: whatever woman you ask, don't let her feel that you are afraid of a refusal. Act as if you were certain. Most women take a man at the value he puts on himself ... But maybe you don't like proposing yourself. In that case I'll be your messenger, if you wish. And I know how to keep my mouth shut, before and after the event.'

'It is very good of you,' said Conall, but there was a note of sadness in his voice.

Sawa looked at him. 'Conall,' said she, 'I feel it's only my duty to help you any way I can.'

'Sawa,' said Conall, 'do you remember the old times?'

'Indeed I do, Conall. The grand old times. But they are gone forever.'

'Sawa, I asked yourself once to marry me.'

'That's past and gone, Conall.'

'It is not too late yet,' stammered Conall. 'If you would care to have me now, Sawa. You know I am always fond of you.'

'Does anyone hear what he is saying?' said Sawa, as if she were talking to a third person. She took the tongs and began to build up the fire. 'Get out of my way,' she said to the dog. 'Never in my life saw a dog like you. Lying there with your paws in the ashes night, noon and morning. Get up, you lazy lump!'

She came across to the middle of the hearth and knelt down on one knee to put the turf on the fire. Conall put a hand on her shoulder ... He drew her head closer to him. 'Sawa,' said he, 'will you marry me now?'

'Oh, Lord, Conall dear, it would be too soon,' said Sawa. 'People would be talking about me. I'd rather wait another year.'

Conall knew he had the game won. The big affair was settled. Of course, there would be minor difficulties (for Manus Roe O'Donnell was dead) but they would be got over in some way.

'Nobody will be talking about you,' said Conall. 'They can't, even if they wanted to. You are a widow for over a year and a half. I would have asked you long ago to marry me – for I had the pity of the world for you, and the hard struggle you had trying to do a man's work and a woman's work. I would have asked you far sooner only I knew that there was sorrow in your poor heart for the man that is gone. For he was indeed a fine man.'

'A fine man,' said Sawa. 'The finest man in the whole of the Rosses, from the ford of Gweedore to the ford of Gweebarra.'

'He was that,' said Conall. 'But you have your own life to live.'

'I have my own life to live until I am called to Eternity,' said Sawa. 'And I must be resigned to God's holy will. All of us must.'

'What day will we settle on?' asked Conall.

'I don't know,' said Sawa.

'Say next Saturday week,' said Conall. 'It can hardly be sooner. I must get a pair of trousers, wherever I'll get them. If I had them now I'd go to the parish priest first thing tomorrow morning.'

'I wonder,' said Sawa, 'would Mickey's trousers fit you – God rest Mickey.'

DENIS THE DREAMER

It was only a nickname. His real name was Denis Doherty but a malicious neighbour had called him Denis the Dreamer. And the name stuck.

When he was a boy there was no school in his native Rinamona. But an ambitious mother found a way to have her son educated. She sent him to Pullanranny school although it meant three miles going and three coming back. He attended school regularly until he was fourteen. At the end of that time not only could he read and write but he was beginning to show a decided taste for literature.

'I am very thankful to you, master,' said his mother one day to the teacher. 'You have done great work with him. Think of the advantages he will have when he grows up and has to emigrate, compared to the poor boys who can't speak a word of English and who can't even write their names.'

'He is a bright boy, Mrs Doherty,' said the teacher. 'It was a pleasure to teach him. And he is studiously inclined. In years to come you will be glad that you sent him to school. The school has mapped out his destiny, if I am not mistaken.'

At the age of eighteen, Denis went across to Scotland. He went to work in Glasgow. He preferred the city so as to have access to the libraries. From time to time, he bought a book or two. At the end of four years he returned home with quite a collection of love literature, including the poetical works of Robert Burns.

He began reading at home. The neighbours said the books would turn his head. Denis paid no heed to their forebodings. He read on. And, according as he progressed, he was getting an outlook on life that was totally different from the traditions and beliefs of his native Rosses. The Rosses people knew nothing about love. With them marriage was based on a mercenary foundation instead of what it ought to be – love and love alone.

Denis made several attempts to convert the young men of Rinamona to his own creed. 'It is altogether wrong,' he would say, 'the way the Rosses people look on life. They know nothing about love. A man comes to marrying-age. He has a bit of land. He looks around him to see where he'll get a suitable wife. He takes lots of things into account. Can the girl knit and card wool and spin? Will she make a thrifty housekeeper? What dowry is she likely to get? ... Sure that is no way to get married.'

'But it seems to work well enough,' someone would say.

'It is against nature,' Denis would reply. 'A pair should be in love with each other before getting married. Nothing else matters.'

'But maybe most of them have a wee notion of one another.'

'How in Heaven's name could they? Sure it very often happens that a man is refused by the first girl he asks. What does he do? He goes straight and proposes to a second one. Aye, and a third and a fourth, if need be. Think of Condy Nanny over there. He asked each of six girls to marry him and the six refused. He managed it only on the seventh attempt. A whole, long winter's night he spent on the quest. At daybreak he asked the one he is married to and she accepted him. Where was the wee notion in that case? Will any one of you answer me that?'

But Denis was making no converts. Tradition dies hard in the Rosses. The young people had no faith in Denis' philosophy of love and marriage. They would require solid proof – something more than mere talk. If Denis believed what he said, why didn't he lead the way? Why didn't he fall in love with a girl and marry her, without asking if she had a shoe to her foot or a shift to her back?

They did not, it seems, understand that this was something that a man could not plan out beforehand. It would have to be brought about by accident or by fate, or whatever you like to call it. Denis was ready to fall in love. His heart was like a powder keg. It needed only the white hand of a fair damsel to set the match to it.

II

At last it happened. The white hand put the match to the powder and a young man's heart was aflame.

It was at a wedding at Bunnamann that Denis met Rosie McCann from Drumnacarta. It was a case of love at first sight. They danced together several times. Between the dances they sat beside each other and talked. At last, they went out for a breath of fresh air and they walked down to the lakeside. And such a night! The moon in all its glory and majesty was sailing across a cloudless sky. The air seemed full of music. The fairies must have come out of the dark shadows of the cliffs to dance on the grassy marge of Loughawillin ... Denis looked up at the bewitching moon. He listened to the fairy music. He was in a world entranced. The drama which he had many times imagined became a reality before his eyes. He felt himself transported to the Banks of Sweet Afton or the Braes of Ballochmile. In other words, he was madly in love with Rosie McCann.

After that night they met often. The winter wore away and the spring after it. One Sunday evening in the early summer Denis felt that the time had come to propose ... Rosie said she could not leave her mother for another two years. But she gave him to understand that at the end of that time she was quite willing to marry him.

Two years was a long time. But they were both young. And Denis had what he considered a definite promise. He could wait.

'I wish it were tomorrow,' said he. 'But I will wait for the two years. I would wait for twenty years. I would spend the rest of my life alone if you did not consent to marry me.'

'That would be foolish.'

'Ah, Rosie! You don't understand how I love you or you would not talk like that. You don't think I could do what Condy Nanny did.'

'Who is Condy Nanny or what did he do?'

'A man from our townland. He asked a girl to marry him. She refused. He asked a second girl. She refused. Six refusals he got, all in one night. The seventh accepted him and he married her.'

'Six refusals,' said Rosie. 'That, surely, is a record.'

'I don't think it ever happened before,' said Denis, 'or that it will ever happen again. The young people of this generation are beginning to see the light. Surely, if slowly.'

Rosie became silent. After a few minutes she spoke. 'But,' said she, 'if a man cannot get the girl he wants to have, I don't see what else he can do but ask another one – that is, if he means to marry at all. For instance, what would you do if I refused to marry you?'

'I have told you what I would do,' replied Denis. 'I would spend the rest of my life alone. Of that I am dead certain. It is the only thing I could do. True love has no other meaning – can have no other meaning. No other woman, Rosie, could take your place in my heart. And the woman that has no place in my heart, she couldn't have a place by my fireside.'

III

Denis was in his glory. He was continually talking about the beautiful girl from Drumnacarta he was going to marry and of how they loved each other. In addition to the pleasure he got from talking about his romance, he wanted to convert as many as possible of the young men of Rinamona to the gospel of marriage based on love and on love alone. His theories had been considerably strengthened. His dream had become a reality.

He decided to begin with Charles McGladdery. Charles was not much to look at but he was well off compared with the other young men of the townland. He had been left a legacy by an uncle who had died in America. With some of the money he put a slate roof on the old house and he built an additional room. He had a horse and two cows and a bull. The parish bull was at the time a hallmark of social superiority in the Rosses.

Although he was not very attractive as far as looks went, it would be easy for Charles to get a wife. Every mother in Rinamona who had an eligible daughter was trying to hook him.

Denis thought it would be a very good thing if he could make Charles his first convert. Charles was more or less a king on account of his wealth. Where he would lead, the rest of the young men would follow.

'The Drumnacarta girls are very good-looking,' said Denis to Charles one evening. 'And, along with being good-looking, they are refined. Totally different from the girls down here.'

'I saw that girl of yours in Dungloe last summer fair,' said Charles. 'Right enough, she is a beauty.'

'They are all good-looking,' said Denis. 'And they have such nice ways with them.'

'I believe your girl will be bringing you a pretty good dowry,' said Charles.

'I don't know,' replied Denis. 'I did not ask. I am marrying her for love. She is marrying me for love. Money does not enter into the bargain at all.'

'I know,' said Charles. 'But, all the same, the money is not to be despised. And I know for a fact that Long Shamey McCann has a pile of money. And Rosie is an only daughter ... But you say all the girls up there are good-looking?'

'They are, and they know it,' replied Denis. 'Every one of them knows that her face is her fortune, as the man said long ago. Every one of them knows that she can get married without a penny piece of a marriage portion. And, as I have said, they are gentle and refined. But you ought to go and see for yourself. There is a dance in Conall More's next Saturday night. If you come along, I'll introduce you to at least half a dozen fine girls.'

The following Saturday evening the two young men went to the dance in Drumnacarta. There was a cordial welcome for them and they enjoyed themselves.

They repeated the visit again and again.

'Well,' asked Denis one night on their way back home, 'have you made your selection yet?'

'No, I have not,' replied Charles. 'They are all nice girls. But I can't find the one among them that I'd like to marry.'

'You are not in love with any one of them,' said Denis. 'But that will come. And it could come when you least expect it. Just like a flash of lightning. That is how it happened me the night of the wedding in Bunnamann. But you must prepare your heart for it as I had done. You must banish from your mind all thought of money. You must believe in love. Then it will come. Make no mistake about it, it will come. For it is one of Heaven's gifts.'

One evening the following winter a group of young people – Denis Doherty included – were gathered in Shewan Aleck's. Someone mentioned Charles McGladdery's name. 'There is a strong rumour that he is getting married before Shrove,' said another.

'Not this coming Shrove, if I know his plans,' said Denis. 'And I believe I do. There is nothing rash about the same Charles. He wants to be sure of himself and of the girl before he says the word.'

'There is no need for him to delay or to hesitate the least little bit,' said Shewan Aleck. 'He has all the cards in his hand. The sworn tricks, as the old gamblers used to say. He cannot fail. He has a fine bit of land and a good house. He has a horse and two cows and a bull. He can have his choice of the girls of the parish for the asking.'

'Not of the parish,' said Denis, 'whatever about this townland of Rinamona. There are girls in the parish who would not marry him for his house and land and cattle.'

'Not until they are asked,' said Shewan.

'Well now,' said Denis, 'I'd be the last person in the world to say anything about Charles McGladdery or to belittle him in any way, for he is my best friend. What I mean to say is this: there are girls in the parish who would not marry a man for all the wealth in the world if they did not love him.'

'That's all nonsense,' said Shewan.

'By your leave, my good woman, it is not nonsense,' protested Denis. 'There was a time when a match was made between a bit of land and a few pounds. We were in darkness here for generations for want of education. But the people are beginning to see the light. The day is not far distant when love, and love alone, will guide men and women in selecting partners for life.'

'That's grand talk,' said Shewan Aleck. 'But I would like to meet the young woman who would turn her back on a home like what Charles McGladdery has to offer her, and choose the open road and the bushes for a night's shelter.'

'I know one woman who would make such a choice,' said Denis. 'A girl who would refuse the wealthiest man in the country and marry the man she loves if he hadn't a penny in the world. When will you otherwise good, Christian people understand that marriages of the right kind are made in Heaven and that the foundation of such marriages is love?'

IV

It was a fine, frosty morning in mid-winter. Denis the Dreamer had just got up and was lacing his boots by the fireside when Condy Nanny came in.

'Are you only getting up now?' asked Condy. 'You're a nice man – lying in your bed till this hour of the day. You are not half as good as Charles McGladdery.'

'Why, what great things has Charles done?' asked Denis.

'The greatest thing that a man can do,' replied Condy. 'Settled himself for life. He is to be married in a day or two. They had the *dáil* last night. Lashings of drink they had too.'

'Don't believe that yarn,' said Denis. 'There isn't a word of truth in it. Charles McGladdery and me are pals. We have no secrets from one another. If he were getting married, I'd be the first he'd tell it to. Somebody has been pulling your leg.'

'In that case,' said Condy, 'it was Charles himself that pulled it. And I only hope he pulls it again and again. As I was passing his door on my way down here, out he steps in front of me and gives me two fine bumpers of whiskey. And you could call it whiskey! The kind that makes you feel that you are walking on air. And two big glassfuls. But sure it is easy for him, he has plenty to spend.'

Denis felt somewhat annoyed by this news. Charles McGladdery and he had been pals. Why had Charles kept his intended marriage a secret from his best friend? ... There could be only one explanation for it: Charles was marrying a girl from his own townland. He was marrying in the old way. A sordid bargain between a bit of land and a few pounds. And so Denis' first attempt at creating a romantic Rosses had failed. But he would not lose hope.

'Who is he marrying?' he asked, at last.

'A girl from Drumnacarta,' replied Condy Nanny. 'Rosie McCann is her name. A daughter of Long Shamey McCann. You know the house. The last house to the right above the bridge. Just before you turn down the road to Meenbannad. I know Long Shamey McCann: I sold a cow to him at Jack's Fair a few years ago and the devil's own screw he was. I've never met the daughter but they say she is a beauty. Long Shamey has lashings of money. A nice penny of a dowry he'll be giving his daughter.'

Denis got to his feet and staggered out of the house. He had to lean against the wall outside to steady himself. What was this frightful story he had been told? Could it possibly be true? No, it could not. Condy Nanny had picked up things wrong. It could not be Rosie McCann. Hadn't Rosie promised to be his? Hadn't she declared time and again that she loved him with all her heart and would till her dying day? … No, it could not be true!

Yet it was annoying him.

Condy Nanny came out after him.

'What brought me down,' said he to Denis, 'is to ask you could you come up and help me to do a wee bit of thatching. I want to take advantage of the good day. There is a bad spot in the roof. Down-drops right over the hearth. Only for that I would wait for the spring. And the Lord only knows when we'll get another good day. This day is only a pet. The white frost never lasts long. Besides, there was a wind-dog on the sky-line this morning. A sure sign of a storm. That is why I want to get my wee bit of thatching done today.'

'Mick will go and give you a hand with the thatching,' Denis managed to say. 'I must go to Dungloe.'

Denis set out on his journey to Rosie McCann's home in Drumnacarta. He would have to meet Rosie and hear from her own lips that the terrible news he had heard was a lie. Nothing else would settle his poor, trembling heart. At times, he imagined that Condy Nanny took delight in telling this awful story. Condy Nanny, the miserable louser who married after having got six refusals! He could have no pity for anyone suffering from the pangs of despised love!

Denis continued his journey … What would Rosie say to him for having come on such an errand? Would she say he was mad to believe a yarn that was manifestly absurd? Would she be vexed with him for being such a fool that a clod like Condy Nanny could make sport of him? … But, oh God, if it were true!

At last, Long Shamey McCann's house came into view … Denis came as far as the end of the lane. He stood there for a while. He was between two minds. Would he go in? What would Rosie think of him? Would she say he was an idiot? … Still, he should have to see her. He could not bear the suspense. The maddening thought was burning into his brain … He went up the lane to Shamey McCann's and into the house.

There was a warm welcome for him from the old pair; but Rosie was nowhere to be seen. Long Shamey was half-drunk. He poured out a glass of whiskey and offered it to Denis.

'Drink this,' said Shamey McCann. 'And drink it quickly till I fill it again and again for you. Aye, and ten times, if you can take it. For you deserve it, so you do. We must be grateful to you forever for bringing luck to our family. Our daughter is getting married to a man from your townland. Charles McGladdery, the best catch from the ford of Gweedore to the ford of Gweebarra. He has lashings of money. That is no hearsay: I saw his bankbook. You know the rest yourself. House and land, a horse, two cows and a bull. Our Rosie will never know a day's hardship. And for that she may thank you. It was you brought herself and Charles McGladdery together.'

Denis managed to say he was a teetotaller. He sat there for a while trying to talk. At times he had a faint ray of hope: Rosie was not married yet. If only he could see her and talk to her. Could she have the heart to go back on her promises to him?

He got up to go. He took a few steps in the direction of the door. Then he came to a halt.

'Is Rosie about?' he asked.

'No,' replied the mother. 'She went to Dungloe this morning. They are being married tomorrow. And we are as busy as we can be. She gave us no time to prepare for the wedding. Young folks nowadays are not like what we were when we were getting married. They keep everything to themselves. And then spring it on you. However, she is getting a good man and that is the main thing. And, as Shamey has said, she may thank you for it.'

'I am out with you,' said Long Shamey as Denis was leaving. 'Black out with you for not drinking the couple's health. I know you have the pledge. But I don't care how many pledges a man has, he should not refuse a wee drop at a time like this. Didn't the old people always say it: two sacred occasions – a marriage and a christening.'

Denis went off. He would go to Dungloe. He would meet Rosie ... Only to see her once. Only to speak one word to her. To remind her of her promise! ... He went along the road, across the bogs of Croghyweal. This way Rosie would return home. Then it occurred to him that the surest way of meeting her was to wait for her at one spot – as he might miss her if he went into the village. For hours he stayed at his post. The evening turned cold. A shower was gathering over the peak of Errigal ... Women came along the road on the way home from the village shops. But not the woman that Denis was waiting for. At last, as the dusk was beginning to fall, he went to the village. He went from shop to shop. But Rosie McCann was nowhere to be seen.

He came back home. That night he lay awake for hours. When, at last, he fell asleep, he had the most frightful dreams. In one of them Rosie fell over a cliff into the sea. She was drowning before his eyes while he was bound to a rock with hoops of steel and could not move hand or foot to save her. Later on, he saw her being put on board a black ship by a gang of pirates. He was left standing helpless on the bleak, lonely shore until the ship was swallowed up by the mist on the horizon.

The following day Denis was shocked, stunned and speechless. Only by degrees was he realising that his darling was gone from him for ever and ever ... He would have to talk to somebody about it or his reason would snap. And he turned for sympathy to another woman – the woman that had tried to soothe his every little ache and pain from the time he was a baby.

'Don't let this get you down, my child,' said the mother. 'You are better without Rosie McCann. She has a deceitful heart and she has proved it. The best thing – the only thing – for you to do is to get married immediately. Get a decent, good-natured girl from your own neighbourhood. A girl that we know and whose people have been known here in Rinamona for generations. It was most unwise of you, my child, ever to dream of marrying a stranger. Didn't the old people always say it: your spouse at your doorstep, your godparents far from home. There's a fine girl over there in Pullanleen – Sally McHugh. A grand girl she is in every way. Better than all the Drumnacarta girls put together. So she is.'

'No, mother,' said Denis. 'I could not think of marrying any other girl.'

The mother's sympathy was consoling. It brought some little relief to a wounded heart. But Denis would not dream of marrying another girl. His mother meant well, he knew. But she belonged to a generation that did not understand love as it was beginning to be understood in a more enlightened age ... 'No, mother,' he repeated, 'I could never marry another. Never, never, never.'

That was all he said to his mother. It was all he could say, to her or to anybody else. The heart was charged too full of sorrow for the tongue to give it utterance. But, after a few months, when he had somewhat recovered from the first shock and got back some of his former eloquence, he expounded his principles of love and marriage to a young man from the neighbourhood. 'For men like me,' he said, 'there rises one star and one only. My star rose and lit the entire world for me, one little while and then no more. It set again and I was plunged into darkness – thick, black darkness. My poor mother thought I could light my way through life with a penny candle. But the candle would only kill me. I prefer the darkness a thousand times. The black darkness, the complete darkness.'

V

Denis the Dreamer was once again in the news in his native Rinamona. They were talking about him one night in Susie Fadawan's house.

'He was here the other evening,' said Susie, 'and for two solid hours he talked about nothing but women. I'll lay a wager he'll be married before Shrovetide.'

'It is a bit late in the day for him to be thinking or talking about marriage,' said Barney Kilday. 'He is fifty-one years. That's his exact age. The one water baptised himself and me.'

'I didn't think he'd ever marry,' said Neil McGilligan. 'I thought he'd end his days mourning for the lass of Ballochmile — as he used to call Rosie McCann from Drumnacarta.'

'He mourned for her long enough,' said Andy Neddy. 'Twenty-five years. When Rosie turned him down we thought he would die of a broken heart.'

'No one does,' said Susie Fadawan. 'As poor Feldy McGulsachan, the Lord have mercy on him, used to say, men die and are eaten by worms, but not because of love ... Poor Denis! He is in a bit of a fix now. Like a man that would sleep all day and get up at sunset to cut his hay or mow his meadow. Why on earth didn't he marry years ago? His mother, God rest her, gave him the right advice. She advised him to get married immediately when the Drumnacarta doll gave him the slip. He would not listen to her. He preferred the thick, black darkness to what he called his mother's penny candle. It will run him tight now to get a rush-light, let alone a candle.'

Maggie McGinty was an old maid who had given up all hope of getting married. Some people would say that no man had ever asked her. That is not true. She had a proposal once, from Billy McNellis of Srathnabratogy. She refused him because he had a wooden leg.

Maggie was getting on in years and she was getting sour. Perhaps she was regretting that she had not accepted Billy McNellis, wooden leg and all. She lived in the old house with her brother Hughie and his family. When their father was dying he divided his little holding in two equal shares between them. If it should happen that Maggie married, the entire holding would go to Hughie on condition that he gave his sister as her marriage portion what would be considered a fair price for her share of the property.

But let us get back to Denis the Dreamer. At the age of fifty one he decided to get married. He had no particular girl in his eye. But, one thing he was determined on, and that was to marry a young one.

Donal Vickey and Johnny Andy accompanied him on his mission the night he went out to look for a wife. Coming on to midnight, they set out. It was always late when Rosses men went on these errands so that nobody would meet them or see them. It was a wise precaution as there was always the danger of a refusal.

They were refused in the first house they went to. They were refused in the second house. And in the third.

'We are not in luck,' said Donal Vickey after the third failure. 'Where will we go now?' he asked Denis. 'Have you any other particular girl in mind?'

'No, I haven't,' replied Denis.

'What about Maggie McGinty?' suggested Johnny Andy.

'Too old,' said Denis. 'Far too old.'

They tried three more houses and they were refused in every one of them.

'It must be near morning,' said Donal Vickey. 'The Carrickfin cocks are crowing their third round. I think, in God's name, we ought to go home. Maybe we'd have better luck the next night. For there is such a thing as luck.'

'No,' said Denis. 'That would ruin any chance I have. We have been in too many houses for the secret to be kept. Tomorrow the news would spread like wildfire throughout the Rosses that each of six girls refused to marry me. Then no woman would have me. In God's name, we'll keep on trying until daylight compels us to give up the hunt.'

'It can't be far off daylight at this very moment,' said Donal Vickey.

'What about Maggie McGinty?' suggested Johnny Andy a second time.

Denis the Dreamer looked towards the east. Was that the first, faint streak of dawn over the peak of Errigal?

'All right,' said he.

They went to McGinty's house and knocked at the door. After some little delay they were admitted. Donal Vickey put forward their proposal ... Maggie, of course, had to be consulted. She got up and dressed and came down a ladder into the kitchen.

Would she marry Denis Doherty? She said she would and that was that. The next thing to be settled was the dowry.

'This miserable little holding is not worth more than sixty pounds,' said Hughie McGinty. 'That means that I give her thirty pounds.'

'It won't do,' said Donal Vickey, 'not by any manner of means. You must be fair, Hughie. Ask any three or four men you wish to name to assess the place and I'll bet you what you like they'll value the land at eighty pounds to say nothing about the house.'

'The devil a red penny more than thirty pounds will I pay,' said Hughie McGinty.

'All right,' said Donal Vickey. 'Have it your own way. It will be easy for this fine man to get a wife any day with forty pounds of a dowry. Come away, lads.'

Maggie McGinty whispered something to her brother.

'Wait a moment,' said Hughie. 'I'll give her thirty-five pounds.'

'It won't do,' said Donal, taking a step in the direction of the door.

'I'll give her thirty-five pounds and a fine, fat sheep along with it,' said Hughie.

'Come on,' said Donal, 'be a man. Make it the forty pounds.'

'Upon my soul I couldn't.'

'Well, that's that. We can't take less. We had better go and let you get back to your beds.'

The negotiations had reached breaking point. At this stage Johnny Andy spoke (as had been planned).

'Listen to me, the two of you,' he said to Donal Vickey and Hughie McGinty. 'What kind of men are you at all? Are you going to break up a good match for a few paltry pounds? Be men and meet each other half-way. Split the difference. That makes it thirty-seven pounds ten.'

'All right,' said Donal Vickey. 'I agree. It is a fair enough dowry – thirty-seven pounds, ten shillings.'

'And won't I get the sheep as well?' asked Denis the Dreamer.

Manus Mac Award, Smoker and Storyteller

People would say that Manus Mac Award was a born smoker. I don't know how true that is. All I know is that, at the age of seven, he was caught smoking turf mould. His mother thought she could beat the habit out of him. But his father's opinion was that brute force would not cure him. So he bought the boy a new pipe and gave him a reasonable weekly ration of tobacco. It will be seen from this that the weed got a strong grip on the lad early in life and that if, when he grew up and got sense, he tried to break the habit, it would be extremely difficult for him to do so.

Whether or not Manus had an inborn tendency to smoking we cannot be sure. But we are almost certain that he was a born storyteller. This gift he inherited from his father, for Shamey Mac Award had a method of telling a story that had died with bygone generations. There were men in the Rosses who could repeat old stories from the folklore – stories about the Fianna or the Red Branch – but Shamey Mac Award had only a poor opinion of their literary talents.

'Just something they have learned by heart,' he would say. 'They have good memories, that is all. But I don't call that storytelling. Listen to the best of them in ordinary conversation. How they ramble from one thing to another. A good story must not have one word that is not necessary. It must point towards the end from the very beginning. It must stop in a way that will make you remember it and have no loose strings hanging out of it. Take, for instance, the stories that Michael Roe had about Colmcille. The story about the casket that Connla Ceard had left unfinished when he died. The story of the attempt made by the saints of Ireland to raise Fergus from the dead to get him to tell the *Táin*. The story of the druid who was shown a vision of hell. And above all – oh, miles above all – the story of how Colmcille will plead for the salvation of the people of Ireland on the Day of Judgement. From the time I was a small boy, I used to take delight in Michael Roe's stories and the way he had of telling them.'

'And your son has taken after you,' his wife would say. 'Already I notice that he doesn't like the rambling way of talking I have. It is not fair. I think that everyone should be at liberty to say what he has to say in his own way.'

'Of course.'

'All the same, during the first years of our marriage you were impatient with me.'

'I may have been sorry – for the children's sake – that you could not come straight to the point. But I never tried to change you. That would be unreasonable. Just as unreasonable as if you were to ask me to get a new singing voice and sing *Mal Dubh an Ghleanna* the way you sing it.'

But young Manus was not as reasonable as his father. He was only sixteen years when he thought it was time for him to reform his mother's habits of speech. A girl from the next townland was being married and she was being discussed in the Mac Award household.

'She is very young,' said the man of the house. 'Nineteen years, I am told.'

'She is more than that,' said his wife. 'I remember well the time she was born. I was going up to Máire Wuiris for a pair of cards that I had lent her. That was Máire's way. If you lent her a thing, she never sent it back, you had to go for it. Well, I wanted the cards anyhow. I was going to card some wool to make a gansey for you or for one of the boys, I don't remember which. On my way up, I met Sorcha Roe and she told me that Nelly Hughdie had a young daughter the day before. That was the summer fair day. Our Annie was five weeks old at the time. That leaves the bride exactly twenty-one years old.'

'Mother,' said the boy, 'could you not have told us that she was five weeks younger than our Annie and, therefore, twenty-one years, and cut out the ramblings about Máire Wuiris and the cards and the gansey?'

'Don't speak to your mother like that,' said the father. 'If you do, you will hear from me. She is perfectly free to tell her story in her own way.'

'Leave him alone, Shamey,' said the mother. 'Leave him alone. The day will come when he will pay for it. We have seen the likes of him before. Often and often. When his day comes, he will get a woman that will make a doormat of him and he won't dare to correct her. That is how life punishes people. So leave him to what is coming to him.'

II

A few weeks afterwards, one of those functions known as a *Feis* was held at Gartan and young Manus Mac Award decided to enter for the storytelling competition. He became his mother's darling once more. She forgot all he had said about her rambling speech. She was praying for his success and was giving him what she considered good advice.

'You should go across to Neddy More and get him to tell you the story of how Oisín was lured away to the Land of Youth by the lady with the golden hair. If you learn that story, you will surely get the prize. I heard Neddy at it a few times. It was like music in my ears.'

'You can go across to Neddy More's a few times because your mother has advised you,' said Shamey Mac Award the following day as he and his son were in the bog footing turf. 'But pay no heed to him. He is no good. I heard him a few times. Just rattles off strings of words he has learned by heart. But he has no idea of a story. You will find out that for yourself if you listen to him for five minutes talking about anything outside the story. Tell your story in your own way. If the judges know anything, you are almost sure to get the prize.'

'But, father, if the judges think that what we call Neddy More's strings of words is the best kind of story?'

'It could happen, son. In fact, the chances are that it will happen. The art of storytelling is dead or nearly dead. The judges will probably be two or three ignorant schoolmasters. A publican from Kilmacrenan may also be on the jury. He will be all for keeping the prize in his own district. He will be afraid he might lose custom if he let the laurels be carried off by an outsider.'

'In that case, what is the use in competing?'

'This much, son: that it is better to fail than give in to a gang of hooligans who hate Irish, and who are in this thing in the hope of getting something out of it – their names in the papers, if nothing else. Don't tell your mother a word of what I am saying to you. It might hurt her. Your mother is a fine woman, an excellent woman. She has her gifts, her great gifts. And, if the storytelling is not one of them, she is none the worse for it. Bear that in mind.'

The day of the *Feis* came round on the day before Manus Mac Award left the Rosses by the midday train. He had his mind made up to tell the story of Colmcille and the Last Judgement as he had heard it over and over again from his father. Having arrived in Kilmacrenan early in the afternoon, he had time to visit the places of historic interest in the neighbourhood. He climbed to the top of the Rock of Doon where kings had been crowned in olden times and where his ancestors, the Mac Awards, had chronicled the event in verse. He went to the flagstone on which Colmcille was born. He visited the ruins of the old abbey where the children first called him the 'Dove of the Church.' He got all the inspiration he could.

The following day he entered for the competition along with six others. There was only one judge – a white-haired old man from Templedouglas who in his youth had spent some years in an ecclesiastical college on the continent, and who, for one reason or another, did not become a priest. He listened with evident interest to all the stories. At the end, he delivered his judgement. They were all good, he said. Between six of them he should find it hard to decide which was the best. But the seventh – Manus Mac Award from the Rosses – had an inborn gift which the rest lacked. He could keep his mind fixed on the main point of a story, bring in no unnecessary side-issues, use not one unnecessary word, and stop at a climax that held his listeners spellbound. He had no hesitation in awarding him the prize.

That evening Manus arrived home with gladness in his heart. His mother flung her arms round him and kissed him tenderly. His father, although he did not say much, was glad too. He was glad that his son had got a prize for what, in his opinion, was real storytelling.

III

At the age of twenty Manus Mac Award left home and went to America. He brought his early habits and interests with him. He was a confirmed smoker and he had an abiding love for stories.

In America he continued to develop both tastes. He sampled the best brands of tobacco. Having discovered that a pipe soon becomes bitter if smoked continuously over a long period, he bought a second pipe and then a third one. He kept adding to his store of pipes until he had seven – one for every day of the week. And he became adept at seasoning them.

Then came a new interest in storytelling. He wanted to read. But he had not gone far with his reading when he discovered that his meagre primary school education did not provide him with a foundation on which he could base his study of the best stories in the English language. Accordingly, he went to night-school. After a time, he became interested in the American short story, notably the works of O. Henry. Later on he discovered that he could get in translation the best short stories of the world – most of which appealed to him, especially the French.

Besides stories and reducing smoking to a fine art, Manus learned something else in America. He became interested in the cause of Ireland's freedom. He began to read the *Irish World* and became very interested in the activities of the various Irish organisations in America. He attended meetings addressed by Parnell, Devoy and O'Donovan Rossa. On one occasion he made a journey of several hundred miles to see and hear Tom Clarke.

After a stay of ten years he came back home to the Rosses with a good bit of money, a trunkful of books and seven pipes.

When he came home he had to say to himself that he was before and after his time. Throughout the greater part of the Rosses the cream of the Irish language was gone and the people were making atrocious attempts at expressing themselves in English. They were floundering between two cultures, having abandoned the old (for valid enough reasons) and not having had time to assimilate the new. As for the freedom of Ireland, the Rosses people were indifferent to it. It was something they could not understand.

Manus built a neat little cottage for himself in one of the beauty spots of the Rosses. He had his books and his pipes. Still, he was not happy. He felt that, in the words of *Genesis*, it was not good for man to be alone. He would have to take onto himself a wife.

That should not be a difficult task, for several mothers in the neighbourhood had their eye on him for one of their daughters. But Manus could not be coaxed or influenced. He would make his own selection and make it according to his own plan. He was not in love with any girl and this gave him a great advantage. He would put a girl in the scales and, if she did not come up to his standard, he would pass on to the next.

The first girl he cast his eye on was one Mary McGee. Mary was passably good-looking but she would have to be examined for other requisite qualifications. Manus listened to her attentively one evening when a number of them were gathered together in a neighbour's house. Mary, without realising what she was doing, exposed her fatal weakness. She talked a lot and Manus thought that, if anything, she was a worse rambler than his mother.

He passed on to the next – a girl named Biddy McHugh. Biddy would not spin out a story in a rambling way. But she had a worse habit – a most exasperating habit. No matter how absorbing the story was that was being told, Biddy would seize on a word and fly off at a tangent with some remark of her own. The man of the house was telling of a near drowning accident that had occurred off the coast some time previously and of the part he himself had taken in the rescue.

'We were coming from Inishbeg, sailing as close to the wind as we could, for we wanted to clear the head of Inishfree with the next tack ...'

'I wonder how Carry Villy likes living in Inishfree?' broke in Biddy. And her fate was sealed.

It soon became known that Manus was looking for certain attributes in the girl he would select for a wife. And, of course, he was being talked about.

'I wonder if a girl were to remain silent,' suggested one.

'That would not do at all,' said Shoney Forker. 'She must talk and talk the way he himself talked the day long ago he got the prize at the *Feis* in Gartan.'

'He'll have a bit of a search,' said Billy Jack.

'He'll have no search,' said an old woman named Shoogey Brennan. 'He is putting them in the scales now and weighing them. Some fine day he will meet a girl that will sweep him off his feet and his poor scales along with him. He'll be caught before he knows where he is. That's how it is done. God gave us women that gift. Only for it our lot in life would be a hard one.'

IV

Sally O'Donnell was known as the Star of the Rosses and all who knew her in her young days would admit that she deserved the title. She was one of three sisters who lived with their parents on a mountain farm in Bunnawack.

Sally met Manus Mac Award one fair day in Cloghanlea. It was whispered that the meeting was more by design than by accident on the girl's part. We cannot vouch for the truth of this rumour. All we know for certain is that as soon as Manus saw her, he fell head over ears in love with her. How did she speak? How did she tell a story? We don't know. All we know is that on this particular occasion she was a damsel of dazzling beauty. On the evening of that day, Manus came home with an angelic vision before his eyes. And, of course, he must talk about it.

'He is caught,' said Shoogey Brennan. 'And I said he would be caught. There were no weighing scales this time. The Star of the Rosses looked at him with her fairy eyes. She shook her golden curls and she burst into a peal of musical laughter that would make an old man young again. She has him in the net. That is, if she wants to have him.'

'You may be sure she wants to have him,' said Nora Villy.

When would Manus see his loved one again? How would he contrive to meet her? The opportunity came sooner than he had expected. One day shortly afterwards, Mickey John Chondy – a young man from the next townland – came to Manus with a request.

'I am getting married next Monday week,' said he, 'and I want you to be best man for me.'

'I never was best man at a wedding in my life,' pleaded Manus. 'I don't know many of the young people after being away in America for ten years. By the way, who are you getting married to?'

'To a girl from Bunnawack – a girl named Ketty McCole. You may remember her. You met her the fair day in Cloghanlea along with Sally O'Donnell. Sally is going to be bridesmaid.'

'Well,' said Manus, trying to conceal his eagerness to comply with the request, 'I don't know many people up that way. Still, I won't refuse your request since you have done me the honour of asking me.'

'He is walking right into it,' commented Shoogey Brennan afterwards. 'And the poor clown doesn't see the trap that has been set for him. He imagines that Mickey John Chondy is conferring an honour on him.'

The Star of the Rosses had her likes and dislikes. She abhorred the sight and the smell of tobacco smoke. A few weeks before the events related, the family came to live in a new house. Before they moved in, Sally made it known to her father that she would not tolerate smoking. It would destroy the curtains. It would blacken the new ceiling. When the father protested that he could not live without his smoke, the daughter dropped a hint that she would go to America.

'What will I do, at all, at all?' said the old man to his wife. 'Sure I might as well be dead as not to have my smoke. And I don't want to see her go to America. It would be the same as if I was banishing her.'

'Don't worry,' said the old woman. 'I'll get your tobacco for you every week as usual. You can smoke away in the old house and in the neighbours' houses when you go for a bit of an *airneál*. We won't have Sally for long.'

'Is she getting married?'

'I believe she is. She can get married any time she likes. I know three here in the hills who have their eye on her. But she met a man from the lower parish lately at the fair in Cloghanlea and I am told that already they have a strong notion of one another. The man is just back from America and he has lots of money (I have that on good authority) ... Sally is going to be Ketty McCole's bridesmaid and the Yankee will be best man. They will decide it one way or the other the night of the wedding.'

V

The wedding-feast was glorious. There was plenty to eat and plenty to drink. The Meenmore fiddlers were at their best. The dancers were lively and gay. On seats ranged along the walls sat the elderly men smoking their pipes. A cloud of smoke rested beneath the rafters for all the world like a morning mist in summer, rising from a valley and resting on the brow of a hill.

Sally O'Donnell did not seem to be enjoying herself. At intervals she would go out and come back in again rubbing her eyes. At last, Manus went down to where she was standing near the door.

'Is there anything wrong with you?' he asked anxiously.

'The smoke is killing me,' she replied.

'Will we go for a walk in the fresh air?' he suggested.

'Wait till I get my coat. In this light dress I could easily catch a cold after coming out of that kiln.'

'Where will we go?' he asked her when they were ready to start.

'Down the glen as far as the head of the lake,' she suggested.

They went down as far as the head of the lake. The moon was full. The water of the lake was as calm as a sheet of glass. That is all that an ordinary person would see. But Manus Mac Award saw the moon smiling down on them. He saw the fairies dancing on the grassy marge. His hour had come. He took his darling in his arms and kissed her. He told her he had no words to describe his love for her. Would she consent to be his? Her answer would bring him lifelong happiness or lifelong misery!

Sally remained silent.

'In Heaven's name, darling, speak,' implored Manus, 'and put an end to my horrible suspense, one way or the other.'

'It is hard to speak at times,' said Sally in a sad voice. 'Very hard … Life is hard at times … People cannot always marry those they love … I don't know how to say what I want to say … May I ask you a question?'

'Of course you may. A hundred questions. What is it, darling?'

'Do you smoke?' she stammered.

'Yes, I do.'

'I thought so … Well, that puts an end to everything. I can't stand the smell of smoke, it would kill me. I am sorry we've ever met, Manus, for I love you. But it cannot be helped. Hard as it is on me as well as on you, we must say goodbye forever,' she concluded.

And, as she looked at him, he could see the sorrow in her face.

If this scene had been enacted in broad daylight, it is possible that Manus might have vision enough to see that it would be the cruellest of cruel punishments on him to give up his pipes … But, at this point, the moon frowned at him. The fairies' light-hearted lilt became a mournful wail. He could hear them plainly singing the saddest of all the world's sad, parting words:

Ae fond kiss, and then we sever
Ae fareweel, alas, forever.

He could not do it. He could not take his last farewell of her. He clasped her to his bosom.

'It is only a light sacrifice to make for you, darling,' he said. 'The day you come to live under my roof I will put away my pipes, never to take one of them up again.'

'Are you sure you won't regret this promise?' she asked after a pause.

'Regret it? I would give up more than that for you, darling.'

It was clear daylight when the wedding party broke up. Manus walked with his loved one as far as her father's house. She asked him once more was he sure he would not regret his promise to give up smoking. The moon had left the heavens. The fairies had retreated to their underground mansions. The morning was raw and chilly. But Sally was still a beauty. Manus repeated his promise and he set out for home.

VI

Shortly afterwards the pair were married and the Star of the Rosses came to live with her husband in Rosbeg by the sea. She had a nice, tidy home in a most beautiful spot.

Manus gave up smoking. He put his seven fine pipes on the top shelf of the dresser. Sally suggested that they should be hidden away in a press. But Manus asked as a special request that they be left where he could see them every day and every hour of the day while he was in the house. It was a small request and Sally granted it. After all, Manus had given in to her on the big issue. And Sally had a wee drop of the milk of human kindness in her that most women have.

Manus wanted his darling to take an interest in the stories he had been reading. She consented. He had not read for long when he discovered that she had the habit of seizing on some word or phrase in his narration and go on talking about something that was miles away from the motif of the story. This used to exasperate him. He tried to get her to overcome the habit by stopping dead and only resuming his reading when she requested him. Sometimes he would put the book away and read no more that day.

'This is a gem of a story by O. Henry,' he said one day. '"The Last Leaf" it is called.' And he began to read about the girl who had got into her head that she would die of pneumonia when the last leaf of the old vine should fall.

'They say the doctors in Dublin have a tablet now that can cure pneumonia in two days. I've read it in the papers lately.'

Manus paused.

'But go on with your story.'

'Are you sure you want to listen to it?'

'Of course I want to listen to it.'

'I have another fine story here that I want to read for you – "The Gift of the Magi".'

He began to read. 'The young woman had a most beautiful head of hair. It was her husband's pride and joy and he wanted to buy her a set of combs ... '

'Do you know that my mother knew a woman from Clochnarone who came back from America with three combs in her hair – one at each side and one at the back ... Do I smell my bread burning? But go on.'

Manus put away the book. He got up and went out. And he cast a longing look at the pipes on the shelf as he passed the dresser.

'I have a pearl of a story here that I want to read for you – a translation from the French. The French are the real masters of the short story. This one is about a goat that escaped from the farm and fled to the mountains. When you have heard it, I think you will agree that the man who wrote it could make a story out of nothing. Listen: "Monsieur Sequin had never had good luck with his goats. He lost them all in the same way; some fine morning they broke their cord and went off to the mountain ..."'

'A man up beside us, Doney John Hughdie, had goats of the same kind. He lost over a dozen of them and had to stop keeping them. One after the other they broke their tethers and they went away off to the mountains of Glendowan ... But go on.'

'I am sorry to refuse you, darling, but I can't go on. It was wrong of me to expect you to become a copy of myself, so I won't bother you any more with my reading. Maybe I am an odd creature. But you have a habit that exasperates me. My mother, God rest her, used to ramble east and west of what she had set out to tell. It used to annoy me. But this habit that you have hurts me. I won't attempt to read any more for you. But, in ordinary conversation, ignore me, contradict me, call me an idiot. Anything you like. But don't fly off at a tangent. As I have said, it hurts. It hurts dreadfully.'

'I would not hurt you for the world, love,' said Sally, coming across to him and putting an arm around his neck.

'I know you wouldn't, darling,' he said. 'Just remember my little weakness and I am sure that before long you will overcome that habit.'

'I'll do my best.'

'I know you will. And, what's more, you will succeed.'

Easter time came round. All of a sudden the newspapers stopped coming to the Rosses. The country was seething with the wildest rumours. A

German army had landed in Kerry. Thousands of men were being killed daily. The city of Dublin was a roaring furnace!

A week passed. 'I think, in God's name, I'll go to the Cloghanlea fair tomorrow,' said Manus to his wife. 'We'll have grazing enough for another yearling and I think I'll buy one.'

He went to the fair. In the evening he came back home without any yearling and he looked very sad and very depressed.

'You didn't buy,' said his wife when he came in.

'No, I didn't,' he replied. 'I didn't see the type of animal I was after.'

He threw himself down on a chair and sighed.

'What is wrong with you?' asked Sally anxiously.

'The papers have come in today. It is all over.'

'What's all over?'

'The rebellion in Dublin. It lasted only the bare week. Now the leaders are being executed. And what they are saying about them in Cloghanlea! Saying that every one of the leaders deserves to be shot. Kept back Home Rule, says the man who drove the police long ago to Gweedore to arrest Father McFadden.'

'Wasn't there a police officer killed outside the chapel in Gweedore that day?'

A pause.

'But continue.'

'And the son of bailiff Narwhal ...'

'What was Narwhal's real name? ... But go on with your story.'

'I nearly lost my temper listening to the heroes of Dublin being called all sorts of names by fools and corner boys when I was having a drink in Brennan's.'

'I wonder is it true that Brennan is going to sell that place?'

A long pause.

'But go on with your story.'

'And when I heard Larry Wally, the bastard son of a peeler, gloating over the execution of Tom Clarke, it nearly drove me mad. Tom Clarke who spent the best years of his life in English jails with only the vilest of England's criminals for companions. I couldn't forget the impression that gaunt, withered, white-headed, old man made on me the day I heard him address a meeting in Madison Square, New York. And to think ... '

'Will you go out and me only after feeding you.'

This remark of Sally's was addressed to two hens that made their appearance on the doorstep.

'But go on with your story.'

Manus did not go on with the story. He got up and went out.

'Are you not hungry?' Sally called after him from the door.

'No, I am not,' he replied. 'I couldn't look at food.'

He went down to the shore and sat on a rock looking out at the tide. If only he had a smoke to soothe his nerves. Would he begin again? 'No, I won't,' he decided. 'I made her that promise because I loved her. And I love her still, no matter how much she exasperates me. So I am keeping my promise.'

As he came back to the house some time afterwards he met Sally coming out. She wore a shawl over her shoulders and carried a basket on her arm.

'If you go out again before I come back,' she said, 'lock the door and leave the key in the usual place. I haven't enough tea for the morning and I must go to the shop to get a grain. And I'll bring a half-stone of linseed meal for the black calf. I won't be long.'

Manus went inside and sat down. There she is gone now, he thought, without a word of apology or a sign of remorse on her face … He looked at the pipes on the shelf of the dresser. But that was all. He was firmly resolved to keep his betrothal promise no matter what happened.

After a while he heard Sally's voice as she came singing up the path towards the door. The gay lilt that had often made him feel she must be the happiest creature on earth.

She came in and put her basket down on the kitchen table. She took off her shawl and hung it on a peg on the lower wall. Then she took the pipe-rack off the dresser and put it on the table beside the basket. What was coming over her at all? Why did she want to torture him that way?

She turned round and faced him.

'Which of these pipes do you want to smoke first?' she asked.

'What do you mean?' he asked in amazement.

'What do I mean? What can I mean? Surely you can't accuse me this time of rambling round in circles or flying off at a tangent? I want to know which pipe you want to smoke first,' she concluded, putting her hand in the basket and taking out a large square of plug tobacco.

He sprang to his feet and took her in his arms. 'Sally, darling, you are an angel,' he said in a voice almost overcome with emotion.

'Fill your pipe and light it before you say anything more,' she said. 'I want to see you smoking. Fill it again and again.'

'Manus,' she said later on, speaking to him through a cloud of smoke, 'that pipe is giving you pleasure. It is making me happy – the first time I was really and completely happy since we were married … Manus, you and I were a pair of idiots. Me first and you afterwards. Each of us in his own way would have our marriage an affair of tyrant and slave instead of an affair of love based on tolerance and understanding. Me first with my absurd no smoking condition, as if a man used to smoking could live without it. And then you, trying to make me think and talk like yourself – as if a woman could be happy without being free to chatter and clatter in her own way ... Two poor idiots we have been, each of us as bad as the other ... This rebellion in Dublin may or may not save Ireland some day. But it has at least saved our marriage.'

Home Rule

At the time my story begins, the only people in the Rosses who took any interest in politics were those who had spent some time in America – particularly the emigrants who had spent their time in the cities where there was a fair proportion of people either of Irish birth or of Irish extraction. Those who stayed at home knew nothing about politics. They did not speak English. They could not read the newspapers. They knew nothing about history – that is to say, history that was modern or comparatively modern.

Of ancient history, mixed with mythology, they had a surprisingly good knowledge – which was due, of course, to the language they had for their vernacular and the folklore enshrined in it. They could discuss the exploits of the Red Branch knights and of the Fianna. They knew that Balor of the Mighty Blows and the Evil Eye was king of Tory once upon a time. But they did not know that a red-haired lad from Donegal was captured at Lough Swilly and brought to Dublin, where he spent three years in close confinement in the Castle, from which he finally escaped and returned to set the heather ablaze on the hills of Donegal. They did not know that at a later date, and nearer home, a French flagship, *La Hoche*, with a young Irishman on board, did for the greatest part of a day, keep up a running fight with several units of the British Fleet, until finally she went up in flames off the coast of the Rosses.

However, there were two men in the district who did not share the general ignorance with regard to modern history and current politics. They were Ned Sweeney and Denis Boyle. Each of them had spent seven years in America in their young days. During their exile they came into contact with more enlightened people of either Irish birth or Irish descent, and they learned something about the history of Ireland and of her struggle for freedom down the ages.

In due course, both of them came back to the Rosses and they got married. Denis Boyle had a large family, the eldest of whom was a boy, named Felim. Ned Sweeney had only one child in his family – a girl named Bella.

When they grew up, Felim and Bella fell head over ears in love with one another. It would be easy to arrange a marriage between them. Felim had neither land nor strand as they used to say in Irish. But he could marry into Sweeney's, an arrangement common enough in the Rosses in those days. This arrangement would almost certainly have been decided upon for Felim and Bella, if the two fathers had not taken the notion to drop into the schoolmaster's every Saturday night, to hear the week's news as reported in *The Derry Journal*.

At that time, the movement that had as its object the gaining of Home Rule for Ireland had at its head a man of extraordinary energy and ability. His leadership and his series of successes gave promise of great things to come. Our two Rosses men followed his career with interest for two or three years; and they were very loyal to him in their hearts. Then something happened. Call it fate, call it ignorance, call it treachery, call it what you will, it happened. The country split into two wild, mad, bitter opposing camps. One sect was for deposing the leader, the other sect for sticking to him through thick and thin. The split reached the Rosses. Denis Boyle was on the side of the chief, as loyal as ever to him. Ned Sweeney was bitterly opposed to him.

In the course of time, the chief was deposed from the leadership by his party. Denis Boyle was heart-broken. Ned Sweeney was delighted.

'The so-and-so has got what he deserved,' said Ned Sweeney one day as a number of the neighbours were on their way home from the local fair. 'Did he think the Irish people were idiots? Did he think they would allow themselves to be represented at home and abroad by a scoundrel with no more morals than a dog? Thank God Ireland has kept the Faith ... We want Home Rule but we won't sell our souls for it.'

'There will be another day,' retorted Denis Boyle, trying to check his rising temper. 'He will come back. Ireland will recover from this spasm. If she doesn't, she'll rue the day when he implored his party not to throw him to the English wolves and they refused. And, talking about morals, some of the lousiest bastards in both England and Ireland are now blowing that trumpet.'

One word borrowed another until at last the two men came to blows. The fight might have been long and fierce, but the neighbours separated them ... They came home. Boyle had a black eye. Sweeney was bleeding from a cut on the lower lip.

'What happened you at all?' asked Bella Sweeney when her father came home.

'Not much, daughter,' he replied. 'Not much as far as it concerns myself – a bit of sticking-plaster will fix me up. But what I have to say concerns you a lot.'

He told the story, and in his own way. 'The next opportunity you get,' he continued, 'you will tell the son of that scoundrel that he will never again darken my door. A nice piece of work I'd be doing before Heaven. Giving my daughter in marriage to one of that cursed tribe. I'd rather see you married to Barney the Tinker who goes round the country stealing hens, than to a son of Denis Boyle. A man who supports a low scoundrel who has been condemned by all the bishops of the country. Tell that to the young fellow the next time that you meet him. Let that meeting be soon and let it be the last one.'

The neighbours in the *airneál* house were all talking about the affair. Here are a few of the comments.

'What the devil business of theirs is it?'

'They have landed themselves where they deserve to land. They couldn't drop into a house of an evening like the rest of us and talk about Cú Chulainn or Conall Cearnach or Oisín or Oscar. No, they'd have to go to the master's and get him to read the papers for them. Knowledgeable men, you know. Think themselves a step above the rest of us. Politics they used to call it.'

'Sure it doesn't matter to us who leads the country, or who doesn't, or will anyone lead it. It doesn't matter to us whether the thing they call Home Rule comes or does not come. We are down here among the rocks and bogs of the Rosses. And that's where we'll be as long as one of our seed or breed is left.'

'I am sorry for the young pair myself. They were all set for getting married next year. I am sorry for the young fellow especially. His father has nothing to give him. He had a nice place there in Ned's, ready to walk into. And nothing would do his idiot of a father but to destroy the whole plan.'

A few evenings afterwards, Romeo Boyle went to a certain spot indicated by a messenger. He sat on a rock and looked out at the grey sea. After a short time, Juliet Sweeney arrived at the same place. She came to where he sat and looked at him with tears in her eyes. What would she say? Would she put a plague on both their houses and declare herself willing to follow her Romeo to the ends of the earth, come what might? No, she did not. She told him, between her sobs, that they must part forever. She was broken-hearted, she said. But it could not be helped. 'If we had any place to go to,' she finally added. Romeo, of course, had no answer to this argument. He had to say goodbye to her … In a few months time, he left for America.

The following October, on a raw and gusty day, a ship came into Dún Laoghaire (then called Kingstown). She steamed slowly up the harbour, and at last she berthed alongside the quay. Soon a coffin draped in black was taken ashore. It was then put in a hearse and driven away. Two days afterwards, the same coffin was borne to Glasnevin on the shoulders of men, as thousands lined the streets along the route. Strong men shed bitter tears; women sobbed. And finally, a cry of heart-felt sorrow rent the air, as the uncrowned king of Ireland was lowered to his last resting place.

He was gone, leaving without a leader the land he had loved and served so well. And leaving Romeo Boyle and Juliet Sweeney with nothing but the memory of a vanished dream. [Romeo, as I had said, had gone to America, Juliet had stayed at home.]

II

Charlie Rodgers from the townland of Shaskinore was better known as 'Charlie the Rover.' He fully deserved the sobriquet, for he was a rover if ever there was one. He was here today, at the other end of the parish tomorrow. He would play the flute for hours on end at the crossroads dancing-boards on summer evenings. He could sing and he could dance, and he would spend whole nights in still-houses drinking poteen. In addition to all these qualities and habits, he was a fine-looking man.

For a number of years he was as gay and happy as the lark in the clear air. At last, he began to realise that the gaiety and the happiness would not last forever; and so he decided to get a wife for himself.

Who would marry him? Lots of girls would if he had any little bit of a holding of his own. But he hadn't. In that respect, he was like Felim Boyle, who was gone from us to America for four years.

Charlie had heard of Bella Sweeney and of the tidy little place he would have, ready to walk into, if Bella were willing to marry him and her parents had no objection. He made his way to Tullybawn and opened his campaign. Ned Sweeney knew that with all his faults, Charlie the Rover was a good worker. But he was a confirmed rake. Would he reform? Above all, would he give up the drink?

Bella Sweeney had no fears on this score. She was certain, she said, that Charlie would give up drinking and turn his attention to their little bit of a farm. Her mother held the same opinion. So the father consented, though he had his doubts at times.

Charlie the Rover and Bella Sweeney got married; and Charlie, of course, came to live in Sweeney's. For a while in the beginning, people were asking themselves how the marriage would turn out. But, before Charlie was a year married, it was plain to the world that he was completely reformed. He put away the flute. He settled down to work in real earnest – blasting rocks, draining bogs, breaking and clearing more land for tillage. He would be out working in winter, on days when other men were inside cowering over the fire. 'The coldest place on a winter's day, sitting in the house with your toes in the ashes,' Charlie would say to a neighbour. 'If you want to be warm, if you want to feel the blood tingling through your veins, get out and work. God meant us to work. "In the sweat of your brow" he said to the first man who was in the world.'

As for drink, Charlie would not taste it under any circumstances. And not alone did he abstain from tasting it, but he was continually preaching against it. He was opposed to it even at weddings or christenings – two functions at which the rest of the Rosses people regarded a drink as a necessary part of their religion.

Five years after they were married, Charlie proved to his neighbours that he was a teetotaller for life. He and his wife were invited to a wedding. Charlie spent the night at the feast; but not one drop of drink did he taste. He resisted all coaxing and all pressure. He was a total abstainer for life; and that was that. In the morning, a number of the guests, including Charlie and his wife, came home part of the way together. Shamey More was one of the group; and it was whispered on the quiet in certain places that Shamey had a suspicion that Charlie's total abstinence was not purely voluntary. Shamey's tongue was a bit loose this morning; and he decided to begin an argument that might either strengthen his suspicions or prove to him that they were unfounded.

'And so you spent a whole night at a wedding, Charlie, and did not take as much as one drink,' began Shamey. 'The wedding of Garry Villy, the decentest man in the parish. I would be ashamed to do it. I'd feel I was insulting the bride and the bridegroom, if nothing else.'

'They knew I wouldn't take a drink. I told them that when they invited us.'

'Do you know what I think, Charlie? I think that I'd be going against my religion if I refused to take a drink at a wedding.'

'You're talking like a lunatic, Shamey, and that is because you have taken too much drink. You are all confused. Against your religion to abstain from drink! What's the next thing we'll hear?'

'What I mean is that there are times for jubilation. There are times for moving out of the dreary rut and singing and dancing and putting on one's best clothes and having a drink. One of them is when a man and a woman become united for life. I would like to see beauty and joy at a wedding. I would like to see the altar in the church decorated with all kinds of flowers. I would like to see the church lit with hundreds of candles. I would like to see the bride dressed like a queen. And I would like to see the gladness of heart that a drop of drink brings afterwards. In the same way, I would like to see a christening celebrated. The big events of life. At such times I feel as if I was in Heaven for a while. I leave the world behind me. I say "to the devil with the blight on the early potatoes; to the devil with the sheep that has the staggers". That is how I feel.'

'I agree with you, Shamey,' said Charlie the Rover's wife. 'Agree with every word you say.'

At this time, the group was standing at the end of the lane leading to Charlie's house. Charlie began his defence. He made no attempt to combat any of Shamey More's arguments. Instead, he launched out into an attack on the evils of drunkenness. And he ended with his favourite argument: 'They talk about Home Rule. But what good will Home Rule be to us if we are a nation of drunkards? Let us all go home in God's name and have some sleep. Good morning, everybody.'

The group broke up. 'You did let him have it,' said his wife to Charlie when they were inside their own house. 'He hadn't a leg to stand on. Of course, the poor man was three-quarters drunk. That is why he talked the way he did. I pretended to side with him. I saw the mad look in his eyes and I was afraid he would cut up rough. When he wakens up sober after a good sleep, he will be sorry for what he has said just now. He will be ashamed of himself. He is a decent man at heart. Which is another argument on your side. Shows what drink can do even to a good, decent Christian like Shamey More.'

III

In the meantime, we will leave Charlie the Rover to work hard on his little mountain farm and to practise and preach total abstinence; and we will cross the Atlantic to see how Felim Boyle is getting along in America.

Felim got over his grief, of course. After two years he married a girl from County Cavan. She was a good, sensible girl. Felim became a steady worker; and he and his wife and family were getting along nicely.

He used to correspond regularly with his sister Margaret, who was married at home. Margaret sent him any and every piece of news that she thought might interest him. One such item, in its own time and place, was the marriage of Bella Sweeney to Charlie the Rover. Felim had, of course, known Charlie in the years gone by.

'Well, I'm blest,' he said to himself when he read the letter. 'I am sorry for Bella. She was, I believe, a wise, thrifty girl and the making of a good housekeeper. But I can't say I am sorry for her old father. He banished me from Ireland because my father differed with him in politics ... Charlie the Rover will drink them out of house and home. Then old Ned Sweeney will sigh from the bottom of his heart and say that even the son of a Parnellite would be a much better match for his daughter than a lazy, rambling boozer. But it is no affair of mine. It is their own doing. Still, I am sorry for Bella: she deserved better.'

The following year he had another news bulletin from his sister. Charlie the Rover had turned out to be a miracle – the miracle of the age. He was out working in all weathers. He had given up drink completely, and, not alone that, but he was preaching a total abstinence campaign throughout the Rosses. 'But nobody pays any heed to him,' concluded the letter. 'And lots of people believe he won't keep it up.'

'Aye, that's the point. Will he keep it up?' said Felim to himself when he had finished reading the letter.

Three of four years afterwards, there was a further letter from the sister on Charlie the Rover: he will never taste it. 'Everyone is sure of that now. A few weeks ago he was at Garry Villy's wedding in Dunmore, himself and Bella; and he didn't taste one single drop of drink. Shamey More and others coaxed and pressed him all roads, but it was no use. On their way home, Shamey said it wasn't right for a Christian to refuse to take a drink at a wedding or at a christening. Bella agreed with Shamey. But Charlie was as firm as a rock. Not even Bella could move him. Isn't it a wonder of wonders?'

'It is,' said Felim to himself. 'I am glad for Bella's sake. Although I wouldn't be a bit sorry for her old scoundrel of a father ... Talking about him, I hope he has found out something since about the honesty and high morals of some of the lousy guttersnipes that downed Parnell.'

Twenty-five years Felim Boyle was in America when he decided he could afford to come back to the Rosses and spend a holiday at his sister's.

In due course, he arrived. He found that great changes had taken place in the Rosses since he had left it. A new generation had taken the place of the old one. His father and mother were dead, as were also Ned Sweeney and his wife.

'Charlie the Rover is a miracle,' said Felim's sister in the course of her replies to the enquiries her brother was making. 'He is twenty years married and not one drop of drink has he taken since – not even at a wedding or at a christening. As for the work he has done, you wouldn't know the place. An additional room built on, a new barn, a new cowhouse, not to mention the improvements he has made on the land ... By the way, you ought to run up tomorrow to see them.'

'I won't go tomorrow,' said Felim. 'Tomorrow is the seventh – the fair day in Ballintemple. I want to see what a fair day in the Rosses is like now. The day after tomorrow, please God, I'll run up to see Charlie the Rover and Bella.'

'The two of them will be very glad to see you,' said the sister.

The following morning, after having taken his breakfast, Felim set out for the fair – about five miles away. When he arrived at the village, he was surprised to see the street almost deserted. He went along to the cattle-market. Things were much the same there as he had seen in his young days – a crowd of men, a few middle-aged women, cows, calves, sheep, etc. But the younger people no longer found pleasure in coming to the village on a fair day and walking up and down the street for hours. That was one of the many changes that had taken place in the Rosses.

Felim had no interest in the cattle market. He had not come to the fair to buy or to sell. How the various prices ranged did not interest him. His lot was cast in another land.

He was about to turn away when he felt a grip on his shoulder. He turned round. A man held out his hand to him.

'Felim Boyle,' said he. 'You don't know me?'

'I am afraid I don't,' Felim had to admit.

'You don't know Charlie Rodgers – him that was Charlie the Rover?'

'Charlie the Rover!' said Felim. 'And how is every inch of you? I'm right glad to meet you after all the years, and to see you looking so well.'

Charlie said nothing. He held Felim's hand in his and remained silent. It was a decidedly awkward moment for Felim. He did not know what to say. With any other man it would have been different. If he could ask Charlie in for a drink, it would relieve the situation immediately. Charlie, however, was the first to break the deadlock. 'This way,' he said in a whisper, holding Felim's hand all the time until he led him into Hughie Neil's pub.

'Two glasses and two pints,' said Charlie to one of the girls behind the counter.

They drank the first drink almost in silence, for Charlie was not inclined to talk.

'Will you have the same again?' asked Felim.

'The same again,' replied Charlie. 'And again,' he added, after a pause.

'I won't take whiskey this time,' said Felim. 'It doesn't agree with me, never did.'

Later on Hughie Neil came into the bar. He looked at Felim Boyle and recognised him after a few seconds. Then he looked at Charlie in blank amazement.

'Come into the snug,' said he. 'You'll have more peace and comfort. There's nobody there at the moment.'

After some time, the publican opened the door of the snug and went in. 'You two are drinking too much and drinking it too fast, if you don't mind me saying it,' said he. 'Take it easy, especially you, Charlie.

Later on, you will come into the kitchen and have a bit of dinner. Then you'll have a drink from me and you'll go home.'

'Taking too much and drinking it too fast,' said Charlie when they were left by themselves. 'Hughie Neil is a decent man, always was. But he doesn't understand. He doesn't know what I am doing here today. He thinks I am just having a drink, but that is not all. I am rebaptising myself in the Faith of my Fathers. Felim Boyle, did you ever look at a shallow pool of bog-water gone dry in the heat of the summer? The bottom of it gets hacked and cracked. That's the way my heart is. Twenty years without a drink. I was at weddings and I refused to taste it. God rest Shamey More. I listened to him put forth arguments that no honest man could contradict. That was on a piercing, cold morning coming home from Garry Villy's wedding. I stood there shivering with cold and I was ashamed of myself. And then the silly rigmarole I came out with! About Ireland sober, Ireland free – as if Shamey More had been advocating drunkenness. Sure an Ireland that would have only men like what I have been for the last twenty years would die of dry-rot in one generation.'

After dinner they had a few more drinks, served at delayed intervals by Hughie Neil himself. Finally, Hughie prevailed on them to start for home.

'Hughie Neil,' said Charlie, as they were leaving, you are the decent man you always were. Please God we'll call again before Felim leaves for the States.'

'You will be very welcome,' said Hughie.

On the way home, Charlie's step was anything but steady. His speech was at times incoherent. But he made no reference to the great function he had fulfilled – rebaptising himself in the Faith of his Fathers.

'And how is Bella?' asked Felim, although he had asked the question already.

'Getting old, like us all,' replied Charlie. 'But otherwise the same. No change in her.'

They walked until they came to the end of the laneway leading to Charlie's house.

'We had a great day,' said Felim. 'I'll see you tomorrow.'

'You're not leaving me like that,' said Charlie. 'Come along with me up to the house.'

'It is too late this evening. I will go up tomorrow.'

'It's this evening I want you,' pleaded Charlie. 'This evening above all times … You needn't stay late. Just about half an hour. Then you can go home and go to bed. And, before you go to bed, get down on your knees and pray to God in thanksgiving for all the favours He has given you. Won't you do that?'

'I always try to say a mouthful of prayers,' said Felim.

'But tonight,' continued Charlie, 'tonight and tomorrow and every night and morning of your life say a prayer that you have never said before. A different prayer. A prayer from the bottom of your heart for the eternal repose of the soul of Charles Stewart Parnell. Don't forget now. You owe it to him ... His love affair may have delayed Home Rule, but it saved you from a life of chains and slavery.'

The Sea's Revenge

'God between us and harm,' said Michael Roe to me one day as we were talking about old, superstitious beliefs. 'But I remember the time when lots of people believed in them. Ignorance, I suppose, was at the bottom of them. Ignorance and want of belief in God. I remember many of the same old pishrogues. Things that in this age would surprise a young man like you. Many things were forbidden. You could not step into a boat before a coffin, you were supposed to push it in front of you. It was dangerous to be out of doors after sunset on May Eve. If you were setting out on a journey and the first person you met was a red-haired woman, it was unlucky to proceed and you were supposed to turn back. The baby was in the power of the fairies between birth and baptism, the young man or the young woman between betrothal and marriage. There were several other superstitions of that nature but they have died out, thanks be to God.'

'And were they all nonsense?' I asked.

The old storyteller remained silent for a little while. Then said he: 'If you believed in them or were afraid of them, it was easy to persuade you that they had some power over you. The best thing is not to think about them at all. The man who said "ignore a *geas* and the *geas* will ignore you" had a lot of wisdom in his head. But, as I have said, they have died out. Where would you find a man now as superstitious that he would not save a person from drowning for fear of the sea's revenge?'

'And did people believe that in the past?' I asked.

'I am afraid they did or, at least, some of them,' replied the old man. 'God protect us from the power of the Evil One but there was a man in this townland – he is still alive – and he fled to the hills and made his home there for fear of the sea's revenge.'

'That man believed in the superstition,' said I.

'He certainly did,' said Michael Roe, 'but he went against it on one occasion. He was every inch a man. He risked his life to save another. And what grander thing could a man do? He saved a man from drowning. Then he remembered the *geas* and he got afraid. Afraid of the sea's revenge. He stopped fishing. At last he fled to the hills and made his home there. Afraid that the sea would take his life to compensate her for the one he robbed her of.'

'That is a most amazing story,' said I. 'I never heard a word of it.'

'Perhaps,' said the old man, 'I ought to tell you how it all happened.' And he did.

II

Murty McRory from the townland of Rinnaweelin was big and strong and courageous. For generations the McRorys had been noted seamen and smugglers.

Young Murty was only a child of five years when his father took it into his head that it was time to begin to teach him to swim. It was proved that day that the boy would follow in the footsteps of his father and live up to their traditions.

'Have you any sense at all, at all?' said his wife to Fergal McRory when he came back after having given their child his first swimming lesson. 'Taking that baby out to swim! Sheer madness I call it.'

'He is five years,' said the father. 'Old enough to get his baptism.'

'But it was dangerous. It could have given the child a fright that he would never recover from.'

'The devil a fright he got. For a while I held him by the shoulders till he got used to the cold. Then I let him go – ready to grab him at any second, of course. He went down and the water closed over him. But, in a few seconds, he bobbed up again like a cormorant. He shook his head and snorted the water out of his nostrils. Then he stretched himself on the wave and began to swim. Never in all my life have I seen a first attempt like it. You would think he had been born and reared on the crest of a wave.'

That was Murty McRory when he was a child. When he grew to manhood he was the talk of the people along the entire coast from the Foreland to Crohy Head. He was a man of powerful strength and of great daring. And he was an expert boatman and swimmer.

Many a time he ran great risks in crossing the sound to and from the island of Inishglass on stormy days and nights. The attraction on the island was a girl he was in love with. Very often it was after midnight when he came back home from one of these trips. But he seemed to believe he was in no danger as long as he did not incur the sea's displeasure or provoke its wrath. For, like the rest of the McRory clan, Murty believed that the sea would have its revenge on anyone who tried to thwart its purposes. He was safe, he believed, as long as he did not rescue anyone from drowning. But he was not callous. He hoped he would never have to do what would wring the very heart within him – pass by a drowning man without trying to save him.

III

Una McGonigle was the most beautiful girl that ever lived. At least, Murty McRory thought she was and that is sufficient for our story. Una was an only child and lived with her parents on Inishglass, an island about two miles from the mainland. It would be an ideal marriage. The two young people were madly in love with one another and there was a home ready for Murty to walk into. And, of course, life on an island was what he was made for, being an expert boatman, swimmer and fisherman.

But, one day, something happened that shaped his destiny, different from what he had planned. He was coming home in his curragh after having set his lobster pots at the Roaring Reef. Another curragh, some distance in front of him, was on its way from Gola to Bunbeg with a cargo of grain for the mill. When the Gola man was in the middle of the sound, his curragh sprang a leak. He could do nothing except jump into the sea and try to keep afloat with the help of his paddle until someone would come to his rescue. He began to scream, hoping he would be heard on the mainland.

The wind was blowing from the mainland and the poor fellow's screams could not be heard there. He was on the verge of despair when he heard a shout coming from another direction: 'Keep quiet and hold the paddle under your chin.'

The drowning man turned his head around. And there was Murty McRory (acting on a noble impulse and forgetting all silly superstitions) ploughing his way towards him – pulling at his paddle for all he was worth. He rescued the drowning man and brought him safe to land.

And then, when he was back home and the neighbours congratulating him on his achievement, a painful thought entered his mind. He began to reflect. What had he done? He had rescued a man from drowning. He had robbed the sea of a victim ... But he could not, he reflected, let a man drown when it was in his power to save him. That would be little short of murder, if not indeed actual murder. The sensible reflection brought him temporary relief. But the maddening thought came back again and again. It was burning into his very heart. He could not banish it from his mind. He recalled all the stories he had ever heard that had a bearing on the case. He remembered the creed of the McRory clan – that the sea would have its revenge!

It is possible that, in the course of time, he would have forgotten about it, had it not been for a fright he got a few weeks afterwards. One day he ventured to sea, not by himself in a curragh, but as one of a boat's crew. They were fishing in Inishfree Bay and the weather looked fair enough. But a sudden storm arose. They made for home immediately and they went within an ace of being drowned when they were crossing the bar. Ever after that day Murty McRory was convinced that the sea was on his track and would get him at the next opportunity.

He could not take the risk a second time. That meant that he could not go to sea any more. What was he to do? He could not live at home without fishing. At last it occurred to him that he would go to Scotland. In the course of time he would send for Una McGonigle. She would go across and they would get married and spend their life in Scotland. It was a cruel fate. It meant living in perpetual exile from the land of his birth. But it was better to live in Scotland than to die in Ireland. Colmcille was supposed to hold the contrary view. But Colm was a man in a million. Besides, he had no Una McGonigle!

Murty decided to emigrate and it eased his mind for a day or two. Then he remembered that there was no bridge connecting Scotland with Ireland. To go to Scotland he must cross the sea. It would be in a big ship, of course. But the big ship was no safeguard. The sea would not let him escape from her a second time – even if it meant drowning hundreds along with him!

What was he to do? If he had a little holding of his own on the mainland, perhaps he would manage in some way. But he was the eldest of a large family and his father had nothing to give him. His case was most distressing. He could not live at home. He could not cross over water to leave home. There was only one line of retreat – retreat to the hills. It was his mother who thought of it. When a crisis comes, when one of life's difficult problems has to be solved, women are far more resourceful than men.

A kinswoman of Murty's mother was married and living in the hills – away beyond Knocksharragh, some ten miles inland. This woman was consulted. Would she happen to know any girl in her neighbourhood with a holding of her own who would be willing to marry Murty McRory? Murty had nothing but the clothes on his back but he was the finest man in the three parishes. It ought to be possible to get a wife for him with a house and a bit of land!

'I happen to know a girl that might have him,' said the kinswoman, mentioning the damsel by name. 'And I think she would do all right, considering that poor Murty is hemmed in the way he is.'

'Is she good-looking? Well, she is not exactly a beauty but I would not say she is ugly ... Her age? Well, there are no grey hairs in her head but I'd say she has all her wisdom teeth got ... She has a good place. There's only herself and her old father. They have plenty of mountain grazing – a good place for raising stock, especially sheep. And she comes of a tribe that is known to be worldly-wise. Too much so, perhaps. But sure, it is a good fault.'

Murty was told about the match that was being made for him. He did not sleep a wink that night ... He would, of course, have a safe asylum in the hills if the girl there were willing to accept him. But Una McGonigle? Oh, God in Heaven, wasn't it hard to part with her for ever and ever!

But, before long, they were as parted as any pair could be in this world. Una thought she had been slighted because Murty stopped his visits to her home. She did not believe the yarn about the sea's revenge. She was vexed. She was sad. She cried for days. Then her pride came to her rescue ... She would let Murty McRory know she was not going to pine for him ... And so she married another – a young man from her own island who was very fond of her. After that disaster it was easy for Murty to retreat to his sanctuary in the hills.

He proposed and was accepted. They were married. Murty McRory said goodbye to his native home and went off to live in the mountains – a good ten miles from the sea.

IV

'Is he still alive?' I asked the *seanchaí* when he had finished his story.

'He is alive and hale and hearty, I am told. He is not very old yet, you know. Can't be more than sixty-four or sixty-five years.'

It occurred to me immediately that I should like to visit this man who had fled from the sea's revenge and, if possible, find out from himself if he still believed in the foolish old superstition.

One summer's day I went to Loughfarragh in the hills to fish for trout. At least, that was the excuse. When I was leaving home my father told me I would have nothing for my journey. The weather was too dry, he said, and the sun too strong. I thought so myself but I did not mind. I had my own motive for going to the hills. The fishing was only an excuse.

About midday I came to the lake and began to fish. For over an hour I kept at it but didn't even get a rise.

At last, I reeled in my line, picked up my basket and set out for Murty

McRory's house. When I arrived Murty was manuring cabbage in a plot beside the house. He raised his head when I spoke to him. 'It's warm, boy,' said he, wiping the perspiration from his face. 'You are a stranger round these parts,' he added.

'Yes,' I agreed. 'I come from the lower country. From a townland they call Rinnaweelin – away down at the edge of the sea. I am a son of Felimy Roe, if you know him.'

'A son of Felimy Roe from Rinnaweelin?' he said, grasping my hand. 'Right glad I am to see you.'

Then he looked at my fishing-tackle and he smiled. 'Tell me this,' said he, 'did you expect to catch trout in that scorching sun?'

I told him I knew very little about freshwater fish or their habits.

'That is evident,' he said. 'We'll go inside for a while. The heat is killing at the moment. It is much worse here than down in Rinnaweelin. No cool sea-breeze in these stuffy glens. Sometimes I feel that I am suffocating.'

We went inside. A rugged, toothless, grey-headed, old woman was sitting in a corner carding wool. There was no one else in the house. Murty introduced me but the old woman had no welcome for me. 'Some people have a fine time of it,' she said. 'Others must work. Must work to earn their living. That's the way things are arranged in this world. By the by,' she asked, addressing herself to her husband, 'how are you getting on with the cabbage?'

'I should be finished by tonight,' he replied.

'Tonight! I thought you would be finished in about an hour. You know the turf out on Drumbawn must be footed. This dry spell won't last much longer. We could have rain in a day or two. I feel it in my bones,' she concluded as she went out to inspect the cabbage plot.

'You are a long time living up here,' said I to Murty when we had the house to ourselves.

'Forty years next Lammas,' he replied. 'Twenty-five years I was then, which leaves me sixty-five now.'

'You are standing the years well.'

'Not too bad at all. In ways, I am as strong as I ever was. Lifting a load or carrying a weight or digging lea-land. But, in other ways, I feel old age coming on me. My step is getting heavy. My breath getting short. I feel it when I climb to the top of Knocksharragh. Even so I like to go up there on Sunday afternoons when the weather is fine. It gladdens me and it saddens me, if you know what I mean. By the way, have you ever been up there?'

I told him I had not.

'You must go up there today since you happen to be here,' said Murty.

'I will go along with you. A beautiful spot is the top of Knocksharragh a day like today. I mean the view from it. No view like it in any other part of the country. You see the whole range of the coast from Horn Head to the Stags of Rossowen. I love to look at it even though … '

The old woman came back into the house. 'You should have put extra manure on the smaller plants,' she said. 'They need more.'

'Put on the kettle and get us a bite to eat,' said Murty.

The old woman made the tea in silence. It was plain from her looks that she had no time for visitors.

'We'll go now,' said Murty to me later on.

'Where in Heaven's name are you going?' asked the old woman in a rasping voice.

'Up the slope of Knocksharragh to show this young man a bit of scenery.'

'And the cabbage to be manured?'

'I was about to stop in any case. The sun is too strong. The leaves are drooping down dead. Must wait till the cool of the evening.'

I picked up my rod and basket.

'Leave your fishing-tackle there till we come back,' said Murty, taking the rod out of my hand. 'As the other man said, a chicken is heavy over a long distance.'

We set out. 'Across this way,' said the old man. 'I must call into Frankeen's. I hear the old woman is not too well these days. I must put my head in and enquire how she is. You can wait here for me. I won't be long.'

He stayed at Frankeen's for three or four minutes. Then I saw him come back out together with another old man. The two of them walked down to the edge of the lake and disappeared behind a huge boulder. In a short time Murty came back carrying a parcel in his hand.

'You would never guess what I have here,' said he.

'It would be hard for me.'

'I have as good a drop of poteen as was ever made, anywhere from Malin Head to the coast of Connaught. None of them can put the flavour on it like Frankeen does. And then the way he matures it. In oaken kegs, buried for a year under the bed of the lake.'

I felt embarrassed. Murty realised it. 'It's for myself as well as for you,' he said. 'Of course, you will have to drink your share of it … It is the least I can do on an occasion like this. It is so seldom I have a visitor from the old, home townland by the sea. But I'll enjoy it myself too.'

As we were going up the slope of the hill, Murty looked back. The old woman was standing on a little knoll outside the house, looking in our direction, with her hand shading her eyes.

'She is vexed with me now,' said Murty, 'vexed because I am not working at the cabbage. How little sense some people have. Sure, cabbage will be grown hundreds and hundreds of years after we're dead. Work will be done and work will be neglected. And the world will go on ... But we'll get over our tantrums, so we will. In any case, it does a man good to take the bit in his teeth an odd time and go his own way.'

V

We reached the top of the hill and we sat down. Murty took two glasses out of his pocket and he uncorked the bottle ... And, sure enough, Frankeen could make a good drop of poteen.

The scenery as seen from the top of the hill was magnificent. Looking down towards the coast I was surprised to see the islands so near the mainland. I said so to Murty.

'The height of your position is the cause of it,' he replied.

'I suppose so. But it looks strange when you see it for the first time. From here the island of Inishglass seems part of the mainland.'

'Ah,' said the old man, 'if only it were!'

'Is Michael Roe still alive?' he asked.

'Alive and kicking. And he is into his ninetieth year.'

'He is a great storyteller,' said Murty. 'I remember one story of his in particular. It was about a man who was in love with a beautiful maiden. But she had murder in her heart for him. She was ever ready to fire a poisoned arrow at him the first chance she got. He loved her all his life. He used to take delight in looking at her from a distance. But he could not go near her as she was waiting to have his life. Cruel, wasn't it?'

'Drink up man,' said he, holding the bottle between him and the light.

'Have you ever heard,' I ventured, 'that people long ago believed that the sea would have its revenge?'

'Long ago!' he replied. 'There are people still living who believe it. And a good reason they have for their belief. The sea will have its revenge, my boy. Always had. In my young days I saved a man from drowning. Of course, I have never regretted it. I am glad that I acted on the impulse and saved him. And I hope God will reward me for it on the Last Day. But the sea will have its revenge. That is why I left Rinnaweelin and came to live up here in the hills. I could not live at home. I could not go to Scotland; the sea was in my way. That is why I retreated to the mountains.'

'So you believed in the sea's revenge?'

'Of course I did. Why wouldn't I? Who could refuse to believe after the lesson I got? One day, about a week or so after the rescue, three or four of us were in Inishfree bay fishing. It was a grand day and, by all appearances, the weather was settled. But, all of a sudden, it began to blow a gale and we made for home. The wind was blowing in the direction of our course. And, although there was a heavy ground-swell, the surface of the sea was fairly even. As long as we did not run into any breakers, we were in no great danger. We came across the sound and up to the head of Illanbo. When we got that far we thought all danger past, for we would be sailing in the lea of the island until we got inside the bar. I was at the helm. Shamey More was sitting on the thwart opposite me, facing me. All of a sudden, Shamey lets one frightful scream and he was as white as a sheet.'

'Look out astern!' he shouted.

'I turned my head around. A huge, green mountain of water with wisps of white foam flying from its crest was rolling in after me. I could not keep any closer to the rocks of the island. I could not lie over to the other side for fear of grounding on the sand-banks of the bar. My one and only chance was to keep the deep.'

'The wave came along until it reached us. The boat seemed to climb backward on to the top of it and then slide down the other side. But the second wave was on the heels of the first, and the third on the heels of the second. I'll never forget that third wave. To this day I can see the boat poised on its crest. There was nothing I could do. There was no steerage: the rudder was lifted clear out of the water. I was there at the helm like a bit of a log, powerless to do anything. I was sure my last moment had come. I closed my eyes and I made an Act of Contrition. But the boat slid down from the third wave and righted herself. The wind filled her sail and we were underway again. I am sure you have often heard of 'The Three Drowning Waves' ... That is what happened to me yon day, crossing the bar. After that, I was sure the sea was on my tracks and that there would be no escape from her next attack. So you see, my boy, it is no foolish superstition the belief that the sea will have her revenge. Once you incur her wrath, she is sure to punish you.'

'But you escaped it,' said I.

He looked at me for a few seconds. Then said he, 'I tell you, young man, the sea will always have her revenge – if not in one way, in another.'

VI

We spent a long time on the top of the hill. Murty told me all about his sea adventures when he was a young man and living 'at home' as he called his native townland. Then he related the smuggling adventures of his ancestors for four generations back. I had great pity for him. I realised that he had loved the sea all his life and that it was breaking his heart that he could only look at her from a distance, often on fine Sunday evenings in summer. He told me he would come up to the top of the hill and sit there for hours gazing down on the distant sea. He was like the man in the story who was crazed with the love of a beautiful woman and whose life depended on keeping far away from her.

'At last,' said he, looking at the empty bottle. 'It is time we were sliding down.'

It was within an hour of sunset when we arrived at the house.

'I won't go in this time,' said I. 'Will you bring me out my rod and my little creel? It is getting late. I would like to be down past Loughkeel before it gets dark.'

'Could you not stay the night with us?' said the old man. 'I would like to have your company ... This house of ours is a lonely house. A dreary house. Never a ray of gladness to brighten it. Never a burst of laughter to make one feel young again.'

'I am very thankful to you for your kind invitation,' I replied. 'But my people at home would be worried. They would be afraid I got caught in a fog and fell down a cliff and was killed. You know the thoughts that come into people's heads when anyone is missing.'

Just then the old woman came out. She was fierce-looking in her anger. She was about to pass us without even looking at us. But her husband spoke to her.

'Where are you going, dear?' he asked, gently.

'Where am I going? I am going to bring home the cows,' she replied in a bitter, rasping voice. 'To bring home the cows two good hours after the time they should be milked.'

'Go inside, my dear woman, and rest your bones and I will go for the cows,' said the old man.

'You will go for the cows,' she hissed. 'If you had any thought for the cows or for your work or for house or home, or for me, you wouldn't have spent the best part of a fine summer's day upon the top of Knocksharragh drinking poteen.'

And she swept past us.

'What did I say to you?' said Murty to me.

I went inside and picked up my fishing-tackle. Murty did not invite me to sit down. He came out along with me and escorted me on my way for nearly a mile.

'Straight across in front of you,' said he, giving me the final directions. 'When you have passed Tullybrack, keep to your left. There is a soft morass to your right ... You have daylight enough to bring you on to the road at Loughkeel.'

'Goodbye and many thanks for a most pleasant day,' I said.

'God bless you son,' he replied, shaking my hand. 'Your visit made me feel young again for a little while. And now you have seen for yourself that the sea will always manage to have her revenge.'

Blagadán

Blagadán was a travelling tinsmith or tinker as we called them in the Rosses. We did not know where he came from. We did not know his real name. He was called Blagadán (which in Irish means 'bald-pate') because he had no hair. It was not that his hair had fallen out, it had never grown. His head from the back of his neck to his forehead was as bare and as shiny as a steel plate.

Blagadán was held in high esteem by the people of the Rosses. He was honest and honourable. He was fond of children. He was kind to old people. He would do his best to help anyone who had got into difficulties and, in addition to all these worldly qualities, he was brave. His bravery had been proved on two occasions. The first was the day he stopped a runaway horse that was madly rushing down the crowded street in Meenaleck on a fair day. The second was when he plunged in fully-clad and rescued a child that had fallen over the pier head in Burtonport.

My father was a good poteen-maker and he was a good strategist as well. For a quarter of a century he had plied his trade and outwitted the police all the time. But, at last, he got a fright: he went near to being caught, despite all his plans. That made him stop the poteen business. This last attempt is part of my story.

One day Blagadán came to a fair in the Rosses with a donkey loaded with tin cans. My father bought a can from him but the can was only an excuse to cover another transaction.

'My old still is nearly burnt out,' said he to Blagadán. 'I don't know the day or the hour she'll burst. I wonder how soon could you make a new one for me?'

'I could make a still for you inside a week,' said Blagadán. 'But, if I were you, I'd give it the go-by for a while. The hunt is very hot since the new crowd of Revenue Police have come to Meenmore. Many a man picked up a still or worm and ran away to a hiding-place when it was only the ordinary police were after him. But these fellows carry firearms and, if a man tried to run away, they'd think no more of shooting him dead than you would of shooting a rabbit.'

'Don't worry, they won't get me,' said my father. 'Do you know that I made a go of poteen inside in my own barn and the police searching the caves of the shore within a few hundred yards of me? That is how it is done. When the police are after you, it is wrong to hide from them. They will get you in your hiding-place. The only way is to make them believe you are operating in some other place. They will keep their eye on that place. At last, they will pounce on it. Of course, they will find nothing and they will give up the chase for a while. So don't be afraid. They won't catch me at this hour of my life.'

'Very good,' said Blagadán. 'I'll make a new still for you. But watch your steps for I can tell you the hunt is hard at the moment. Away beyond Dungloe they've stopped making it altogether. They are afraid. The most daring of them are afraid since this new crowd has come to Meenmore. They say their officer is a born sleuth-hound.'

In due course, my father got his new still and he hid it away in a sand-bank. Then he began to work his plan. He let out the information in one of the village shops that he intended going to a certain cave near the foothills to make a go of poteen. He was seen a few times going in that direction carrying a bag on his back.

But the police officer did not fall for this ruse. He came to the conclusion that my father would go to one of the islands. And he had an agent that my father knew nothing about – a local informer. The informer was instructed to keep a constant eye on the boats in the townland and report as soon as any one of them was missing from the usual mooring-ground.

One day my father and two other men set out for the island of Inishfree with all their equipment and material. That night, six police, armed with rifles, came to the little harbour of Bunbeg. Six or seven fishing-boats were moored there but the police did not take any of them. They were afraid to navigate the sound on their own at night. They knew at least that it was dangerous. They would have looked for a pilot but they were told it would be impossible to find one. The men of Gweedore had remembered little scraps of their history, had remembered such personages as Father McFadden, Pat O'Donnell and James Martin.

The only thing the police could think of was to send for the coastguards. Two of them went to the coastguard station while the rest remained on guard at the harbour to make sure that no other boat would put to sea before them.

Blagadán happened to be in the neighbourhood. He heard that a force of police from the Rosses had come to Bunbeg harbour and that two of them had been seen going to the coastguard station. He concluded they were preparing to raid the island and he decided to act on his own and to act quickly. He went to a creek in Magheralosk where he knew there was a curragh. He launched it and set out for the island.

A skilful pilot would have taken a roundabout way to avoid the sunken reefs. But Blagadán knew nothing about the reefs and he took a straight course from the mainland to the island. He got there long before the police.

'Merciful Lord!' exclaimed my father when Blagadán had told his story. 'You ran a terrible risk. In broad daylight a skilful pilot would not dream of coming that way. Imagine it,' said he to the other men. 'Out the Black Bar and across the Yellow Reef at this stage of the tide. You don't know the danger you were in.'

'It is better at times not to know where the danger is,' said Blagadán. 'But here I am and that's that. The police will be here in about an hour's time. What are you going to do?'

'There is only one thing to be done,' replied my father. 'We must empty the barrels. We'll hide the gear in a sand-bank. Then we'll take your curragh in tow and slip up the channel when we hear the sound of their oars coming across the bar.'

II

We were not expecting my father when he returned home that night. He told us all that had happened. I remember it well. I was eight years old at the time.

'There must be an informer in this very town,' he said. 'For how else would the police know we had gone to the island? However, I'm finished with poteen-making. Never again will I put a still on a fire ... It is easy enough to baffle the police. But you are helpless against the informer, for you don't know who he is.'

'In a way I am not sorry you are finished with it,' said my mother. 'They are on your track for years and, if you were caught, you would be fined the full amount.'

'I know that,' replied my father. 'The fine is a hundred pounds. They can reduce it to six, and they nearly always do. But there would be no reduction in my case which would mean that we'd be turned out of doors and there would be nothing for us but the poor-house. But Blagadán saved me this time. With God's help, I'll save myself for the rest of my life.'

'Isn't Blagadán a great man?' said my mother.

'Blagadán!' said my father. 'There is not another man like him in Ireland. How he crossed the sound, God only knows. It was the first time he had a curragh paddle in his hand. He did not know the way. He took straight course from Magheralosk to the islands and went over five sunken reefs. If any one of them happened to break under him, it was all over with him. We can never forget him.'

'Let us all pray for him, every morning and every night,' said my mother, 'that God and his Blessed Mother will protect and guard him.'

The following day six armed policemen came to our house. They searched the barn and the cow-house. They came into the kitchen and tossed and turned everything. They even lifted the baby out of its cradle, but they found nothing.

Many a time afterwards my father went over the whole story and told us of the danger he was in when Blagadán, at the risk of his own life, came to his rescue. 'We'd have been banished from the soil of Ireland,' he would say. 'Banished for ever only for him. We must never forget him. And now, Jack,' he would say to me, 'when you grow up to be a man, watch out for Blagadán. Find out where you are likely to meet him. If he ever happened to be in trouble or difficulty, be sure to help him. If you find him hungry, you must share your last crust with him. The obligation is on you; you must fulfil it if ever the occasion arises.'

I used to imagine myself a big, strong man and paying Blagadán the debt we owed him. In my imagination I came to his rescue several times. He was attacked by a band of robbers in the darkness and loneliness of the Black Gap. I came to his aid in the nick of time and the two of us beat the attackers until they cried for mercy ... I brought his runaway horse to a stand-still and saved him from a terrible death ... He was marooned on a lonely island in stormy weather without food. I put to sea in a curragh and brought him safe and sound to the mainland.

Blagadán stopped coming to the Rosses. We did not know why. We did not know where he had gone to but I was firmly resolved that when I grew up I would seek him out and offer him my heart-felt gratitude and my help if ever he should need it.

I did grow up. I was a man and it was time I began to show my gratitude and discharge my obligations. I went to the summer fair and made enquiries, but without result.

'I'll tell you where you'll meet him if he is in the country at all,' said my father. 'At the Lammas Fair in Glenties. All the tinkers of the county come to that fair.'

When the date came round I went to the Lammas Fair. There I met an old man who had known Blagadán. 'He left the country years ago,' said the old man, 'but I don't know exactly where he is. The last time I was talking to him (and that's years and years ago) he said to me he was thinking of going to America. 'A tinker's trade,' says he to me, 'is hardly worth anything now. No poteen, no stills. And,' says he, 'the times have changed. The people have stopped using tinware. Nobody takes his tea out of a tin mug now.' That is what he said to me ... In any case, he is gone from the country. Of that I am certain and I'm nearly sure it's to America he went for he was always talking about it. Did you know him?'

'I saw him a few times when I was a boy. My father knew him well and was very fond of him.'

'Everyone who knew Blagadán was fond of him. He was a fine man every way you took him. He was straight and honest. He was as gentle as a lamb and as brave as a lion at the same time. Did you ever hear of the night he crossed in a currach to one of the islands to save the Rosses man who was in there making poteen?' And he told me the story I knew so well.

'That man was my father,' said I when the old tinker had finished his tale ... 'I am dying to meet him and pay back the debt of gratitude I owe him ... I am thinking of going to America but my chance of meeting him isn't one in a thousand millions. Imagine the vast American continent.'

'I think we could narrow the area a bit,' said the old man. 'If he is in America – and I am almost certain he is – you will find that he is in New York. More than once he told me that he had two brothers living in that city. Now, wouldn't you know the back of his neck among a million without one single particle of hair on it? Remember the old Gaelic proverb: the people meet, the hills and the mountains don't.'

There was a ray of hope left. Enough to make me decide to go to America.

III

I went across to Scotland to earn my passage money and got work in the shale-mines near the town of Broxburn in Mid-Lothian. I was saving every possible penny. There was nothing else in my mind but America and Blagadán.

And then, all of a sudden, I decided not to cross the Atlantic. The whole project seemed absurd to me. What chance had I of finding Blagadán in America, even if I could be certain he was in New York? Why, I didn't even know his name, let alone his address. I said to myself, what chance would I have of meeting him at a street corner in New York? It was a mad idea ... But if ever he comes back – and I hope in God he does – I will fulfil my father's wish.

Who made me see reason? A beautiful girl of eighteen years whose name was Nora Sweeney. Her father kept a small hardware shop on the

Edinburgh Road, Broxburn. One day I went into the shop to buy a penknife. That was the first time I saw Nora. Inside a fortnight I had an assortment of articles of hardware, including a screwdriver and a tin opener.

After a time, I got to know Nora so well that I could drop into the shop of an evening and make no purchase. I got to know her father too. He was a big man with a shock of white hair. His eye was keen and piercing. At first sight he gave the impression that he was not a very sociable person but, when I got to know him better, I found that he could be pleasant, even friendly at times.

In due course I began to walk out with Nora on Sunday afternoons. I often called to the house for her. Both her father and mother were friendly and seemed quite pleased with our courtship.

St Patrick's Day came. I met Sweeney in the street as I was on my way to his house. He asked me to turn back with him and have a drink. I would not, of course, refuse his kind invitation, although I should much prefer to be in the kitchen looking at Nora and talking to her. But then, another thought occurred to me: sooner or later I should have to ask this man for his daughter's hand. Why not today, after a few drinks?

We went into the Shamrock Bar and we sat down. When we were nearly through the third drink I plucked up courage to say the word: 'I want to marry your daughter. I love her with all my heart. I will do everything in my power to make her happy.'

'What age are you?' he asked gently.

I told him.

'Well, now,' he said in a very friendly tone of voice, 'both you and Nora are a bit young yet. If you take my advice, you will work for three or four years as you've been doing, and earn all the money you can. It is most unwise for a man to get married on nothing. You can take that from me, I am telling you from my own experience. You are very young. Put a bit of money by and then get married. For one thing, you will need a house ... Love is all right in its own way but it needs a bit of financial backing.'

This was a setback. But still, the situation on the whole was good. I had what amounted to the father's consent. The only condition attached to it was that we were to wait for three or four years. Nobody could say that it was an unreasonable condition, considering that I was only twenty-two years of age and Nora not quite nineteen.

After that day saving money was the one and only thought in my mind. I gave up smoking. I worked every hour of overtime I could get. I got a post-office book and I lodged every penny I could spare.

One day I got a letter from a cousin of mine who was in New York. He asked me if I still had a notion of going to America. If I had, he would help me: he would lend me some of my passage money.

I wrote back thanking him. I said I had abandoned the idea of going to America and that I intended to make my home in Scotland. I was going to marry the sweetest girl on earth. Nora Sweeney was her name.

Then I remembered what first put America into my head. I meant to go in search of Blagadán. What a crazy idea, I said in my own mind. Going to America in search of a man whose name, even, I don't know. But, if ever by accident I should meet Blagadán – and it must be by accident if I am to meet him at all – I will have a hearty welcome for him and I will do all in my power to help him if he should need my help.

IV

One evening the following August I was on my way to see my love and I met her as if she had been looking out for me. The moment I saw her, I knew there was something troubling her. Her face was dark. Her expression was disturbed.

'We'll go down here along the canal,' she suggested.

We walked along in awful silence for a few minutes. Then the thunder-clap! She could not marry me, she said. Her father would not give his consent.

'And why?' I stammered when I recovered my speech.

'He wants me to marry another man, the man who owns the public house at the bottom of the Main Street.'

'What do you say yourself, Nora? Where does your heart lie?'

'I could not go against my father's wishes.'

'Your father has no right to dictate to you in this matter. We'll get married and we'll tell him afterwards.'

'You can't do that. You must remember that you are in Scotland and that I am still a minor. My father would have you arrested and tried and you would get penal servitude … In any case, I would not go against him in the matter.'

'But there is another side to the question. Last Patrick's Day he gave his consent to our marriage. I will go straight up to the house to him now and ask him why he is going back on his promise.'

'He won't be at home until late tonight; he's gone to the city on business. If you must talk to him, let it be tomorrow evening. I won't be at home. I hate scenes. But I must tell you, his mind is made up.'

I spent hours that night lying awake, suffering tortures that I cannot describe. When at last I fell asleep, I dreamt that Nora and I had made a runaway marriage and that we were fleeing frantically towards the shores of Lochgyle, pursued by her father with a band of armed soldiers.

I woke with a start. I looked at my watch. It was only three o'clock. I lay awake for the rest of the night. Many thoughts rushed through my frenzied brain. I asked myself many questions. Was this marriage being forced on Nora or was it by her consent? Was Nemesis punishing me for having abandoned my search for Blagadán?

The following evening, after my day's work, I went to Sweeney's to have it out with him. The woman of the house opened the door and brought me into a small parlour. Sweeney was sitting at a table with a pile of papers in front of him. We talked about different things for about ten minutes. But I could feel a terrible tenseness in the atmosphere.

At last, I came to the object of my visit. 'I want to marry Nora and I thought there was no objection to me.'

'Nora is going to marry another man,' said Sweeney, 'and that's that. There's no more to be said.'

'Pardon me, Mr Sweeney,' I replied, 'but I think there is quite a lot to be said. I understood from you last Patrick's Day that your daughter had your consent to marry me.'

'I never gave any such consent. I said you had nothing to get married on. I gave you a bit of fatherly advice. That was all.'

'You gave me to understand that I could marry your daughter when I had enough money saved to get a house for her.'

'I am sorry if you took a meaning out of my words that I never intended them to have.'

I felt my anger rising. 'It is unjust,' said I. 'Unjust to your daughter in particular. Even though you are her father, you have no right to make her marry against her wishes.'

'Who told you she was marrying against her wishes? In any case, whether she is or she is not, you will permit me to say it is no concern of yours.'

'But you promised her to me.'

'I tell you again I did no such thing and I find it hard to believe that you failed to understand what I said.'

This was too much for me. My temper got the better of me. In any case, the game was lost. And I decided to tell this heartless, old schemer what I thought of him.

'You are a mean, old man,' I said. 'You know in your heart last Patrick's Day you promised me your daughter in marriage. And now you are going back on your pledged word because another man comes along who has more of the world's goods than I have. Why didn't you say that straight out? You didn't, because you are a coward – a mean, despicable coward. That's what you are.'

'Well,' said Sweeney, running his fingers through his white hair, there was a day and the man who would call me a coward to my face would have either to prove his words or swallow them. But that day is past and gone. I am an old man now. You are a young man. You can call me a coward without any danger to yourself – if that is any credit to you.'

Then a terrible look came into his eyes. He put his hand to his head, pulled off the wig he was wearing and flung it on the floor. His head was as bare as a cannon-ball.

'Your father was a better man than you,' he began, in a voice choking with emotion, 'and he would not dream of calling me a coward. And, if I am not far mistaken, he would not be too pleased with you if he knew what you have just said. The night I went across in a curragh to the island, to Inishfree, to warn your father that the police were coming, neither he nor any other man would call me a coward. I risked my life that night to save your father. Little did I dream that I should live to see the day when your father's son would call me a coward.'

Single Combat

Pinkeen was small but he was not a weakling. He was a good little worker for his size and weight. When his time came to marry he would have no difficulty in getting a wife. For, along with a bit of land, he had a nice penny of money – a legacy left him by an uncle who had died in America.

Yet, for all that, he was not satisfied with his lot in life. Far from it. 'Pinkeen' was only a nickname but, much as he disliked it, it was the only name by which he was known. If you knew him, you would say the name suited him as if it had been made for him. You would come to that conclusion whether you understood the meaning of the word or not. It was not necessary to understand it. All you had to do was to look at Pinkeen and you would say to yourself: 'That is how languages are made.'

As a baby, he was very tiny, and there lay the origin of the nickname. 'My poor pinkeen,' his mother would say. 'And the size of him. But he won't be always small. The day will come when he will be a big man. I've often heard the old women say that Big Toal Gallagher down here was the smallest baby they had ever seen. Not the size of my fist, they say. And look at him now. One of the biggest men in the Rosses. So your day will come, my little pinkeen.'

But that day never came. As a baby, Pinkeen was a pinkeen. As a boy and as a youth, he was a pinkeen. As a man, he was a pinkeen and nothing but a pinkeen.

He would give anything to be big. It was his life's ambition. It was his ruling passion. When he was a young stripling, his mother bought him a man's shirt. At that time, the boys in the Rosses used to wear shirts of unbleached calico. The men wore shirts of coarse cotton with alternate red and white stripes. It was always a day of joy and gladness for a youth the day he got into a man's shirt.

Pinkeen got a man's shirt and it made him work harder and more constantly than he used to work when he was in calico. On cold, frost days in winter he would go out and strip off his coat and spend hours cleaning drains or delving lea-land. It was a type of work that could wait for longer days and warmer weather. But Pinkeen wanted to let the neighbours see that he was wearing a man's shirt.

The next event of note in his life was the legacy. People thought it would have the effect of making him foppish – that he would buy fine clothes with a view to make himself attractive in the eyes of the young girls of the neighbourhood. But these people were wrong in their forecast. Pinkeen's first resolution regarding the legacy was to hoard every penny of it.

The years passed and Pinkeen decided to get married. He passed over several eligibles in his native townland and selected a huge woman from Bunnawack known by the name of Nabla Wore. The neighbours had their own comments to make on the match.

'He'll think himself big because he is married to a big woman.'

'No, that's not it. Because he is small himself he wants compensation by having big sons. He must have heard the old proverb: "Select your wife and your children the one and the same day."'

We do not know for certain what motive actuated him in making his selection. All we can say is that he married Nabla Wore, the biggest and strongest woman in the three parishes.

Pinkeen was forever talking about fighting and fighting-men. 'Black Jimmy Boyle has a powerful right,' he would say. 'I saw him fighting with a Highlander a few years ago in Edinburgh. A powerful right, so he has. But his footwork is weak. The man that is slow on his feet will never make a first-class boxer. That is one of the tricks of the game and the best of them. Keep your man running round after you until you wear him down. Then, when you have him tired out and confused, let him have it. And down he goes.'

And then came the day when Pinkeen himself went into action. He was at the harvest fair in Mullineeran. At that time a little man known by the name of Smiglum used to attend all the fairs in the county. Smiglum was a tinsmith by trade but he used to supplement his earnings with a pellet gun and target on fair days. He wore an old coat that had been made for a big man. He shortened the sleeves but left the body of the coat as it had been originally. It was far too wide for him and he seemed lost in it. It came down below the knees which made the wearer's legs look still shorter than they were. Taken all in all, Smiglum was a poor specimen to look at. But he was a game little fellow and ready to defend his good name and his profession.

Pinkeen, after repeated failures, said the gun was designed to shoot wide of the target aimed at. Smiglum replied in terms that made it impossible to continue the argument in words. And so the two of them went at it. It is not easy to say for certain – though we can make a good guess – what the final result of the contest would have been had they been allowed to fight it out. Two or three of Pinkeen's neighbours were standing by and they separated the combatants. From which we are inclined to conclude that they were anything but hopeful of Pinkeen's chances of victory.

Perhaps it was best so. There was no victor. But then there was no vanquished. Pinkeen could say he had fought. He did talk and he had his own version of the story. 'If we had been allowed to fight it out, I'd soon settle him. He thought he could get in on me with his head down – the biggest risk a man can take. I gave him one uppercut and, I can tell you, it straightened him. He reeled and he staggered. He shook like an aspen leaf. I was just about to finish him with one on the pit of the stomach. But just at that very moment, my hands were caught from behind and I was held tight. As soon as your man saw his chance of escape, he picked up his gun and target, and off with him as fast as his legs could carry him. He didn't stop running until he left the Gap of Glengesh behind him. I'll bet you what you like you'll never see him again in this part of the country with his crooked, old gun.'

II

Pinkeen spent that winter talking about fighting. Some of the neighbours were of the opinion that his wife, Nabla Wore, ought to tell him to have sense, that she ought to point out to him that whatever gifts he had or had not, he wasn't a fighter. Others alleged that Nabla Wore was as bad as himself, that she was supposed to have said she was glad that neighbours had separated himself and Smiglum for that Pinkeen had a wicked temper and could kill a man when he was roused. But those who said that did not know all the facts. They did not know that Pinkeen was very close-fisted and that the only way his wife could wangle an odd shilling out of him was to play up to him and pretend to believe that he was a real fighter.

His mother-in-law was living with him. She had no illusions about Pinkeen's prowess and one day she made that clear. It happened like this. It was the springtime of the year and the early potatoes were sprouting in the ground. And then, the source of many a Rosses feud – the hen with a clutch – went into action. A hen with a brood of chickens can do untold damage in a plot of potatoes that are just sprouted. This is only natural: very often the hen with a clutch has as many as a dozen hungry mouths to feed. One day a man from the near neighbourhood came to Pinkeen's door and complained angrily about the destruction done to his early potatoes by Nabla Wore's hens. It was Pinkeen's mother-in-law who answered him. Tempers became frayed on both sides.

'If you don't keep your hens away from my potatoes,' said the man, 'I'll kill every one of them I get my hands on.'

'Donal,' said the old woman, 'it is easily known we haven't a man in the family to send out to settle with you. If we had, you wouldn't come barging to our door like a raging lion. Alas for those who are helpless.'

Pinkeen was away in the bog for turf with the donkey and cart. When he came home he was told about the hen and the neighbour's potatoes. Later on he was told by some busybody what the mother-in-law had said: 'If we had a man in the family that we could send out to settle with you.' This clearly meant: 'We have a thing that wears trousers but that is all we have. We have no man that one could call a man. We have only Pinkeen.'

Pinkeen jumped to his feet. 'I am going straight over to him now,' he said. 'First of all, I'll pay him for whatever damage the hen has done to his potatoes. Then I'll beat him for coming barging to my door when he knew I wasn't at home and that there was nobody to face him but women.'

'Don't go near him till your anger cools down,' said his wife. 'You know what a wicked temper you have. You might do something you would be sorry for afterwards. Sit down there for a while and smoke your pipe.'

'I won't sit down,' said Pinkeen. 'I will go over to the house to him and I'll smash his brocky face on his own doorstep.'

'I implore you!' said the wife, and she put her arms around him.

'Let me go, woman!' said Pinkeen.

Nabla Wore tightened her grip. Pinkeen felt his ribs hurting him under the muscles of his wife's arms. 'Very good,' he gasped. 'Maybe you are right.'

'Of course I am right,' said his wife, letting go her hold. 'I know your wicked temper.'

Afterwards Pinkeen said to the neighbours he was glad he had taken his wife's advice. 'I might disable the man for life,' said he, 'and then I'd be very sorry. But that's me for you. I go clean mad when I am roused. And, while the fit lasts, I could half-kill a man. It's a good thing I have a sensible wife. Only for her patience and good advice, the Lord only knows what I might do at times.'

Of course, the neighbours laughed and sneered at him when they got his back turned.

'It's the mercy of God he has a sensible wife to advise and restrain him or he might have killed Donal Andy.'

'It's the mercy of God, rather, that he has a strong wife. She put her arms around him and she caught him like the grip of a vice until he was gasping for breath and ready to fall (so the old woman tells me). Only for that he would go over to Donal Andy. And we know what would happen then: Donal Andy would put him across his knee and give him a good spanking.'

'It is a pity she didn't let him go. About ten yards from his own house he'd go. Then he'd cool down all of a sudden and come back. And he would say that it would be the height of folly to draw Donal Andy's blood for the sake of a little bit of scraping that a hen had done in a potato plot.'

In due course, Pinkeen was told all this (for there will always be mischief-makers in the world). He felt humiliated beyond words. There was a stain on his honour. Nothing would redeem him but a feat of outstanding bravery.

III

Big Ned of the Glen was well over six feet in height and he was broad and heavy in proportion. He was a powerful man but a peaceful man, as long as he was left alone. Of him it could be said that he had a giant's strength but that he would not use it as a giant unless he had to. Many a man attacked Big Ned for no other reason than to be able to say afterwards that he had been fighting with the champion. For Ned was not dangerous. That the punishment should fit the crime was not one of his theories. According to his code, the punishment should fit the capacity of his antagonist. And very often a fighting man's reputation depended on the amount of beating Ned found necessary to give him. For that reason Ned was not dangerous. If he had opened a gash six inches long in the forehead of the first man who attacked him or smashed his jawbone, he might have peace for the rest of his life. But that was not Big Ned's way. If you attacked him, he gave you what he thought you could stand in the way of punishment, and no more.

What I have to tell now may seem strange. But strange things happen and have happened from the beginning of time. Pinkeen decided to fight Big Ned of the Glen.

It was a desperate remedy. But then the disease was desperate. Poor Pinkeen's heart was sad and sore ever since the day of the clutch hen. The neighbours had been saying cruel things about him. And then what his mother-in-law had said was gall and worm-wood to him every time he thought of it: 'Donal, it is easily known we haven't a man in the family to send out to settle with you, etc.' It was a cruel blow. It was a most painful humiliation. Nothing would redeem him except a deed of undoubted bravery.

Once the thought of fighting Big Ned occurred to him, he could not put it out of his mind. He used to sit by the fireside at home and shut his eyes. The whole scene would appear to him in his imagination. The next fair day in Dungloe he would walk up to Big Ned and hit him. The fight would not last long. But that did not matter. Before twenty-four hours it would be talked about from Gweedore to Gweebarra. Nobody would say: 'Big Ned beat Pinkeen.' This is how the conversation would go – as imagined by Pinkeen.

'I hear Pinkeen and Big Ned of the Glen were fighting in Dungloe on the fair day.'

'Were they really? What was the cause of the fight?'

'Well, now, I can't give the exact details. Something about the buying of a cow. Pinkeen was buying a cow and Big Ned is supposed to have butted in on the bargain and offered more. Of course, that may not be true. But, in any case, they fought, of that I am certain.'

Then Pinkeen imagined and rehearsed his own comments. 'Damn on him anyway. Even if he is big and strong, he has no right to ride rough shod over the people. I suppose he thought he had only to look cross at me and that I would take fright and run away from him. But I faced up to him and I fought him while I lasted. And maybe, if the truth were known, he was tired enough of me ... If every man did what I did, Big Ned would not walk on the people the way he does.'

IV

The summer fair day came – the national festival of the Rosses at the time. Most of the people in two parishes were gathered in Dungloe that day. Big Ned of the Glen was there. So was Pinkeen. They passed each other a few times in the street – one going up, the other coming down. Big Ned did not see Pinkeen, but Pinkeen saw Ned.

Big Ned of the Glen is a powerful man, thought Pinkeen. The size of him! Never in all his life was he as big as he is today. I hope he won't hit me a heavy blow. Just a light tap that would peel a bit of skin off my face. I could put sticking-plaster on it. People would say: 'I saw Pinkeen with a patch of sticking-plaster on his forehead.' And, in reply: 'I suppose you did. Himself and Big Ned of the Glen had a bit of a scrap. Do you know what I am going to tell you? Pinkeen is a bully man. That's what he is and no doubt about it. For none but a bully man would put them up to Big Ned of the Glen.'

He and Big Ned passed each other again. Ned was getting bigger and bigger. Getting bigger and fiercer in his looks!

Pinkeen went into Brennan's public house and drank a glass of whiskey. It did him no good. He called for a second glass. He gulped it down quickly. It made him shiver and he felt a burning sensation in his throat and chest. He came out and walked across to the cattle market. On his way back he took another drink. But his courage was as low as ever.

He sat down on the wall of the bridge and tried to think. Should he give up the adventure and not bother with Big Ned? It might be the best thing to do. But then, like a steel dagger through his heart went his mother-in-law's cruel words: 'Donal, if we had a man in the family to send out to settle with you … ' There was a stain on his name and honour that nothing but blood would wash away … The ordeal would have to be faced. But oh, that it were over! That he were going back to the public house – this time with one or two of his neighbours – and a patch of sticking-plaster on his face!

He came back up the street. Big Ned was standing with his back to a seat in front of the hotel. He appeared to be expecting someone for he was looking down in the direction of the bridge. We do not know what he was thinking of at that particular moment. But we can be certain that for one solitary second it did not enter his mind that Pinkeen was about to attack him.

It must be now or never, thought Pinkeen to himself. He went round and climbed on to the bench behind Big Ned. Ned's back was as broad as a curragh, he thought. And his neck was like the trunk of a tree! Pinkeen jumped up on the giant's shoulders and began to beat him with his fists on the back of the neck.

For a few seconds, Big Ned seemed dazed. He could not make out what was happening to him or what was wrong with him. Had he burst a blood-vessel? Was he losing his reason? Or was he being attacked from the sky overhead by some unseen and unknown force? He opened his mouth wide like a dog waking from his sleep. Then he recovered his senses. He put back his hand, caught Pinkeen by the leg, pulled him over his shoulder and threw him on the ground. Pinkeen came down on his backside without a hurt or a scratch. And he sat there as if he were glued to the ground.

Big Ned of the Glen looked down at his assailant and identified him. He did not utter a single word. He spat at Pinkeen. Then he turned away and walked down the street with his hands in his pockets.

Pinkeen got up and hid himself somewhere until he should get an opportunity of slipping out of the village unseen by those of his neighbours who were at the fair.

That evening, as the dusk was beginning to fall, he was seen going out the Black Cow's Gap with bent head and heavy step – a living picture of sorrow and despair.

At Sunset

I was wandering along the shore on a Saturday after my first week as a teacher in Cleenderry. I was asking myself what the people would be like. Were they a friendly people? Would I be at home with them when I got to know them? Would they have stirring stories to tell about their struggles with the sea for generations? Was there a *seanchaí* among them?

I came as far as the pier. An old man was there mending a net. 'Good day, master,' he said. 'You are welcome to this part of the country.'

I got him talking about the sea. 'Yes, it was a hard life, master, sometimes dangerous. But we were used to it. Another thing, we thought there could be no other life in store for us. But times are changing. Not so long ago some of the young people took it into their heads to go away. Before twenty years, you won't be here, master. There will be no children. Therefore, no school. The rest of the story is soon told.'

'Tell me this – by the way, what is your name?'

'Michael Gallagher,' he replied. 'They call me Mickey Neddy.'

'Well, tell me this, Mickey,' I asked, 'if you were young again, would you decide on leading the same life?'

'I would, master, if I thought of nobody but myself. I loved the sea and do still. I love this place. I think there is no place in the world like it. But when I think of herself and the agony she suffered over the years. We might be out fishing and a sudden squall would come. We would run for shelter to the nearest island and maybe have to spend a whole night there. And the poor women at home trying to console the children, trying to give them hope which she didn't have herself. It was when I got old and stopped fishing (this net belongs to one of the sons) it was only then she told me all. It was cruel to make a woman live in such a frightful way during the years that she should be getting any little pleasure out of life that is in it.'

'Ah, master,' he continued, 'I have seen some terrible days and nights in my time. Also days that brought me great pleasure. The curragh-races used to be great sport. I won it four times in succession, racing against the flower of the men of three parishes. The fourth time, I had to put all

I had into it to keep my crown. There was a youth – one of the Buckies of Inishmacdurn – that put me to the pin of my collar that day. The other craft were hundreds of yards behind us on the last lap. Young Buckie and myself were just abreast until we were within about a hundred yards of the winning post. Then I put every ounce of strength I had into ten strokes and passed him by about two lengths. He made a spurt of the same kind. But I kept the short lead and came in first.

'There was great jubilation in Cleenderry that day. But, although I was the champion, I didn't feel any cause for gladness. I had a feeling that I was near the end of my reign. One other man felt the same thing: that was Black Hughdie O'Donnell. By the same token, I see him down on the rocks at Portnamoe, himself and his old woman. Poor Hughdie, he was worth listening to until he got old. Now he is doting. But that's another story. Where was I? At the curragh-races.'

II

'A few weeks after my victory,' the old man continued, 'I met Black Hughdie and we began talking about the race. I could lay bare the secrets of my heart to Hughdie. We were always great friends. "Hughdie," says I, "I am afraid Cleenderry will lose its crown next year."

'"I think the same thing," says Hughdie, "only I didn't like to be the first to say it. That Buckie youngster," says he, "is only nineteen years. You managed to get ahead of him in that wonderful last spurt of yours," says he, "and you kept your short lead to the end. But I am afraid you won't beat him next year."

'"Listen, Hughdie," says I. "Would you take him on yourself next year? I always thought you were as good a curraghman as myself. Maybe you are a wee bit better. What about testing one another in all kinds of weather?" says I. "With the wind, against it, with a side wind, with wind and tide running in the same direction and, again, running against one another."

'This was agreed on. Every opportunity we got, we raced against one another. And, mind you, master, I did my level best every time. I wanted the victory to come to Cleenderry the following August but I also wanted to be the man who would bring it. But, in the end, it became clear that Black Hughdie was the better man. For a few days I felt a trifle sad. But, thank God, I got over it.

'Well, the fifteenth of August was coming and for weeks before it, the curragh-race was the talk of the three parishes. Here in Cleenderry some of my friends and relations kept saying that I was a better curraghman than Black Hughdie and that I was the townland's only hope in the coming race. But I paid no heed to them.

'At last the day came. There were fourteen in for the curragh-race and from places as far apart as Bloody Foreland and Rosbeg. We got ready and took up our places. A shot was fired and we were off. After some time, twelve of them fell behind – far behind – and Black Hughdie O'Donnell and young Buckie in front and side by side. At last, the young lad put on the final spurt. But Black Hughdie made the effort at the same time. He ploughed past young Buckie and beat him by about twenty yards.

'We all gathered round him when he landed. We wanted to carry him to the tent where there was a bar for that day. "No," says he. "I'll walk. And you'll walk along with me," says he to young Buckie, taking him by the hand.

'Later on, as we were having a drink, Black Hughdie caught the young man by the hand a second time. "You'll do it yet, my lad," says he, "and that before long. In three years time there won't be a man from Fanad to Glen Head to match you. You can take that from me," says he.

'"I won't do it," said the young lad. "Today was my last chance, my only hope. I am going to America next fall," says he, and he did go.'

'That is great stuff, Mickey,' said I. 'And you tell me that's Black Hughdie O'Donnell over yonder on the rocks?'

'That is himself and his wife.'

'I must have a talk with him the first chance I get.'

'Sometimes he is very interesting,' said Mickey. 'But he is doting. At times he forgets that he is old and he rambles away. Talks about what happened over fifty years ago as if it had happened only yesterday. Some people feel very sorry for him. I don't. But I feel very sorry for his old woman. The poor creature is broken-hearted over it. Although she shouldn't, if she had the sense to count her blessings ... '

'But,' he resumed, after a pause, 'I remember the time when Black Hughdie O'Donnell was not doting. I remember the time when a whole houseful would sit and listen to him for a long winter's evening. That is how he made the first impression on the girl he married. He used to drop in for a bit of an *airneál* to the house she stayed in. She happened to be in the kitchen the first night he came in. Ever after that, as soon as she heard his voice, she used to come out of her little room and sit in the kitchen along with the rest.

'You know Black Hughdie would put a spell on anybody, especially when he used to talk about the pictures that he used to see in the sky at sunset in good weather in summer. For a while at first I thought myself he was making it up. Then, one evening, he and I happened to be on the height. It was near sunset and he told me to look through the broken clouds. For a while I could see nothing. Then I could see everything he mentioned.'

'By the way, master,' continued Mickey, 'you are a man of learning and you might be able to explain things to me. One summer I was boating an Englishman who was staying in the hotel in Portnoo. He told me that what we saw was caused by the way the light played on the vapour of the clouds. He was a man of powerful learning, they said. A professor in a college in London. When I came back home I dropped into Black Hughdie's house one evening and told them what the London professor had said. "I prefer to call it the Isle of the Blest," says Hughdie. "The clods," said his wife, "it is no wonder they have failed to rule us after trying it for seven centuries."

'But I am wandering, master. This girl took a notion of Black Hughdie. He had his heart set on her too. But he thought she was as far away from him as the stars. He never dared to hope she would marry him. But the day of the curragh-races opened the gates of heaven for him, as he used to say himself. The following spring they were married. So you see, master, not alone did Black Hughdie O'Donnell win the curragh-race that day but he also won the hand of a beautiful bride.'

'That is a great story, Mickey,' I said. 'A great story entirely. But you said something about the house she stayed in. Is she not from Cleenderry?'

'No, she is from Dublin,' replied the old man. 'She was a teacher. She taught here in Cleenderry for forty years. Not where you are now. The old schoolhouse was on the other side of the height as you go out towards Moycross.'

III

'I am sure she'll soon invite you to their house,' continued the old man. 'And I hope you will visit them as often as you can. It will do her good to talk. The poor thing is very sad. You have only to look at her face to know it. I have never seen a more sorrowful face in all my life.'

'Has she had any great cause for such sorrow?' I asked, thinking that, for one thing, she might have had children and that some of them had died. Perhaps, I thought, she had one child and one child only and that it was stricken down by some deadly disease. That today it was smiling in her face, that a few days after it died in her arms. I told old Mickey Neddy what had run through my head.

'She had nine children,' said the old man. 'All of them alive. When she married, her parents were not at all pleased. They couldn't understand why she consented to bury herself in the wilds of Donegal and marry a fisherman into the bargain. But she was an only child. And when they were dying, they left her all they had. She did well for her children. Gave every one of them a college education. They are all gone from here years and years ago. They are all married, one or two of her grandchildren are married. She had everything one could ask for in life until she got this bit of a cross to bear. But, I suppose, master, everyone gets it sooner or later. If it is not one thing, it is another.

'But, Lord,' he went on, 'there was a time when she was not sad or sorrowful and that up to a few years ago. And, in her young days, could she sing! Very often on her way to school on a summer morning she would start singing. And you would think it was a burst of music from the lark at dawn, it was so cheerful. As the old people used to say long ago, if you were within an hour of death and knew it, you would have to listen to her singing. And the songs she had, "My Lagan Love", "Bantry Bay" and "The Kerry Dancing". Especially "The Kerry Dancing".

'I have a story to tell you, master,' said the old man as if he meant to change the conversation.

'Go ahead, Mickey, your stories are excellent,' I replied. For, by this time, I had discovered he had his own method of placing events and that, although he deviated from his main theme at times, he had his own way of coming back to it.

'I was on the salmon-fishing this particular summer,' he began, 'on Shamey More's boat, myself and four others. This evening, we were to leave at six o'clock, just at the turn of the tide. About an hour or so before we were due to leave, I took it into my head to take a run up in the curragh and have a look at some lobster-pots I had set beyond the Grey Rock. I thought I had more than enough time to go there and back before the boat would leave. Instead of that, I was over an hour and a half late. The men were on the slip waiting for me.

'"Where the blazes have you been?" said Shamey More, and he had eyes like the eyes of a tiger. Never saw such fury in a man's face.

'"I went up to the Grey Rock to have a look at my lobster-pots," says I. "And I got a sudden stitch in my side. I had to put into the creek and lie there for an hour and a half. I thought," says I, "my last hour had come."

'Shamey More's face softened at once.

'"Go home and go to bed," says he.

'"No," says I. "I am all right again."

'They all wanted me to go home, but I wouldn't. So we went on board and out into the bay. By this time we could see the white sails of more than a score of boats away out near the horizon.

'"It is too late to go where we meant to go," said Shamey More later on. "When it gets dark," says he, "we'll cast just outside the headlands."

'It was the only thing we could do and we did it. Shortly before dawn we hauled. And what would you say master! The biggest catch of salmon landed in Rosbeg for years. And the boats that went out for miles and miles, every one of them came back without a tail.

'"That was a lucky stitch you got in your side yesterday evening," said Shamey More to me as we were having a drink in Rosbeg after selling our fish. It was then I told the truth,' he said, and he stopped as if his story was finished.

'And what was the truth?' I asked.

'The truth was, master,' he replied, 'that I got no stitch in my side. I was on my way to look at the lobster-pots and I had plenty of time. Mrs O'Donnell was sitting on the grass with four or five of her children grouped around her. As I was coming on to the Red Cliff, she began to sing "The Kerry Dancing". I put the paddle across the bows of the curragh and rested my elbows on it. And I was there under a spell. Honestly, master, I thought I could see the boys as they began to gather in the glen of a summer's night. She sang one song after another and ended by singing "The Kerry Dancing" a second time. I'll never forget that evening, master, never, never, never.'

'I wonder could we get her to sing that song now?' I asked.

'Sometimes she sings a few lines of the last verse,' he replied. 'But the voice is old and feeble and where there was joy and gladness before, there's only sadness and sorrow now. In a way, I think she hasn't much sense for an educated woman like her. One would think it ought to occur to her that things could be much worse. Suppose Black Hughdie were an invalid and not able to leave his bed, or suppose he was dying of cancer and couldn't be cured. Or, for that matter, that he was dead and that she was alone by herself down here, it is then she would have the cause for sadness and tears. I said that to her one day last year (we were always great friends, you know). But it was no use ... But look! They are coming up in this direction.'

They arrived at the pier. The old woman was the first to shake hands with me. 'You are welcome to our townland,' she said. 'I hope you will be happy.'

The old man in his turn welcomed me. Then he began to talk about various things. Was I fond of boating or fishing? Were the people beginning to emigrate from my part of the country? Had I much knowledge of the Land War in Gweedore? He talked very intelligently about different subjects for over ten minutes. And I could not for the life of me understand why Mickey Neddy had said that this man was doting.

The old woman was sitting on one of the lower steps of the breakwater staring out at the open sea. From time to time I looked sideways at her and, without doubt, I had never seen a sadder face. At last, she stood up and she spoke to me. 'Have you anything special on tomorrow evening, master?' she asked me.

'Nothing, Mrs O'Donnell,' I replied.

'Will you come and have tea with us? Say, six o'clock.'

I was very glad to get the invitation. I wanted to have a talk with this old woman. Perhaps, I thought, old as she is and young and inexperienced as I am, I would have some little influence over her.

IV

About half-past five on Sunday evening I arrived at Black Hughdie's. The old man was asleep in a chair in the chimney corner. The old woman pointed to the sofa. She sat down opposite me and we began to talk.

'How long are you here now, Mrs O'Donnell?' I asked.

'Fifty-four years next January,' she replied. 'I'll never forget the day I came. The journey took two days. The first day from Dublin to Strabane. The second day I came on the old train from Strabane to Fintown. And from Fintown down here on the mail-car. That alone took the best part of three hours. I'll never forget that journey. The mountains covered with snow and miles of dreary moorland on all sides of me. I was frozen to the marrow of my bones. Well, do you know what I had in mind, master? I was firmly resolved to go back home the next day.

'However, I got there. I called on the manager Canon Brennan, Lord have mercy on him, and the first thing I said to him was that I was leaving again for Dublin the following morning. He looked at me. "Well, Miss Tracey," said he, "in a way I find it hard to blame you, considering that you have been born and reared in Dublin. But," he added, "I am now in a bit of a fix. It did not occur to me that you mightn't stay. If it had, I would have selected one of the other applicants. So that now I think I am justified in asking you as a special request to stay for a period of three months." Considering everything, I did not think his request at all unreasonable. So I consented. Before the three months were up, I had got to like Cleenderry. Later on, I got to know Black Hughdie O'Donnell. In due course, we were married. I haven't gone back to Dublin since except for an occasional visit. And not even that since my father and mother died.

'There aren't many visitors down this way yet,' she said, as if she meant to change the conversation. 'Of course, it is early in the season. I am told there is nobody at the hotel but two elderly priests and a honeymoon couple.'

'I passed the honeymoon couple down at the rocks yesterday evening,' I said. 'You could hear their bursts of laughter a mile away.'

'The laughter won't last long,' said she. 'Poor little children, they don't know what is before them.'

I did not like this old woman's outlook. I thought she should remember that she had a lot to be thankful for. Why should she conclude that the lot of mankind on this earth was unrelieved misery because her husband in his old age suffered from occasional fits of mind-wandering? I would like to say that to her but it was hard to say it. She looked so sad. Her voice sounded so sad. I would have to lead up to it gently. Ever so gently.

'The scenery here is beautiful,' I remarked.

'It is,' she sighed. 'But it takes time to see the heavenly part of it. I remember the first time I saw it. It was a beautiful evening in August. There had been a regatta in the bay earlier in the day. Cleenderry won the curragh-race and there was great jubilation. Black Hughdie and myself were standing on the height. "Look at the clouds above the sunset," said he. I did. For a while at first I could see nothing wonderful. Then, all of a sudden, it burst on me. I saw – but why should I try to describe what cannot be described? Is it any wonder it has been called the Isle of the Blest? Oh, if I could see it once again as I saw it that evening! But I can't. That gift has not been granted to me.'

At this stage the old man woke and sat upright in the chair. His face beamed with happiness. There was a look of gladness in his eyes. And, without addressing himself to either of us, he began to talk. 'It was beautiful beyond words yesterday evening,' said he. And he poured forth a torrent of the most lurid and fantastic language I had ever heard, describing the sight he had seen at sunset the evening of the day before.

'Yesterday was a great day for me,' he continued. 'I will remember it to my dying day. And I know Margaret will remember it too. And yesterday was also a great day for Cleenderry. It was a very tough battle. There's great stuff in that youngster from Inishmacdurn, great stuff entirely. Short, quick strokes he pulls when he puts on the final spurt. I noticed this stroke of his last year and I practised it for months. When we were within two hundred yards of the winning post I knew I had him beaten. He won't compete next year, he is going to America in the fall. Some say he intends to come back after five years. If he does come back and if he competes again, he will beat me. When that day comes, I hope I'll be a man and wish him many more such victories. I don't mean just shaking his hand and congratulating him. I've known men to do that and at the same time their hearts were burning with envy and spite. No, I hope I will be able to admire and honour a man better than myself. That is the best thing a man can do. And I have the example of Mickey Neddy. Last year Mickey knew it was the last time he could beat young Buckie. He came to me and wanted each of us to test himself against the other. We did, and in all kinds of weather. "Hughdie," says he to me, "you are the better man. You will defend Cleenderry's crown next August." They were the very words he used … There are men – and some of them in this townland – and they would rather see the stranger having the victory if they could not get it themselves. But that's not Mickey Neddy. Yesterday evening he was the gladdest man in Cleenderry.'

He became silent. After a few minutes he lit his pipe. Then he began to talk sensibly. The wandering spell had passed and he made no further allusion to what he had been talking about.

We took our places at the tea-table. The old man was in great humour for talking. He talked about the decline of the fishing. 'The big boats are one cause of it,' he said. 'The big boats that keep far out to sea and prevent the shoals from coming inshore. We here can't afford such expensive boats and gear. Then again, some of our young people are getting discontented. They are beginning to emigrate, especially the girls. That is always a sure sign that decay has begun to set in in a district – when the young women begin to leave. That is what I see in store for Cleenderry. And it is a pity. For it is one beautiful spot. Even strangers get to like it.

'This lassie here, when she came fifty-three years ago, was wondering how anyone could live in such a place. Coming across the bleak moorland from Fintown on an old outsider, she had her mind firmly made up to go back home to Dublin the very next day. And, after the first summer, she wouldn't leave it for the world. Isn't that so, Margaret?'

'That is so,' said the old woman feebly, and she said no more.

'I think I'll give that cow a drink,' said the old man, getting up. 'I will leave you two to talk. You will have lots of things to say to one another that the likes of me wouldn't understand.'

I have a few things to say, said I in my own mind, if I can pluck up courage to say them. And it won't be about teaching or school programmes. I hope I'll get the words out some way, that I'll manage to tell her that she has no cause for sadness or sorrow. That her husband is still a fine, sensible, companionable man and that an occasional lapse of memory in an old person is nothing to worry about. What way would I get her to listen to me? What would be the best approach? Would I appeal to feminine vanity? I would.

'Mrs O'Donnell,' I began, when we had the house to ourselves, 'I believe you have a beautiful singing voice.'

'Who told you that?'
'Mickey Neddy.'
'He would. Mickey was always a generous soul.'
'He told me he sat spellbound in the curragh one evening long ago listening to you sing "The Kerry Dancing".'
'I heard that legend. That was the evening of the miraculous draught of fishes,' she added, making a feeble attempt at smiling … 'It was one of my favourite songs when I was young,' she continued. 'I believe I could sing it fairly well too. At least, they told me so in Dublin and the Dublin people have an ear for music.'
'Well, now, Mrs O'Donnell. One request. Will you sing "The Kerry Dancing" for me?'
'I am sorry, very sorry, master, for having to refuse your request. I couldn't sing that song now. It would break my heart,' she added, and she changed the conversation.
'That is the way his mind works,' said she, referring to her husband. 'He could read a novel today and tell you the whole story in detail tomorrow. But, in far-off things, he gets mixed up. He told you just now of a regatta, of a curragh-race that he took part in, of the pictures that he and I saw in the sky at sunset. The whole thing was correct in every detail. But he thought it had occurred yesterday. Fifty-two years slipped out of the picture unknown to me. It was all yesterday with him. He lived that bright day of his youth again while the spell lasted … He mightn't have another lapse for a week or longer. It is very often according to the way his mind is stimulated by what he sees or hears, especially if he is only half-awake. But he doesn't mind. He never tries to explain, never asks to be excused afterwards.'
'Why should he ask to be excused? If a person gets a headache or any other ache, why should he be expected to apologise for it? Then why should your good man be expected to ask to be excused for an occasional lapse of memory?'
'I didn't mean it like that,' she replied and, at this stage, the tears were gathering in her eyes. 'No,' she explained, 'what I meant is that he pays no heed to it. He is happy. As happy as anyone can be at his age.'
Then she burst out crying. The tears flowed down her cheeks. Her whole frame shook with emotion.
There was nothing for it, I thought, but to let her cry her fill and then, when she had calmed down, try to make her see reason. Hang it all, there wasn't that much wrong with her husband. A lapse of memory for a few minutes and that not oftener than once a week. I knew old women who could laugh at it!
'Will you listen to me, my dear Mrs O'Donnell,' I began when I

thought she had sufficiently calmed down to heed me. 'I want to give you a few words of advice, a few words that I hope will do you good.'

'I appreciate the kind intention very much, master,' she replied. 'But you are too young to say any words of advice to me. Fifty years too young. You don't understand old age. You don't understand the cause of my grief. I know you don't ... When I think of the past, the past that for me is gone forever. And when I see Black Hughdie O'Donnell in one of those lapses, I feel my heart frozen within me ... Maybe I am a mean, miserable soul and that I am sadly lacking in the virtue of resignation. Maybe I am wrong in presuming that I have as much right to happiness to the end as anybody else ... They say that real love should have for its aim, above all things, the happiness of the other person. But I haven't risen to that height. When I see him lapsing completely and cancelling out half a century, when I see him today living over again a scene he lived fifty years ago, and when I see the light of gladness in his eyes, I envy him. And it makes me sad beyond words that I am not like him. I am sad and I cry for hours because I too haven't the gift of becoming young again, if it were only for a few minutes, once a week. Oh, how I wish I had the gift that Black Hughdie has. The gift of recapturing,

> One of those hours of gladness
> Gone, alas, like our youth, too soon.'

Mayday Magic

In the Rosses in my young days there was a *geas* on Mayday. Dinneen defines *geas* as a solemn injunction, especially of a magical kind, the infringement of which led to misfortune or even death.

At the time about which I am writing, no Rosses man would put to sea on Mayday. No matter how settled the weather was or how calm the sea, there was always the danger. If any young man were to say it was a silly superstition and should be ignored in a more enlightened age than that of their grandfathers, he would be told a story. It was the story of Billy More from Inishglaise who ventured out to the mainland on Mayday. The weather was settled. The sea was as calm as a duck pond. Billy decided to cross to the mainland. The islanders came down to the beach as he was preparing to leave. They implored him – some of them with tears in their eyes – to remember the *geas* and not to put to sea. Billy laughed at them. He was going to put an end to that silly superstition. Before many years, he said, everyone would put to sea on Mayday as well as any other day if the weather was suitable. He launched his curragh, knelt in the bow and pulled out from the shore. The islanders stood looking after him. He got half-way across the sound and nothing happened. He came three quarters of the way. After all, was the *geas* only a silly superstition? And then, all of a sudden, a squall struck him and capsized his frail craft. He was, of course, drowned.

This and similar stories were always told if anybody said he did not believe in the Mayday *geas*.

Carry Villy had his own peculiarities. From his early boyhood he had a craving for the limelight. He wanted to be different from other boys of his age. He pretended not to believe in the old legends. The Isle of the Blest which lay on the rim of the ocean, on the western horizon, was, he said, nothing more or less than the way the light played on a certain formation of cloud at sunset. On a ledge in Tormore, said the folklore, no one ever had been known to have been refused the granting of his wish. That was true, said Carry, in the sense that no one ever had ventured out on to the same ledge. As for the Stags being three druids that Colmcille once turned into rocks, that was the silliest piece of nonsense that could be imagined. And so on with the rest of the *geasa*.

Of course, it is to be expected that the Mayday *geas* would come under Carry's condemnation. Time and again he said it was only foolish nonsense. He was always answered by being told of the tragedy that had overtaken those who had contravened it. It was only a coincidence, Carry would say. It could happen any day.

'It is easy to talk,' said old Murchadh Antoin to Carry one day. 'Very easy. Nothing easier. I am over eighty-four years of age and I have heard a lot of talk in my day. For four generations I have been listening to young men saying that the Mayday *geas* was only a silly superstition. But that was all the far they went. None of them ever risked putting to sea on that day.'

This was a challenge to Carry. He was up against it. He would have to act according to his alleged beliefs or else keep silent forever on a lot of issues. This he did not want to do. He wanted to be talked about. He wanted publicity. In a subsequent generation he would become a successful politician. But, in the days of our story, there were unfortunately no opportunities of this nature.

Murchadh Antoin's words were burning into Carry's brain. He would have to defy the *geas* or else stop talking about it. It was about the middle of April at the time. Carry made his decision. If the weather was settled at Mayday he would put to sea in his curragh and cross to Illanala.

II

Sally O'Donnell was a very fine, young girl and each of two men wanted to marry her. One of them was Big Murty McGrenra, admittedly the finest young man in the parish. He was an able boatman and often took risks that no other man would take. As for his strength and skill in handling a curragh, he had no peer in his day. His name was always linked with that of Oweneen Harlais, the ace curraghman of a bygone generation.

Would Sally O'Donnell marry him? There were certain factors in his favour. First of all, Sally liked him. Secondly, he was favoured by her grandparents. If Sally married him they could make their home in the old couple's house and, in due course, have the holding to themselves. That was a consideration that no young pair contemplating marriage could dismiss lightly.

The second suitor was Shamey McGarrigle. Shamey was a very well-behaved young man and a diligent worker. And he was of a gentle disposition.

What would Sally's final decision be? Each of the two aspirants to her hand had very good points to recommend him. Which of the two would be the lucky one? Which of them had the warmer corner in Sally's heart? Nobody knew. In fact, Sally herself did not know for certain. She would wait. Time might reveal a good quality in one which the other lacked, or reveal a fault in one from which the other was free.

Sally was a first cousin, on her mother's side, of Carry Villy. Carry intended to put to sea in his curragh on Mayday if the weather was reasonably good. Old Murchadh Antoin's words were burning his heart. He would have to defy the *geas* and show that it was only a silly superstition, or keep his head down and his mouth shut forever. But he would not breathe a word of his intention to anybody. Especially from his cousin it would have to be kept a secret. Sally might tell it to her father and Carry Villy knew well what Manus O'Donnell would say: 'The conceited little prig. I was ten times as good a curraghman as he is or ever will be. I have done things that he could not do if he lived to be a thousand years. Yet I would not dream of going to sea on Mayday.'

It is true that Manus O'Donnell had been a first-class curraghman and that he had often taken risks that few men would take. Many a fright his poor wife got when night was coming on and the sea and the sky had an angry look and no sign of her man returning from the fishing-ground. But it was their life and it had to be lived. At last, Manus met with an accident. One day he climbed up the face of a cliff in Gola to release a log of timber that had been washed up by a huge wave and got wedged in a cliff. Manus broke his leg that day. For the rest of his life he limped about with a stick, tending to his little bits of crops as best he could and, of course, he never afterwards went to sea. The family felt the pinch of poverty when the fishing stopped. But the neighbours were good. And in her heart of hearts Manus' wife was glad. She had been told that the fall was as near fatal as could be. A few inches either to the right or to the left and his skull was smashed.

III

Mayday dawned, fresh and glorious. Carry Villy got up early. He went out and looked on all sides of him. The sun had risen clear off the peak of Errigal. The morning mists were rolling up its slopes.

Carry looked in the opposite direction. The sea was as calm as a sheet of glass. There was not even the thin, white hem that even in good weather one sees in the lip of the Big Strand. The moan of the distant bar was scarcely audible which went to show there was hardly any ground-swell. Carry imagined the day had come for himself. It was a day for breaking the Mayday *geas* if there ever had been one. Henceforth he could talk. He could speak with authority of a deed accomplished. What would old, crabbed Murchadh Antoin say? What could he say to Carry's boast: 'I have been always saying that the Mayday *geas* was a silly superstition. Now I have proved it.'

He put to sea in his curragh and headed for Illanala, an uninhabited island about a mile and a half from the mainland. The curragh was seen going down the bay. Who could it be at all? Who was the lunatic that was defying the Mayday *geas*? It soon became known that it was Carry Villy. People gathered in groups on the heights along the coast. They felt that tragedy was hanging over the Rosses. *Bealtaine* had been defied, her decrees ignored, her ordinances flouted. *Bealtaine* would punish!

Carry Villy went across to Illanala and landed. He walked up to a height in the middle of the island. There he collected a heap of dry fern and set fire to it. The people on the other islands and on the headlands from the Foreland to Crohy would see the smoke. They would know that some man had put to sea on Mayday. Later on they would find out who he was. Old fogies would disapprove. But the young people – and it was the young people that Carry wanted to emancipate and enlighten – would declare him a brave man, a man of intelligence.

After some time Carry put to sea again and set out for home. There was no change in the weather except a murky belt in the sky, on the north-western horizon. But the sea was as calm as ever and there was not a breath of wind.

When he was half-way across the sound, on the return journey, Carry heard a rumble like the sound of distant thunder. It was getting louder and louder. Carry looked round. There was a white strip spreading towards him from the Stags. He knew what it was.

Carry did not panic. The wind would blow him straight to the creek where he had left in the morning. But, as he carried no ballast, he should have to keep the bow of his craft in the storm and let it drift sternwise to the shore. That would mean, of course, that he could not see where he was going. But he would be sure to strike the coast at some spot and there would be men on the beaches who would help him to land. It would be a rather humiliating end to his exploit. But anything to save his life!

About three hundred yards from the spot where the storm would blow him on to the shore lay Lacknarone. Lacknarone is a big rock with a flat surface several yards in extent. At low tide it is visible. At high tide it is covered under six or seven feet of water.

The storm was blowing the curragh straight in the direction of the rock. The men on the beach were frantically shouting to the lone sailor. But, of course, he could not hear them against the wind. At last, he was dashed onto the rock.

He made an attempt to hold on to the curragh but it slipped from his grasp and was blown in towards the shore. There he was on the rock with the waves dashing over him. The tide was rising. No man could go out against the force of the storm to rescue him. Death was inevitable.

Shamey McGarrigle was on the beach along with scores of others. He noticed Murty McGrenra standing by himself some distance away from the crowd. Shamey ran across to him. 'Murty,' he asked, 'can you do nothing?'

'Nothing,' replied Murty mournfully. 'If I could, I would not be standing here. No mortal man could break his way through that storm. Oh, God, what took possession of the poor boy at all?'

Just then they heard a sharp, piercing cry. It was the cry of a woman. When they looked in the direction it came from, they saw Sally O'Donnell running down the sand-banks. She came to where the two men were standing. 'Murty,' she implored in a heart-rending voice, 'can you do nothing?'

'If I could do anything, I would not be standing here,' Murty replied in a choking voice.

Sally made no appeal to Shamey McGarrigle. She did not even look at him. She turned away and ran across the beach, yelling frantically.

And then happened one of those things that are very often impossible to explain because they are outside the compass of reason and logic. Shamey McGarrigle was off like a shot. He ran to a creek where a curragh was beached, got in under it, carried it to the water's edge, launched it and got into it. All eyes were turned on him.

Shamey kept alongside a tongue of land that jutted into the sea until he was about a hundred yards from Lacknarone. Then he put all his strength into an effort to reach the rock. He knew he could not rescue his man by approaching him from the lee side. The only way was to go round to windward of the rock and try to get in between two waves.

Shamey managed to get to the storm side of Lacknarone. But, just then, a huge mountain of water came rolling in on him. It lifted his curragh and carried it onto the rock. Carry would have been swept away but he had the presence of mind to throw himself down on his face and get a grip of a small jut in one of the crevices of the rock.

Shamey kept a firm grip on the gunwale of his curragh. When the wave subsided, he tilted it and emptied the water out of it. Then the two went aboard. The rest of the task was comparatively easy. Shamey could keep the bow of his curragh facing the shore, the craft being ballasted by the weight of the second man in the stern.

When they landed, Sally O'Donnell ran to Shamey and held out her two hands to him. He put an arm round her and kissed her affectionately on the cheek. Murty McGrenra came across to them. He took Shamey's two hands in his. 'Shamey McGarrigle,' said he, 'nothing like your deed has been done in the Rosses since the day long ago that Oweneen Harlais rescued the Rannafast crew off the cliffs of Owey. Your name will forever be linked with the name of that great hero and the two stories will be told by the firesides of the Rosses for many and many a generation.'

Having said that much, he turned and walked away leaving Shamey and Sally together. It was a magnificent gesture from a man who was a rival in love and who had shrunk from the deed which the other man had faced and accomplished.

IV

Shamey visited Sally's home on the evening of that hectic day. The old woman kissed his hands and burst into tears. Old Manus O'Donnell sat in a low chair in the chimney corner with his stick by his side. Sally sat opposite him, knitting. Two or three men from the neighbourhood completed the circle.

'It was a magnificent piece of work,' began Manus O'Donnell. 'Nothing like it since the days of Oweneen Harlais. But, when I think of the conceited little monkey who took it on himself to break the Mayday *geas*. *Geasa* have been broken in the past, we are told, but always by great men. Cú Chulainn broke a *geas*. So did Goll Mac Móirne. So did Fionn. So did Diarmaid. But, as Shaneen Nelleen said: "Little Paddy Bonner that never did any fighting." Little Carry Villy who could never handle a paddle nor never will.'

Shamey wanted to change the conversation. Sally's mother was present. And 'little Carry Villy' was her own flesh and blood – her brother's son. 'The poor boy has no sense. And I am sorry for him, apart altogether from the fright he got.'

'It must have been a stiff pull going out to Lacknarone against the storm,' said one of the neighbours.

'It was a bit tough all right,' said Shamey. 'I had to put everything I knew into the last hundred yards.'

'Were you afraid?' asked another of the men.

'Well, no, I was not,' said Shamey. 'A man's life was in danger. At the rate the tide was rising, it would be all over in an hour. To tell the truth, I did not spend any time weighing up my chances. My heart moved me to act and I did act. That's all.'

'But when the wave dashed you onto the rock?'

'I wasn't prepared for that,' replied Shamey, 'but I kept my presence of mind and held on to the curragh. The rest was easy. It is really not worth talking about.'

'It will be talked about when you are dead,' said Manus O'Donnell. 'And why wouldn't it? You are a man to your fingertips. That's what you are.'

Shamey was glad this evening. He had accomplished a wonderful feat of heroism. He would be talked about throughout the Rosses for many a day. There was, of course, a little secret in his mind. He had his own stratagems. All was fair in love and war. Once married, little details would adjust themselves.

The summer passed, and the autumn and winter after it, and Sally did not seem in the least inclined to choose between the two men that wanted to marry her. One would think that Shamey's heroic act on Mayday would tip the scales in his favour. But it did not look as if Sally would be swayed by that consideration. She seemed as far away as ever from making a decision.

The following spring Sally announced her intention of going to America. Each of the two lovers approached her separately and put his proposals before her. To Murty McGrenra she replied that she liked and admired him. That he would be a very good husband to her. But that love was an affair of the heart and could not be regulated by the decisions of the head. She was sorry, very sorry, she said, but that was how it was. To Shamey she said nothing about her head or her heart. She said she had made up her mind never to marry and settle in the Rosses. And, she added, with a tear glistening in her eye, that she was sorry that it could not be otherwise.

V

When I came back from America, an old man Murty McGrenra was still alive with some of his children and grandchildren around him. The conversation came round to Shamey McGarrigle. Murty was as generous as ever. 'He was a great man,' he said. 'His name will live in the Rosses for generations. He did a man's work the day long ago he rescued Carry Villy. He got an impulse that only heroes get. I was there on the beach looking at the poor devil on the rock with the waves of the rising tide rolling over him. I was in agony. I made my calculations. I decided that the poor fellow could not be rescued and that it would be suicide for me to try to attempt it. But, apparently, Shamey made no calculations. It was as if he got a ray of light from Heaven and he was off like a shot.'

'Is he still alive?' I asked.

'He is, but he is not here in the Rosses.'

'And where is he?'

'Up in Cloghernagore – away beyond Fintown. He married a girl from up there a few years after you left. He is a widower now; his wife died two years ago.'

'I must make my way up there.'

'He'll be glad to see you. I meet him an odd time at the fair in Dungloe. He always asks is there any news from you.'

One day the following week found me in Cloghernagore. I enquired where Shamey McGarrigle lived and I was directed to his house. He was sitting on a stone seat outside the door doing something to a piece of harness.

When I came up to him he looked at me but he did not recognise me. I told him who I was. 'I am glad to see you there, Jimmy,' he said, grasping my hand. 'It was very good of you to come all the way from the Rosses to visit me. I am always glad to see a Rosses man. My heart is still in the old Rosses. Wonderful grip that wild district by the sea has on its children. We must leave it. Yet, for the rest of our lives, it is calling to us to come back.'

'I often heard that call myself,' I replied. 'I did, as far away as the shores of the Pacific.'

The following day he went out to the moors to look for a strayed sheep and, of course, I went along with him. When he reached a height overlooking Lough Finn, he sat on a rock and I sat beside him. 'Strange, very strange, Jimmy,' he began. 'Often when I am wandering through the moorland, I sit on a rock as I am sitting now and I see things and hear things. I see the coast of the Rosses and the headlands and the islands. I hear the lapping of the waves on the White Strand and the moan of the bar away in the distance. Sometimes I see myself in a curragh going out to the fishing-ground. It is not the same as a dream. Dreams are very often rambling affairs without head or tail. But this is real. And, when the spell passes, I feel sad.'

'Strange that you left the Rosses,' I ventured.

He looked at me for a few seconds before replying. 'I've never told anybody why I left,' said he. 'But I'll tell you now. One has to tell these things to somebody. I left the Rosses because I was afraid to live there.'

'Afraid of what?'

'Afraid of the sea.'

'You, afraid of the sea? You, who performed a feat of skill and bravery that will be talked of in the Rosses for generations? I mean the rescue of Carry Villy.'

'You were there that day, I think.'

'Yes, I was standing on a sand-dune and I saw it all.'

'Well,' said Shamey, 'that was the day that scared me out of the Rosses. I could not continue to live there where a man makes his living partly by fishing. I defied the sea that day. She spared my life but she gave me such a fright that I ran away from her and hid up here in the mountains. I cannot describe it to you. It was not going out against the storm but when my curragh was dashed onto Lacknarone and upturned, and when the huge wave passed over us and I saw the other poor devil crouching down to keep himself from being swept away, I got a fright that I feel since. Of course, that evening I said I wasn't a bit afraid. I wanted to be a hero in the eyes of the woman I loved. And, of course, I could not swallow my bravado and tell her the truth afterwards.'

'I think I know the girl you mean,' I interrupted. 'Sally O'Donnell.'

'Sally O'Donnell,' he agreed. 'She went to America the following spring. Three years afterwards she got married. She is a widow now. I am told there's talks of her coming back on a visit this summer.'

He lapsed into silence for a while. Then he resumed. 'If she comes back, I must go down to see her ... I wonder ... But no. Time has chalked up the years against us and we can't rub out the figures.'

'Well, to come back to the Mayday long ago,' he resumed. 'I was on the shore along with scores of others. I was standing at the foot of a cliff along with Murty McGrenra, looking out through the spray at the poor creature on the rock. I asked Murty could anything be done. He shook his head in despair. That was enough for me: if Murty could not do it, no other man could. Just then, we heard the piercing cry of a woman. It was Sally. She ran to us. 'Murty,' she said, 'can you do nothing?'

'If I could, Sally,' he replied, 'I would not be standing here.' And I saw the tears in his eyes. 'Sally turned away from us, still screaming. She did not look at me at all. I felt I wasn't a man in her eyes. And, without thinking, I ran to the creek and launched a curragh. You saw the rest.'

'Well, that evening in Sally's father's house everybody was praising me. At last one man asked me if I was afraid. I wasn't afraid at all, I said. I wanted to appear a hero before Sally. But I knew I could not keep it up. Every day that passed I was getting more and more afraid of the sea. I was avoiding it as much as possible. Going out to fish only in settled weather, and never by myself. Then Sally went off to America ... Well, people must live and they can't live on the dreams of the past. In due course I made my way up here. And that's my story to you.'

VI

The following week I was back in the Rosses, staying with relations. Going down to the sea-shore one day I saw two women at some distance. One of them was walking out towards the top of a cliff. The other called after her.

'Hi, Joan! Do you want to break your neck? You can't get down to the strand that way.'

'And what way do I go, mammy?' asked the other.

'Round to the big rock on your left. There you will see the steps.'

I knew they were mother and daughter. I knew also that the mother had been there before for she knew in detail the paths and steps leading down to the strand.

When I came to where the old woman was, she spoke to me.

'You seem to have been here before,' I said to her.

'Here before! I was born and brought up in this very townland. See the long, thatched house on the brae face?'

'You are Sally!'

'I am Sally that was. And the girl gone down to the strand is my daughter. But I don't know who you are.'

'I suppose you don't,' I replied, and I told her.

'Ah, Jimmy Elimy!' she said. 'I am delighted to meet you.'

We sat down on a rock and began to talk. 'Not many of our generation left now,' she began. 'Still, I am glad to have been able to come back and see the few survivors. I called on Big Murty McGrenra yesterday. He has got very old. Murty was a fine man. There was always something big about him. I still remember his generous praise of Shamey McGarrigle the day long ago that Shamey rescued Carry Villy on Lacknarone ... By the way, does Shamey ever visit the Rosses?'

'Seldom. People sometimes meet him in Dungloe on a fair day. I spent three days with him last week.'

'Well, did you really! His wife died a few years ago, I am told. How is he at all?'

'He looks very well indeed.'

'I'd like to meet him. In fact, I must go to see him although I know it will only be a meeting of two ghosts ... This may surprise you, Jimmy, but I fully intended to marry him. But his rescue of Carry Villy and his attitude afterwards separated us.'

'I must confess I am puzzled,' I said.

'I suppose you are,' she replied. 'But I was afraid of the sea and I had every reason to be so. You remember my father. He would take risks that very few men would take and my poor mother lived in dread. He kept on taking risks until he fell down a cliff and broke his leg. In her heart of hearts my mother was glad of that accident. We knew hard times as a result of it. But we pulled through. We had great neighbours – the best in the world.'

'I'll never forget one night. I was about twelve years at the time. It was in the month of October and my father went out to the Blowers to fish. Coming on to nightfall it blew a sudden squall which lasted nearly four hours. My father managed to run before it and to land in Umpin and, of course, he had to remain there till the storm was over. And such wind! The very walls of the house seemed to tremble. Sometimes the storm would die down to a whisper and, just when you thought it was over, a fresh gust struck the house and made it tremble.

'None of us went to bed. After midnight the small children lay down on the flags of the floor and fell asleep. My mother was crying and praying by turns. There was a picture on the chimney-breast – a cheap print that had been bought at a mission stall. It was a picture of Our Lord walking on the water and the waves that had been dashing against the disciples' boat falling away to a calm at His approach. I will never forget the expression on my mother's face as she looked up at that picture.

'After nearly four hours the storm settled. It was all over, one way or the other. I helped my mother to put the small children to bed. Then we sat silently over the ashes of a dying fire. About an hour before dawn we heard footsteps coming along the path leading to the house. I ran to the door and drew back the bolt. My father came in. My mother rose to meet him. She stumbled towards him and collapsed into his arms.'

'I could never forget that night. Later on, when I grew up, I made a firm resolution never to marry a man that would take such risks as my father took. I might fall in love with such a man. But the vision I had of that night of horror would always keep me from marrying him.'

'Well, that brings me to the day that my poor, foolish cousin took it into his head to make a name for himself by breaking the Mayday *geas*. You were on the beach yourself, Jimmy. I remember seeing you as one sees a person in a dream. I came running down the sand-banks and saw poor Carry on Lacknarone with the waves rolling over him. Murty McGrenra and Shamey McGarrigle were standing together some distance apart from the crowd. I ran across to them. I asked Murty if he could do anything. He said no man could. I turned away. I didn't speak to Shamey at all. I didn't look at him ... And I may as well tell the whole truth since

I am at it. I did not want him to take the risk, no matter what happened.'

'Well, you saw the rest. You saw how Shamey dashed off and launched a curragh. How he went out against wind and wave and took poor Carry Villy off the rock. It was magnificent although it frightened me. Still, I thought he had acted on a generous impulse, a kind of inspiration, and that he would never again take such a risk. But that evening, he came to our house. He dismissed what he had done as a thrilling adventure and no more. He did not want to talk about it. But what struck terror into my heart was the reply he made when someone asked him was he afraid. 'Not in the least,' he said. Then I understood that he did not see the danger, that he did not understand the sea although he had been nursed in her lap, so to speak. In his ignorance he would take risks again and again and get lost in the end. And, even if he were to come safe out of every danger, I could not reconcile myself to such nights of terror as my mother endured the night my father was blown on to Umpin.

'I decided to go to America. How hard the decision was nobody knows but myself.'

She lapsed into silence and looked out towards the sea. After a time, she resumed: 'I must make it my business to see Shamey before I go back to the States. He may still think I went off to America because my affection for him was not strong enough. I want to tell him what separated us – fear of the sea on my part, on his part, the want of it.'

I, who knew the two sides of the story, found myself asking myself could not something be done yet to repair past mistakes and misunderstandings. But I suddenly remembered something that each of them had said. Shamey a few days ago: 'I wonder ... But no. Time has chalked up the years against us and we can't rub out the figures.' And now Sally: 'I must go to see him although I know it will only be a meeting of two ghosts.'

So, I said nothing.

A Dog's Life

In my young days nearly every house in the Rosses kept a dog. The people had lots of stories about dogs. Dogs formed part of their folklore almost on the same scale as they are to be found in the literature of the Fianna of ancient Ireland. There was the story of the dog that would watch children all day and keep them away from cliffs, streams or other dangerous places. The story of the dog that went out to the hills to collect ten sheep. For a long time he could collect only nine. He searched and searched for hours until he found the tenth. There was the story of the dog that was brought by sea from the Rosses of Donegal to Sligo and made his way back home by land.

The owners of such dogs were proud of them, of course. But the greatest quality a dog could have was to be a good fighter. A dog might be useless for all kinds of domestic tasks and purposes. He could be the biggest idiot of a dog that ever lived. But, if he could fight, all his shortcomings would be forgiven – especially by the menfolk. The women were not quite so indulgent. When vexed or annoyed by a dog, a woman could complain bitterly: 'That dog has my heart broken. This morning he scattered my clutch hen and her little birdies all over the place. Yesterday, he chased the cow right into the potato plot. Two whole ridges destroyed. He is a heart-scald of a dog if there ever was one.'

'Aye,' the men would reply, 'in ways he hasn't much sense. But he has his good points. After all, he has something to his credit. Look at the stump in the place where his left ear should be. He lost that ear in Mullaghderg two years ago – the day he let them know he was king over the dogs of the Rosses.'

At the time that our story commences, Johnny McGinty of Crawbawn had the champion dog of the parish – a dog called Rover. Like most champions, he had to fight every bit of his way to the top and it was a tough struggle. However, in the end, he was victorious and, for a while, he reigned undisputed.

Red Hughdie Ward from the same townland had a dog that suffered a crushing defeat in the early stages of Rover's campaign. Red Hughdie was a young man and thought he felt himself humiliated through his dog's defeat. He wanted at all costs to have revenge. But how could he? His dog would never make a come-back. He would not come within a mile of Rover. There was nothing for it but to get a new dog.

The following winter, after a season's work in Scotland, Red Hughdie came home with a pup of about two months old. He had bought him in a kennel in Kilmarnock. He was a dog of a fighting breed and it was commonly believed that Hughdie had paid more than half his season's earning for him. He was called Cameron.

Cameron continued to grow and gave every promise of being a big, strong dog. The men of the townland were talking about him. Yes, he would be big and strong all right, but would he be a fighter?

'A dog needs something more than strength,' said Jimmy Elimy one day. 'To be a good fighter, a dog must be wiry. He must be determined. In a way, he must be like a man, that is, he must have it in him to feel ashamed at being defeated.'

Cameron went into action sooner than had been expected. He was scarcely a year old at the time. It happened in this way. A number of men were on the White Strand digging for sand-eels. Johnny McGinty's young son – a lad of about twelve years of age – was there and he had Rover with him. There were several other dogs there chasing seagulls, barking aimlessly, running around in circles. But none of them would come near Rover. They were all afraid of him.

In due course Red Hughdie Ward got his bucket and spade and set out for the White Strand. Cameron followed him. Several times Red Hughdie shouted at the dog to go back home. Cameron would retreat for a bit, then stand and finally sneak back to his master. Hughdie did not want the test to come for some time yet. He is too young, said he to himself. If he tackles Johnny McGinty's Rover today, he could get a fright that he'd never get over. I had better go back home. There is no other way out of it.

Just at that moment, Cameron let a fierce growl and ran down the strand with every hair on his neck and back standing erect like the bristles on a hedgehog. Rover heard that growl and understood it. He seemed to realise that he was up against a definite challenge to his reign of supremacy. It would have to be now or never. The issue could not remain in doubt. There was no place for two kings among the dogs of the Rosses.

Rover ran to meet his oncoming enemy and, of course, all the men were at his heels. This was too much of a good thing to miss.

The two combatants made for each other's throats, without any preliminaries. In the first encounter, Rover fell but he managed to get up again and ran away as fast as his legs could carry him. Cameron made after him but could not overtake him. If Cameron had won the fight, Rover won the race.

Johnny McGinty would not believe that his famous dog could be defeated in a few seconds. He had a most satisfactory explanation of the affair. When Rover saw all the men armed with spades running after him and his own master nowhere to be seen, he got afraid and he ran away. But there would be another day and that before long. In fact, Johnny McGinty was arranging for a pitched battle on the plain of Magheramore the following Sunday afternoon.

But the pitched battle never came off. It was abandoned on Saturday night. Red Hughdie, accompanied by Cameron, happened to pass by McGinty's house. Just as they were passing Cameron growled for some unknown reason, as dogs sometimes do. Rover was inside, lying on the hearth in front of the fire with his muzzle resting on his forepaws. The moment he heard the growl outside, he recognised it. He leaped up in a panic and ran from one corner of the kitchen to the other. At last, he went in under the bed in the alcove, howling dismally all the time. Several times during the night he repeated that howl, as if he had been dreaming that Cameron was at his throat. He was beaten. He was crushed. He lived in daily and hourly dread of the victor.

II

Red Hughdie was delighted. For weeks on end he kept talking about Cameron's great victory. But the recording could not go on for ever. Cameron's great victory was not the only issue in Hughdie's life at the moment. It was time for him to get married and his mother was talking about making a match for him with one Sara Gallagher from Derrymore. Sara was not exactly a beauty, conceded Mrs Ward. But then she was not positively ugly. And she would have a nice penny of a marriage portion to get – at least forty pounds. Mrs Ward was a hard-headed, efficient woman. She had made enquiries and obtained useful information. She was about to undertake the preliminary stage of her negotiations when, all of a sudden, a startling item of news burst on herself and on all the people of the Rosses. Johnny McGinty was getting a legacy from America. He had had a communication from a solicitor in Letterkenny. He showed the letter to the neighbours. The issue was beyond doubt.

Johnny McGinty had a brother Dan who went to America forty years before that. He never married. It was said by certain persons that he had piles of money, for he had saved every penny he had earned, they said. He died without making a will and an attempt was now being made to trace the next of kin through a few bits of papers found among his belongings, as well as from scraps of information supplied by a few people in America who had known him.

'It's Dan all right,' said Johnny McGinty to his wife and family. 'May the Lord have mercy on his soul,' he added in a more tender tone. 'But it's him. Not a doubt in the world on that point. Dan McGinty from the County Donegal. Went to the States such a year. Had two brothers, Johnny and James. Three sisters, Mary, Bridget and Delia. That is the only point of difference. There were only two girls in our family, Mary and Bridget. (It makes me sad when I think they are all dead but myself.) There was no Delia. But I don't mind that. They didn't like the name Bridget in America. Lots of our Bridgets when they went across called themselves Delia. That is what happened in this case. Talking to some of his neighbours in America, Dan referred to one of his sisters as Bridget. Later on, he changed it to Delia. People thought there were two where there was only one ... Of course, there is no address given. Nothing but County Donegal. No townland, no parish, no post-town. But that does not matter. In a million years you would not get the same number of particulars in two families.'

It was the common opinion throughout the Rosses that Johnny McGinty was the man that the lawyers were trying to trace. With Red Hughdie Ward's mother, it was a certainty. Consequently, she changed her objective. She decided to get Johnny McGinty's daughter Fanny as a wife for her son. Didn't the news come at the right time, she said to herself. A few days later and all was lost. For, if she had made any overtures towards a match with Sara Gallagher, she would find it very hard to draw back, that is, provided Sara and her parents consented to the match.

Mrs Ward decided on her plan of campaign. There was to be no mention of marriage for months to come yet. There was plenty of time for preparing the ground. In those days, it took a letter three weeks to get to America. Three more weeks for a letter to come back. Between the slow transport and the 'law's delay' it might take the best part of a year before the legacy was finally settled.

Mrs Ward's plan was that her son would become a frequent visitor to Johnny McGinty's. He would be polite to the daughter, slightly flattering to the mother and deferential to the father. In addition, he would give McGinty a helping hand now and again with turf or hay or any other kind of work that a man cannot do easily by himself.

As time went on, however, Johnny McGinty was doing his own bit of thinking. Red Hughdie Ward was a good worker. In due course, he would have a neat, little holding. McGinty would be quite pleased to give him his daughter in marriage under ordinary circumstances. But the expected legacy showed things in a fresh light, called for further consideration. The amount of the legacy might be considerable. He had heard it stated once that his late brother had money in what was called Funds – whatever that was. It could happen that his daughter would have two or three hundred pounds for her dowry. In that case, he would not dream of giving her to Red Hughdie Ward or to any man of his class. He would marry her to one of the wealthy shopkeepers in Dungloe.

But that was not all. There was in the drama another character whose destiny Johnny McGinty was resolved to decide. That character was Cameron. Ever since 'the day of the White Strand', Johnny felt humiliated. There was his dog Rover about whose exploits in the past he had made many a proud boast. And look at him now! Afraid to go a hundred yards from the house without the protection of his master. Jumping up from his sleep at all hours of the night and howling like a lost soul. The forthcoming legacy could be big or small, but one thing it could do if properly handled: it could seal Cameron's fate. How would he go about it?

He got his inspiration sooner than he had expected to get it. One day, going out towards Ardbane, he came upon a dog attacking a sheep. He yelled at him for all he was worth and the dog ran away. Johnny recognised him at once – a big, black dog with a white breast and a curly tail. It was Paddy Frank's dog. When Johnny came to the scene of the attack, he discovered that the sheep was his own. It lay there in the heather gasping, with blood spurting from the gashes in its throat.

Under the circumstances, all Johnny McGinty had to do was to go to Paddy Frank and tell him the story, the truth of which could easily be proved. Paddy would pay the price of the sheep and then destroy the dog. That was the custom. But Johnny saw his opportunity of disposing of Cameron and, sad to relate, he made full use of it.

A few evenings after that, Red Hughdie was visiting in McGinty's, according to plan.

'One of my sheep was killed last Tuesday,' said the man of the house. 'Killed by a dog.'

'Whose dog?' asked Hughdie, rather uneasy.

'Your dog.'

'Cameron?'

'Cameron.'

'Did you see him kill her?'

'No, but I have it on very good authority.'

'Who is the authority?'

'I can't tell you. But you had better destroy the dog. That is what the law says. Needless to say, Hughdie, I won't bring you to law. But if I don't, some other person will some fine day. Of that you may be sure. Once a dog gets the taste of blood, nothing can cure him. You could beat him to within an inch of his life, it would be no use. When the rage grips a dog, he could kill as many as six sheep a day. Just for the mad pleasure of killing them.'

'What do you say the sheep is worth?' asked Red Hughdie, and he felt his tongue going dry in his mouth.

'We'll not talk about that,' replied Johnny. 'I am only telling you for your own sake. After that, you can do what you like.'

'I find it hard to destroy my dog,' said Hughdie, 'until the person who saw him kill your sheep comes along and tells me.'

'Please yourself,' said McGinty. 'As I've said, it's for your own sake I am telling you.'

The daughter Fanny was listening to this conversation. She did not share her father's mean, spiteful character. She knew nothing about the wicked plan he had hatched. Therefore, she thought Red Hughdie was being unreasonable. After all, if he were brought to court, he would be made destroy the dog. And brought to court he would be. Cameron had got the taste of blood and, after that, nothing could stop him!

Red Hughdie did not stay long after that. He made some excuse to get away. When he was leaving, the girl accompanied him down the lane as far as the road.

'I think, Hughdie, you ought to destroy the dog,' she pleaded.

'But why doesn't your father tell me who his informant is?' asked Hughdie.

'That might breed bad blood between neighbours,' replied the girl. 'You may be sure my father wouldn't say it unless he was certain he was right. I think that, for all our sakes, the best thing is for you to destroy the dog.'

Hughdie had to do a bit of quick thinking. It was hard, very hard indeed, to destroy Cameron, and on such flimsy evidence. But, if he refused, he was running the risk of ruining his marriage plans. In this matter he was not moved by any romantic or sentimental considerations. For that matter, he would prefer to marry Sara Gallagher from Derrymore. But his avarice got the better of him. Two hundred pounds dowry ... Five hundred? ... A thousand? As much as would keep himself and a wife and family in comfort all his life, without ever again having to go to Scotland to earn a few pounds as a harvester.

'All right,' he consented. 'I'll take out the dog tomorrow and shoot him.'

III

When he arrived home there was nobody in the house but his mother. He sat by the fireside and began to smoke his pipe in silence.

'You look like a man who is worried,' said the mother.

He told her the whole story.

'Johnny McGinty could have made up that yarn,' said the mother. 'I wouldn't put it past him. He is burning with rage in his heart ever since the day Cameron silenced himself and Rover. However, it cannot be helped now. In any case, what is a dog but a dog?'

'But when you love a dog, mother!'

'I know, I know. But there is another thing that deserves to be loved far more than any dog – a bagful of money the day you get married. Enough to keep you in ease and comfort all your life. Take out the dog tomorrow and shoot him. But don't breathe a word of it to your father or to anyone else who might tell him.'

'Why, mother?'

'Because your father hasn't much sense in ways. Never had. He could never see what was in his own interest. He could easily take a fit and go up to Johnny McGinty and say: "Very good, Johnny, take your case to the law court and get that hidden witness of yours to take the Holy Book in his hand and swear that he saw my dog killing your sheep." That is what your father could do when the fit works him.'

'But how can I kill the dog unbeknownst to him?' asked Hughdie.

'Nothing easier,' replied his mother. 'You will leave in the morning to go to the mountains to shoot rabbits. You will take the dog along with you, of course. When you come to a lonely spot out, say, at the foot of Grugan, you will shoot him. Later on, you will come home by yourself. You will ask has Cameron not arrived. He strayed from you in the mountains. We'll keep talking about him and pretending to expect him for a week or so. He'll never come back, of course. Strayed in the mountains and got lost. Not the first dog that happened to!'

The following morning Red Hughdie took down an old shotgun he had and he put a handful of cartridges in his pocket. His mother made up a piece for him and he set out on his journey to the mountains. He did not bother looking for rabbits. Delaying the execution would only prolong his agony. The longer the dog frisked and gambolled around him and barked affectionately at him, the harder it would be to shoot him.

At last he came to a grassy hollow. He sat down on a boulder and put two cartridges in the breech of the gun. He then made a ball of grass and threw it some distance away for Cameron to fetch. But the dog would not stay long enough in one place or position for Hughdie to take steady aim, and it would be disastrous to inflict only a slight wound on him and let him get away.

Hughdie put the gun across his knees and looked up at the sky. The dog ran to him. Hughdie took up the gun and began playing with the dog as he had often played with him using a stick. He poked him lightly in the chest a few times with the muzzle of the gun. Cameron was enjoying the game thoroughly. It was great fun ... At last Hughdie pressed the trigger. A shot rang out. The dog spun round once or twice. Then he fell. From where he lay on the grass, he cast the last look at Hughdie. And all was over.

Hughdie looked down at the dead dog. Oh, God! That last look! He felt the tears gathering in his eyes and trickling down his cheeks. He had done that terrible deed at the prospect of a handful of money. But if Cameron were alive now, he would not shoot him for all the gold in America.

Towards evening he came home with a heavy step and a heavier heart. Then there were the questions and answers as had been decided on. Had Cameron not come? No. When was he missed? Last seen running up the slope of Grugan chasing a hare ... He would be home the following day ... Dogs were sometimes led astray by all kinds of distractions, etc.

But, of course, Cameron never returned.

IV

Four or five months passed. Then, one day, the postman brought Johnny McGinty a letter. They recognised the envelope, having received several of the same kind before. The letter was from the solicitor in Letterkenny.

Johnny McGinty could not read. Neither could his wife. They would have to wait until their daughter returned from the shop to find out how much money was coming to them ... Would they call in a neighbour's youngster? No. This was something they must keep to themselves until they were certain of the amount. They began to guess how much might be coming to them.

'Five hundred pounds, perhaps,' ventured Mrs McGinty.

'Maybe a thousand,' said her husband. 'Maybe more. Along with saving every penny he had ever earned, except what he needed to keep him, he had money in the Funds. There's a man over there in Shaskinarone, Anthony the doctor, and he made a fortune in the Funds.'

'By all accounts,' said the woman, 'he was a fine man. Of course, I never saw him. But I heard people who knew him in America talking about him.'

'A fine man in every way,' said Johnny McGinty. Would the daughter never come?

At last she arrived and, before she had time to take off her shawl, she was handed the letter.

'Letterkenny,' she said, looking at the postmark.

'Open it quickly and read it for us.'

The girl opened the letter and began reading to herself. What was that frown on her face?

'All a washout,' she said at last in a husky voice. 'No legacy for us,' she said, flopping down on a chair as if she fell on it.

It was a cruel letter. It began by thanking them for their kind assistance in the task of tracing the next of kin of the late Dan McGinty. The said Mr McGinty was a native of the townland of Cashelard, in the parish of Kilbarron, post-town Ballyshannon. The names of the family were Dan, John, James, Mary, Bridget and Delia. The surviving members were John, living in Cashelard, Ballyshannon, and Delia, living in New York, USA. The evidence produced by Delia, including passports and extracts from the baptismal register in the parish church in Ballyshannon, has established the identity of the family beyond the shadow of a doubt, etc.

'Damn on Delia,' said Johnny McGinty. 'She has ruined everything on us ... Shocking, so it is.'

'Serves us right,' snarled Mrs McGinty. 'Serves us right for expecting anything off him. Since the day he left Ireland, he never sent as much as one dollar to anyone belonging to him. Never even wrote to ask if we were alive. If he is alive himself, he is in the poor-house. If he is dead, we may be sure he died a pauper.'

'We must keep this terrible news to ourselves,' said Johnny McGinty. 'The neighbours would be only delighted to hear how we've been let down.'

'We can't keep it a secret, father,' said his daughter. 'It will be in next week's *Donegal Eagle*, the whole story. I have seen such news items before. Just an account of how the next of kin of Dan McGinty of Cashelard, Ballyshannon, have been traced. All the names and particulars will be given. We'd be only making ourselves ridiculous by trying to keep it a secret.'

The news spread like wildfire through the length and breadth of the Rosses. Malicious people said cruel things about Johnny McGinty and his wife. Charitable people had pity for the daughter who, they said, was sensible, and had put on no airs and graces when the legacy appeared a certainty. Red Hughdie Ward's mother took no part in the discussions.

One game had been played and lost. It was time to prepare for the second one. Consequently, Susan Ward opened her campaign to get her son married to Sara Gallagher of Derrymore.

The negotiations were brought to a successful conclusion. Hughdie was to get half his father's land. Sara would bring him forty pounds as her marriage portion.

The night before Hughdie was married, he was sitting at home with his mother, silently smoking his pipe and looking into the fire. The mother began to talk to him. He neither agreed nor disagreed with her remarks. He merely replied from time to time in meaningless murmurs, like a man who was only half-awake.

'Why aren't you bright and cheerful on the eve of your marriage?' the mother began. 'Just think of how lucky you are. It was the mercy of God you didn't marry Fanny McGinty on the strength of the fairy legacy. You would have her now and not one red penny along with her. And you would be the laughing-stock of the parish. Think of the terrible things some of them would say about you. Mary Feggy Tammy would say that the Ballyshannon McGinty was sending you a few pounds for pity's sake. Old Shoogey Brennan would say that the Delia one deserved hell's red, roasting damnation for having ever been born. Think of those things, my son, and cheer up.'

'How he barked joyously into my face and him looking up sideways at me as we were going out Glenfadda.'

'Will you stop your foolish raving and listen to your mother. You have a good girl and a handsome penny along with her. I grant you she is no beauty, but neither is Fanny McGinty. Anyhow, who wants a beauty? What good are pretty little dolls, either inside in a house or outside in the fields?'

'And the way he thought it was playing with him I was when I had the muzzle of the gun against his breast.'

'Do I have to tell you again to give over your lunatic ravings and listen to me? Thank Heaven that you've been so lucky. With the money she is bringing you, you will be able to build a tidy, little house. We are giving you the red polly along with the land. And you are getting a wife who is wise and thrifty and has a splendid pair of hands. She can card and spin and knit. And, in the harvest field, she can handle a reaping-hook as good as any man could. A gem of a wife you are getting. So, shake off your gloom and thank Heaven for your luck.'

'And the way he looked up at me for the last time, as he lay on the grass dying.'

THE BEST LAID SCHEMES

It was the first time I visited Clochglas in the end of the Rosses farthest from where I was born and brought up. I thought the view from the same spot was superb. From a little knoll at the end of the promontory you have, on one side, a full view of the Atlantic and of the islands and headlands from Tory to the Stags of Rossowen and, on the other side, the range of mountains from Muckish to the Blue Stacks. But, on this particular day, it was not the scenery that so much attracted my attention. No, it was a cottage the like of which I did not know to exist in the Rosses. It was situated in a sheltered spot with a southern aspect. Roses and woodbine trailed around the trellised door and windows. In front of the house was a beautifully laid out garden with flagstone walks and rockeries and all kinds of shrubs and flowers.

I came off my bicycle and stood admiring this rare combination of natural beauty and human achievement. It was, I thought, an ideal spot to live in. And I concluded at once that it was owned and occupied by one of those wealthy Englishmen who, in their sight-seeing trips, take a fancy to such places and decide to settle in them.

I was about to move off when an old woman emerged from behind a bush and came along one of the walks leading to the gate that opened onto the road. She wore leather gloves reaching to her elbows and carried a small garden fork in her hand. She was old and withered and wrinkled. Her hair was bleached almost as white as snow. Yet, despite her evident age, there still remained traces of beauty in her face and features.

I was trying to think of something to say but I was saved the trouble of opening the conversation. The old lady spoke first. 'Admiring my flowers?' she said.

'And they are to be admired,' I replied. 'I did not know that such a fairy flower-garden existed in the Rosses.'

The old lady was inclined to talk. 'When I came here over fifty years ago, the place where the garden is now was a wilderness. I was first attracted by the scenery. I bought the site and had the cottage built. Then I wanted to have a garden laid out and to have shrubs and flowers planted. I was attracted to the idea by pictures I had seen in illustrated magazines, particularly by pictures of villas on the French Riviera ... You may open the gate and come in, if you wish.'

I went into the garden.

'I am sure you have wondered how I managed to do it.'

'Yes, that thought did occur to me, madam. I expect it had an absorbing interest for you.'

'Yes, after a few years it became most interesting. I began it to escape from the boredom of life. To get out of that state of flat indifference in which one finds oneself when a dream has vanished.'

I thought she was going to embark on what, to me, would be the makings of a story. But she did not continue in that strain. She returned to the garden. 'Of course,' she said, 'I could not have done it by myself. I had no knowledge or experience of such work. But I was fortunate in securing the services of an old gardener who had worked for half a lifetime on the Glenveagh estate. It was he who planned and laid out the garden and the walks and the rockeries. It was he who planted the roses and the vines and most of the shrubs. Of course, as time went on, I became interested myself and I learned quite a lot. I often experiment with shrubs and flowers which some experts would tell you would not grow at all in this soil. And very often I am successful. Take, for instance, this one,' she continued, pointing to a particular flower. 'The *Gladiolus Cinquecentus*. I got it from the Botanic Gardens in Dublin. Experts told me it would not grow here at all. They said that the salt in the sea air would kill it. But I tried it. And look at it now.'

She went on to describe the nature and peculiarities of different kinds of shrubs and flowers, which made me feel embarrassed. For then, as now, my knowledge of botany and floriculture was near to nothing. My embarrassment, however, was soon relieved. A neatly-dressed maid emerged from the cottage and came down the walk to us. She begged to be excused and told the old lady that luncheon was ready. And I noticed that she addressed her mistress in the third person. Later on in life, I came across, in the course of my reading, such forms of address, particularly in French society. But it was new to me this time and I could not understand it.

The old lady, pulling off her leather gloves, begged to be excused. She then added that any time I was passing I could come into the garden and spend as much time in it as I wished. I thanked her, of course, for her kind invitation but I hadn't the slightest intention of coming back. As I have said, I didn't know the first thing about flowers or shrubs. I was not interested. I would be interested in her life story. But beyond a passing reference to vanished dreams, she told me nothing. From her hurried return to the shrubs and flowers, it was evident that she intended keeping her secrets to herself. At least she would not tell them to me.

II

I put her out of my head and I turned my attention to another individual who, as had often occurred to me in the past few years, might have a story to tell. He was an old Rosses man and it was believed he had seen a good deal of the world in his day. He had been twice in America – for a spell of about three years in his young days and afterwards for over a quarter of a century. When I saw him first he was badly stooped. Still, he was tall and broad-shouldered. His name was Mickey Mulligan and he came from the townland of Rinamona in the Lower Rosses.

He lived by himself in a miserable cabin and he was a born miser if there ever was one. And local tradition had it that 'he did not pick it off the bushes,' for that the Mulligans had been misers for generations back.

As long as he could work he tilled his little patches of land. And he kept a cow and sometimes a calf in addition. He was reported to have plenty of money. Some of the neighbours – the kind that know the full uses of keyholes – alleged that he kept a pot filled with gold coins hidden under a flagstone in the floor and that, at night, having bolted the door and screened the window, he would spread out his treasure on the table and, in the light of a flickering candle, contemplate it for hours. Others, and I believe their guess was right, maintained that he kept only small sums of money in the house. It was known for a fact that he had an account in the bank in Cloghansuarach. And the local postmistress, without stating any figure, let it be understood that he had a considerable amount in the Post Office Savings Bank.

If he had plenty of money – and there was every reason to believe he had – why didn't he spend some of it on himself? Why hadn't he the wretched hovel that he lived in made more comfortable and a little bit more pleasing to the eye? He could have got a solid, comfortable bed with suitable bedclothes for the different seasons. He could procure at least one comfortable chair. He could purchase a plentiful supply of good turf before the beginning of winter instead of trying to boil his wretched pot with damp clods and fragments of driftwood.

Outside the hovel too he could, if he were prepared to spend a few pounds, have made several improvements that would make the place look like a home. Choked drains could be cleared. A lawn could be laid out in front of the house. Without going to any great expense, old Mulligan could do a lot to make his wretched hovel look a little bit more decent and comfortable. No reasonable person would expect him to spend his entire life's savings on a fairy cottage and a fairy garden like what I had seen in Clochglas a short time before that. But there is a medium in all things.

The next question is, why didn't Mickey Mulligan marry in his young days? On this point different opinions had been expressed from time to time. Some would say that he was too miserly to share his worldly goods with a woman. Shoogey Brennan maintained that his star rose once, when he was a young man, and set suddenly again, plunging him into darkness.

I visited him a few times but could get nothing out of him. At last I thought I noticed that he seemed to resent my visits. So I decided not to molest him further.

To a man on the quest for stories it was annoying to be baffled twice inside a week or two – first by the old lady with the enchanting garden and cottage, and now by this sordid, old miser. But I felt there was no hope of success in either quarter. If I was ever to get one or other or both of their stories, I should have to direct my research to other sources.

III

Andy Divir was a Rosses man who made his home in the townland of Shallogan on the banks of Lough Finn. What took him up there? He went via America. When he was a young man he left his native Rosses and went to the States. There he met a girl from Shallogan and they got married. The following year they were invited by the girl's parents to come back and make their home on the mountainy farm by the Finn side which was to become theirs after the old pair died. The farm, while it did not contain much arable land, was excellent for sheep-raising, and the young pair gladly accepted the offer.

From Andy Divir's viewpoint there was one little drawback in the arrangement: the property would belong to his wife, left to her by her parents. That could have as a result that the wife would claim more of her own way than, under other circumstances, Andy would be pleased to concede. However, it was a good home. And, if small sacrifices had to be made, there was consolation in the thought that he was getting a holding where he could bring up a family in comparative comfort.

In due course the children arrived. They had four sons, one after the other. Fine lads they were too. But Mrs Divir was becoming discontented. She longed for a daughter. She prayed for a daughter. She had her own plans for bringing her up, for dressing her, for having her educated.

At last, her wish was granted. She had a fifth baby, and this time it was a girl. According to the opinion of the women of the district, it was a bonnie baby. They said that when she grew up to womanhood there would be no beauty to match her in seven parishes.

The first thing Mrs Divir had to do was to select a suitable name for her child. In her earlier years she had been reading romances and had taken a fancy to certain names. When her baby girl was born, she weighed up several of these names in her mind. She considered, rejected, accepted, rejected again. At last, she decided on the name Florence.

Andy Divir did not relish the idea. In the first place, the name was strange; he had never before heard it. But the principal objection to it was that it would break a sacred Rosses custom – that of calling the first girl after her paternal grandmother. Andy Divir's mother's name was Biddy. For that reason his eldest daughter should be called Biddy. But, of course, the child's mother would not, could not, consent. The surname Divir was bad enough. That could not be helped. But to have her daughter called Biddy Divir was an outrage that the poor mother could not stand.

Andy Divir had to give in. In her own quiet way, without putting it in so many words, his wife conveyed the idea to him that the least he could do in return for a good home was to allow her to choose a name for their daughter.

The child was duly christened Florence. Florence Divir! The Divir part of it was 'a bit thick'. But that could not be helped. The name Florence was in itself a mark of distinction, no matter what came after it.

IV

Florence was growing up. She was admittedly good-looking. At school she was bright and intelligent. She was her parents' pride and joy and her father had become reconciled to her name. He imagined there was something elegant and distinguished about the sound of it. It was, he thought, a much more fitting name than Biddy, although that had been his mother's name.

At the age of fourteen Florence left the national school. 'She must have a lot of learning now,' said her father. 'I wish I had had half as much when I left home.'

'It is not much in the way of learning in this age,' replied the mother. 'Times have changed. The struggle is much tougher now than it was. Much harder to succeed.'

It was all she said on this occasion. Just enough to break the ice. But she would return to the attack.

Later on, she disclosed her plans. They should, she said, send Florence for a few years to the convent school in Assaroe. Andy Divir opened his eyes in wonder and looked at his wife. What had put that silly idea into her head?

'How much will it cost?' he asked, when he recovered his speech.

Mrs Divir pretended to be doing an exercise in mental arithmetic. But she was only pretending. She had all her calculations already made.

'So much,' she replied.

'So much!' gasped her husband.

'But that includes everything. Board, tuition, books, uniform, music, and a little pocket-money.'

'But, woman dear, we can't afford it. You know we lost nearly half of our lambs in the snowstorm in March. It's going to take us some years to pull up on that.'

'All we have to do is to write to my brother Patrick in America. He has plenty of money.'

'We know that he has made a lot of money, especially since he went into the fur trade. But he made it the hard way. He may not be too willing to part with it. And maybe he doesn't believe in sending country girls to convent schools.'

'Listen to me, Andy,' said Mrs Divir. 'I have the money to pay for Florence at a convent school. Every penny of it. All my American savings for four years in addition to what I won in the lottery the year before we came home. That should settle the case.'

It did settle it too. Once again Andy Divir knew what his wife was thinking. She had brought him home to her father's farm and handed it over to him. The least she might be allowed in return was the privilege of spending her private savings on their daughter's education.

On the evening of that day, Mrs Divir was day-dreaming. She saw her daughter grown up, educated and polished. Able to play the piano. Singing at the annual concert in Letterkenny.

Later on, when putting away her daughter's national school-books, she opened the senior reader and sat down to look through it. She kept turning the pages until she came to a poem written by one Aubrey de Vere. All of a sudden she got a flash of inspiration. De Vere! De Vere! It was surely the original of Divir. Florence de Vere! She repeated the name to herself three or four times. It was a vast improvement on Florence Divir.

She did not fully realise the cachet value of the new form of the name. She did not know that the prefix *de* had been inserted by famous Frenchmen, including Balzac. She could not foresee that, in her own country, the day would come when separating the *de* from a name in which it was incorporated would give a similar mark of distinction. So, there and then, without the aid of genealogies or heraldry, she decided that henceforth her daughter should be known as Florence de Vere.

Her husband was amazed at the idea. He could trace his ancestry for seven generations, back to Black Jack Divir, the famous smuggler from Inishmacdurn. But it would not do. The name Divir sounded badly. And, in any case, what adornment would the name of a smuggler be to a talented, young lady who was destined to have a lady's education?

V

In due course, Florence de Vere – for so we have consented to call her – went to the convent school in Assaroe. Her new environment, associating with girls from the towns, and especially her new name, all went to her head. She made a pal of a girl about her own age, a solicitor's daughter from Ballyshannon. The Ballyshannon girl went in for reading romances. She used to smuggle them into the convent, read them on the sly and hide them under the mattress of her bed. And, of course, she lent them all to Florence.

This type of reading would never have any lasting effect on the Ballyshannon girl. She was plain and unimaginative. She had the mentality and outlook of a small town where twopence ha'penny looks down on twopence. When she returned home, after having finished her schooling, her only care and that of her mother would be to find a suitable husband in the twopence halfpenny class.

But with Florence, it was different. She was extremely good-looking. She had a most vivid imagination, born with her to begin with and then stimulated by the wild and rugged grandeur of the hills of Donegal. And then her name counted for quite a lot. The fact that, but for the grace of God, she could be Biddy Divir instead of Florence de Vere went a long way towards making her imagine that she was different from her school companions.

She read avidly and the reading made a deep impression on her. She often imagined herself as the heroine of one of these hectic tales. She is being held captive in a castle. A champion comes along, fully armed and accoutred. He challenges, of course, the captor to single combat and vanquishes him. Then he and Florence get married.

In one respect, Florence de Vere, during her years at the convent school, closely resembled the notorious Emma Ronault – but with this difference. Unlike the French demoiselle, Florence's imaginary escapades would fail to draw the slightest reprimand from the sternest moralist. Florence always married the hero of her story and remained faithful to him all her life.

In her last year at the convent school, Florence read a story that got a powerful grip on her. It was about a girl who had an immense fortune and kept the fact hidden from everybody. Her idea was to find a man who loved her for her own sake although she was penniless. The marriage took place. The couple came home to the bridegroom's little cabin. They were poor but they were happy because they loved each other. And then, all of a sudden, the bride presents her young husband with proofs of her fortune.

This was precisely what Florence wanted to do. And it was becoming more than possible that, in due course, she would see her dream fulfilled. Her uncle Patrick in America was known to be very wealthy. He had never married. It was almost certain that he would leave Florence the bulk of his money. Moreover, he was known to be in failing health for some time. Florence hated herself for letting her mind dwell on this aspect of the expected legacy. Several times she said to herself she hoped her uncle Patrick would live for many more years. But somehow, she felt she was not sincere.

VI

After five years at the Assaroe boarding-school, Florence came home with her education finished. She was then nineteen years of age and very attractive.

She was not long at home when she had an offer of marriage. It was from a shopkeeper in Letterkenny who was supposed to be fairly well off. He presented proofs of his assets and asked that Florence be given a certain sum of money as a dowry. Andy Divir thought the claim unreasonable and wanted to settle for so many pounds less. Mrs Divir came to the rescue. She would, she said, pay the difference between what was asked and what was offered out of her own private resources. She had not spent all her savings on her daughter's education.

Mrs Divir was pleased at the prospect of having her daughter marry in a town. In Letterkenny, Florence would be in the limelight. She would have repeated opportunities of showing off her accomplishments whereas she would be lost on a mountainy farm beside Lough Finn. Imagine this talented and polished lady in her bare feet carrying a load of sedge grass on her back to the huts in the lambing season! She would become a Florence Divir again. A Biddy Divir, if God hadn't said it!

Florence refused point-blank. Her alleged reason was one that could not be opposed. She did not like the man, she said. But the real reason for her refusal was that the man asked for a dowry.

The next proposal came from a school-teacher in Ardard. He, too, wanted money. He said they could live comfortably on his salary but he wanted to build or purchase a house that would be in keeping with his social status.

Florence refused again and for the same reason as on the first occasion. She did not like the man, she said.

'And what do you intend doing with yourself, my daughter?' asked her father. 'Only one of you can have this holding – Michael, the eldest of the boys. All we can do for the rest of you is to give each of you what money we can afford when your turn comes to leave.'

Florence would not be moved by that argument. She would marry no man who insisted on having a gift of money along with her hand.

A few weeks after the second proposal, Florence got a letter from a second cousin of hers in New York. 'Your uncle Patrick is dead,' the letter began. 'Died last Saturday. Lord have mercy on him ... According to the law of this state, your uncle's will cannot be admitted to probate until he is a year dead. But this much I can tell you – and keep it a dead secret from everybody – there is a rosy future before you ... '

Florence was very glad. The image of the girl posing as penniless until she found a man who loved her for her own sake had become a reality. She could wait for years now. The man would surely come along someday. All that was necessary was to keep the secret hidden in her own bosom. The day would come when her rosy dreams would be realised.

VII

The Harvest Fair in Glenties. It is the big day of the year in this part of the country. As big as, if not bigger, than the summer fair of Dungloe is in the Rosses.

Florence de Vere went to the fair accompanied by two girls from the neighbourhood. Her beauty and the contrast of her dress with the homespun worn by her companions would make any young man stand and look at her.

There was a huge crowd of people gathered in Glenties. Out at Mullineeran the horse fair was being held. Nearer the town was the cattle market. In the town itself there were the usual attractions. There was the man with the air-gun offering 'three shots a penny and every time you ring the bell, you win threepence.' There was the man with the roulette table offering 'one to one on the red, two on the black' and so on to a 'shilling on the anchor or on the crown.' But, for many people, the greatest attraction in the town that day was Felimy the Fiddler, believed to be the best traditional player in the country.

Felimy played several airs – some fast ones and some slow ones – and, from time to time, he stooped down to pick up the pennies that were being thrown at his feet. At last, a young man walked up to him and asked him could he play the 'Foxhunt'. Felimy could and did play the air requested of him. The crowd was held spellbound. They imagined they saw the pack setting off in full chase. The fox ran this way and that, trying to elude his mortal enemies. At last, the audience thought they heard the last, desperate yells in the face of inevitable death. Then the last feeble squeals as the victim's life ebbed out.

The young man put a silver coin in the old fiddler's hand, thanked him and praised his performance generously. The people around were looking at him. He was a stranger. But that was not to be wondered at. At that time people came any distance up to fifteen miles to the Harvest Fair of Glenties.

Florence de Vere looked at the stranger. He was a fine man – a man that any young girl could easily take a fancy to. He was dressed in a fine suit of the latest American cut and he wore patent leather shoes.

How many times Florence's eyes and those of the young man met, I do not know. Nor do I know how the pair got introduced to each other. All I know for certain is that within two hours of the time Felimy the Fiddler played the 'Foxhunt', the two of them were together in the Highland Hotel drinking tea.

The young man was most interesting. He had, he said, returned from America a few days beforehand after having spent a few years in that country. There was, he said, money and plenty of it to be earned in America. But he would not like to live there for long. America was a country where the creed of materialism reigned supreme. It had no past, no traditions, no culture. Nothing to worship but the almighty dollar. That was why he had left it. That was why he would never go back … 'How many times,' he concluded, 'how many million times would you go up Broadway before you heard a fiddler playing the "Foxhunt"?'

The stranger began to visit Florence in her own home. Andy Divir was making enquiries and he was not too pleased with the courtship. After eight or nine months, the stranger declared his undying love for Florence and proposed to her. Florence was pleased with the proposal. She was willing to accept but, on one condition. 'You know,' she said, 'the custom here and, I suppose, in your part of the country, is for her parents to give a girl a dowry when she is getting married. I have no dowry to get, not a penny piece. Between paying arrears of rent, which nobody expected would be demanded, between that and the flooding of the meadow two summers in succession, and the loss of lambs in the snow-storm last March, my parents are left without a penny. Therefore, the man that marries me must take me as I am with nothing but the clothes on my back.'

The young man took the girl's two hands in his and looked lovingly at her. 'Florence, darling,' he declared, 'it's yourself I want, not money. I offer to share my little home with you, such as it is. God will bless us for we are beginning the right way. Please don't mention the word dowry to me again.'

The following day Florence told her parents of her betrothal. Her father stared at her in blank amazement. 'Are you mad?' he began. 'He is a fine-looking man all right, I grant you that much. But what has he? A *screabán* in the Rosses that would no more than feed a goat ... '

Florence, however, could not be shaken in her resolution to marry the man she loved and who was prepared to take her without a penny. As for the future, she was not, of course, worried in the least. She was sure of a considerable fortune from her uncle's legacy although she did not know the actual amount. She had kept her secret from everyone, including her parents. When the time came she would spring a pleasant surprise on them ... In the course of a few days she would have definite news!

On the morning of the day before that fixed for the wedding, the postman brought Florence two letters. The address on one of them was typed and the envelope had an official look about it. Florence opened it. It was from a firm of New York solicitors, and what heavenly news it contained! It stated that under the will of her uncle, Patrick Timony, deceased such a date, when death duties had been deducted and all legal expenses paid, the residual was 27,000 dollars, which amount was due to her as the testator's sole legatee. She was, at her earliest convenience, to instruct her solicitor to whom the above sum would be remitted, in her name, as soon as he had communicated with them.

Florence read the letter three times. Her heart was on the point of bursting with joy. Her dream had become a reality. Twenty-seven thousand dollars! She reduced it to sterling in accordance with the current rate of exchange. Enough to keep them in comfort all their lives. When would she tell the news to her husband? On their way back from the church after the wedding? Would she wait for a few days or weeks or even months? Some day, when they would have no money to buy food or fuel? Then she could, like a fairy godmother, present her husband with a cheque for 27,000 dollars!

When she got time to settle somewhat after the first wave of pleasurable excitement caused by the legal document, it occurred to her to read the second document. She took it up and opened it. She read and reread it. Then she locked herself in her little bedroom and cried until she was exhausted. When she came out of the room, her eyes red, her face tear-stained, her parents got a shock. They could not understand what had happened their daughter – on the eve of her wedding!

The mother, however, recovered. 'Listen to me, my daughter,' she advised. 'Wash your face and eyes in cold water. Then lie down and rest for a while ... You are not the only girl that that happened to on the eve of her wedding. Just strung up, that's all. Every woman feels it, more or less. I knew a girl that cried for two days. It's the way we're made. It will be all over before you are back from the church tomorrow.'

The future bridegroom called in the afternoon. He was staying in Glenties for a few days. He came to tell Florence and her people that the final arrangements had been made. 'We are to be in the church at nine o'clock,' he said.

'I won't be in the church at nine,' said Florence in a husky voice.

'Is nine o'clock too early?' asked the young man. 'I thought we had agreed on nine and I have made that arrangement with the priest.'

'You had better cancel your arrangement.'

'And what time do you prefer?'

'I am not getting married at all tomorrow, or the day after tomorrow, or any day.'

'In the name of God, Florence, what is the matter with you?'

'What is wrong with me? The cherished dream of a lifetime vanished.'

'Florence, darling, will you tell me, in Heaven's name, what has happened to you?'

'That is what has happened me,' she replied, handing him the letter which she had received from her kinsman in America that morning:

> ... I expect that by now you will have got a letter from the solicitors in charge of your uncle's estate. It is in the region of 27,000 dollars, after deducting tax and expenses. I congratulate you on your great, good fortune. You will remember a year ago I gave you a hint of the rosy future that lay before you. It was all I could say at the time. I knew the total of your uncle's estate because I witnessed the will. The second witness was a man named Mickey Mulligan from the Rosses ... A week or so afterwards Mulligan left New York for Klondike. I am not surprised. From what I am told, I am led to believe that get rich quick is the policy of the same Mulligan and of all his tribe. Again, my dear Florence, I congratulate you on your marvellous fortune, etc.

Florence remained with her parents for a year during which time she was getting a home made for herself in Clochglas. At the end of the year her eldest brother married and brought home his bride. The remaining brothers emigrated.

Then Florence, with a maid, moved into her neat cottage and she devoted the remainder of her long life to the cultivation of flowers and shrubs.

Mickey Mulligan went back to America almost immediately after his scheme went 'agley.' After about a quarter of a century, he returned to the Rosses to spend the remainder of his days in the way that suited his nature and disposition.

Fair-Haired Mary

She was fair-haired and, for that reason, the only name she was known by was fair-haired Mary. It is only a very poor translation of Máire Bhán. But what can I do? If I am to tell my story at all, I must tell it in the language of the people of Ireland.

Fair-haired Mary was extremely good-looking. Even her rivals admitted that much. She was also calm and gentle. But, notwithstanding her beauty and her disposition, she passed the most charming period of a young woman's life – from eighteen to twenty – and no young man in the Rosses seemed anxious to marry her. As the old woman would say, there was the bad drop in her. Her mother had come from Moorloch, a townland in the parish of Kiltywag. For generations the women of Moorloch had the reputation of bossing their husbands and, on that account, they were known as the 'holy terrors'.

For a long time it had been believed that a marriage between a Rosses man and one of the 'holy terrors' could not survive. The Rosses men were a bold, hardy race of men, used from their earliest years to struggle against the natural forces they had to contend with. They had to blast rocks and dig up heather and gorse roots to make little patches of land that could be cropped. In addition, they had to fight against the wind and the waves in their efforts to provide themselves and their family with a scrap of fish whenever possible. 'No Rosses man would allow himself to be ruled and bossed by one of the holy terrors,' the old women used to say. 'Hang it all, our men are men. But the men up yonder – the men of Moorloch, did you ever notice them in Cloghansalach on a fair day? Long, lifeless *streachláns* in sleeved waistcoats and marteens. Sure it is easy for the women to boss them. But it could not happen down here. No Rosses man will ever go to Moorloch to look for a wife.'

But this prophecy proved false. One man did go to Moorloch to look for a wife and that man was Fergal O'Boyle. Fergal was a very popular young man in his native Rosses. He could dance and sing and play the fiddle. His company was appreciated at weddings and christenings and other festive gatherings. Added to his other qualities, he had a marked capacity for drink. He could spend a whole night in a still-house and turn up for a day's turf-cutting in the morning. He always held, with the poet, that drink gave him health and strength and that the want of it would be the death of him. And he would clinch his argument by citing the case of 'the bird with the long, smooth neck who had got his death from the drought at last'.

In the end, Fergal took a fancy to a girl – not a Rosses girl, but a maiden from Moorloch whose first acquaintance he made at a wedding in that district. In due course, the pair were married and Fergal O'Boyle brought his bride home to the Rosses. Speculation was rife on how the marriage would work out. 'They'll never make a go of it,' said Biddy Vickey Andy.

'I wouldn't agree with you,' said Shoogey Brennan.

'Then one of them must give in to the other.'

'Agreed,' said Shoogey.

They made a go of it all right, despite Biddy Vickey Andy's gloomy forebodings. The Moorloch woman turned out to be a good worker and a thrifty housekeeper. She could card and spin and knit and make the children's clothes. In fact, she and her husband became a model pair. Fergal drained bogs and blasted rocks. He would let no opportunity pass without putting to sea in his curragh and he became a noted fisherman. As for drink, he would not taste a drop of it if you paid him for it.

They had a family of three sons and two daughters. The eldest of the daughters was fair-haired Mary, the subject of our story.

II

Mary grew up to womanhood and was, by common consent, very good-looking. In addition to her looks, she had other attractive qualities. She was mild and gentle and retiring. She would rather agree with another person's opinion than contradict it with any marked emphasis.

Who would marry her? For a while at first the young men seemed to fight shy of her. But nothing can withstand the power of beauty and charm, not even the tradition of the 'holy terrors'. Prejudices were gradually overcome and, before she had completed her twenty-first year, the names of two men in the parish began to be linked with hers. One of the men was Shoney Forker from Bunnawack, the other was Charlie Daney, a young man from her own neighbourhood. We don't know how anxious Shoney was to marry her but we know for a fact that Charlie was head over ears in love with her.

Again, speculation was rife. Which of the two would Mary marry?

Charlie Daney was the finer man of the two. But Shoney Forker was supposed to be the owner of what was considered a good, mountainy farm.

Fair-haired Mary seemed unwilling to choose between the two of them. Her mother favoured Shoney on account of the land. But would the land be his? He had three sisters and each of them would have to get a portion out of the holding. Shoney decided to do what had often been done under the circumstances: he would go to America for a few years and earn a bit of money.

As we have said, Mary had been keeping the two of them on a string and was content to await developments. But when Shoney had gone to America, she did a bit of thinking. America was far away, as the Rosses folk used to say in those days. Out of every seven who went away, only one ever came back. So Mary decided to be more responsive to Charlie's love-making. At last, one fine evening, about an hour before sunset, on a grassy knoll overlooking Coolbawn Bay, he declared his love for her. She closed her eyes and leaned her head on his breast. The usual silence. A sigh or two. A protest that this declaration was sudden and had taken her completely by surprise. And finally, consent.

That night Charlie Daney came home walking on air, so to speak. He was too happy for words. The following day he seemed surprised at a question his mother asked him: 'What's wrong with you today?'

'Nothing, mother, nothing,' he replied. 'Why do you ask such a question?'

'You are behaving in a very strange way this morning. For over half an hour you stood up there on the height looking out to sea. Four times I suggested that you should go to the bog and see if the far bank is ready for footing. You never answered me. You didn't seem to hear me. You know that when a man behaves like that, he shouldn't be surprised if his mother asks him what is wrong with him.'

He had to tell. He might as well tell her now as on another occasion. 'I have made an important decision,' he stammered, and he told her about his betrothal. The mother was spinning at the time. She wound the length of yarn in her hands round the bobbin and knotted the end of it. Then she came up and stood facing her son.

'Going to marry fair-haired Mary?' she exclaimed. 'To marry one of that tribe? The women of Moorloch. No wonder they have been called the 'holy terrors'. They are good-looking, I admit. But for generations they have made doormats of their husbands.'

'That is not true, mother, not wishing to contradict you,' said Charlie. 'It is just a malicious lie invented by some evil-minded people. The lie has made its way down this far and has come to be accepted by people who know nothing about the women of Moorloch.'

'So the story of making doormats of their husbands is a lie?' said the mother bitterly. 'But for proof of it you need not go past fair-haired Mary's own father. You don't know Fergal O'Boyle. You know only a cowed and subdued old man without a spark of life in him. But I knew him when he was full of life and joy. The brightest and the gayest man in the sixteen divisions of the Rosses, from the Ford of Gweedore to the Ford of Gweebarra. And look at him now. The shadow – no, not even the shadow – of himself. She has just made a dishcloth of him. Never in all their married life did she let him go by himself to Jack's Fair, to sell as much as a goat's kid. As for taking a drink! He would not dream of it, not even at a wedding. And that's not enough as regards the drink. He must go around preaching a temperance crusade in the Rosses. No one should taste drink, he says. And the silly, snivelling way he goes on talking. "Fanny says this, Fanny says that, Fanny can't be wrong."'

She paused for a moment as if for breath and looked into the fire. Then she resumed. 'Do you know what I am going to tell you, son? If there was no middle course, I would rather be married to a man who would kick my behind once a week than be married to a spineless creature like what Fergal O'Boyle has become. And the same thing will happen you. She will put the petticoat on you and you will have to wear it. On Sundays she will gallivant round the townland and you will stay at home to mind the babies – aye, and wash their nappies. Take my word for it. That is the life that lies ahead of you. You may not believe me now. But I am telling you that the time will come when you will rue the day you decided to marry one of the "holy terrors" of Moorloch.'

She said no more but went back to her spinning-wheel. Charlie went out and strolled down to the sea-shore. His mother, he thought, was a hard woman, a cruel woman, an unjust woman. Mary was the very opposite to what his mother had described. In any case, if it were a fact, which it was not, of course, but if Mary were in reality a 'holy terror', he was a man and he would stand for his rights. He would let no woman wipe her feet on him. 'And,' he added a second time, 'Mary would not attempt it. It is not her nature.'

III

The pair would get married but it would be some time – at least two years – before they would. The poet could offer his loved one 'flour and mead and red, juicy apples off the bough, and a heathery couch on the slopes of Céin Mhic Cáinte' but, for bed and board, the rude Rosses man must have a thatched cabin, potatoes and salt fish and a noggin of buttermilk. Such are the social grades in life.

The courtship went on smoothly and pleasantly for about a year. Then Charlie noticed a change in Mary. It was only slight at first. But, as time passed, it was becoming evident that the fair one was discontented. She would talk about the women of the Rosses and of their hard lot in life. At last, she went as far as to say that no girl should get married to settle down to a life of poverty and drudgery in the Rosses.

The following Sunday Charlie began to talk about the place where he intended to build their home. In a cosy spot overlooking the bay and sheltered by a height from the north and north-east winds. It would be heavenly to sit there on a summer evening, to watch the turf-boats going down the bay to Corfin, to listen to the lowing of the cows of Braad as they were being driven along the White Strand on their way homewards to be milked. And they could hear the sound of the church bell coming to them across the bay from Kilclooney.

Mary remained silent.

'What is wrong with you?' asked Charlie, not without anxiety.

Mary's voice became very sad. 'It is sometimes hard to say what one has to say,' she murmured. 'But it has to be said. I can't settle down and make my home here in the Rosses ... It is hard to say it. But I must say it. I have my mind made up to go to America about the middle of July. My cousin, Annie McGee from Moorloch, is getting a place for me.'

This piece of news gave Charlie a great shock. He would not mind crossing to Scotland occasionally to earn a few pounds at the harvest in a bad season. But to go to America was like going to another world. Still, he could not part with his loved one. Her decision to emigrate was a cruel one. But, without her, life would not be worth living. So he decided to leave the home of his childhood and all it meant to him and to accompany his darling across the Atlantic. But that could not be in July. He needed time to settle with them at home about his passage money and to make other preparations.

'Maybe you are right,' he said in a sad voice after a period of silence. 'Maybe you are wrong. In any case, I won't go against your wishes. I have only one request to ask of you, that you wait till the fall so that we can go off together. And I think we should get married first. They say it is much more difficult for emigrants to get married in America than here at home.'

The truth had to be blurted out. It came in bits. She told him she had no intention of getting married in the near future ... It was too bad, Charlie said. But he would wait.

Then the final blow fell. She could not marry him at all!

'But, Mary, your promise!' he began, in a choking voice.

Mary was becoming more logical and more eloquent now that the ice was broken. 'I know I promised,' she pleaded. 'But I did not understand. Now I do understand. I realise that we were not made for one another. That is no reflection on you. You are too good for me. Miles too good. And I know that you will meet some other girl who will make you happy, as you deserve. But, as I have said, you and I were not made for one another, of that I am convinced. And it is better to have found that out now than to find it out when it would be too late. So, in God's name, let us say goodbye,' she concluded, holding out her hand to him.

And Charlie? He said nothing. He could say nothing. Like Diogenes Teufelsdröck when his fair Blumine made a similar dread announcement, 'thick curtains of night rushed over his soul, as rose the inevitable Crash of Doom, and through the ruins as of a shivered universe, he was falling, falling towards the abyss.'

The neighbours were, of course, talking about him. 'He is in a bad way,' said Owen Roe. 'Going about talking to himself. Poor fellow, you'd be sorry for him.'

'That or some other calamity was bound to be his fate,' said Shoogey Brennan, 'since he got in tow with one of the 'holy terrors.' If she didn't make him rue his folly in one way, she would in another. And maybe the more merciful way was to leave him alone on the rocks of the Rosses and to clear off to America.'

'Women are contrary creatures,' said Black Hughdie Boyle. 'I think the less a man has to do with them the better. Take the Slasher out there. Never did a woman cross his threshold and he is the happiest man in the country. I spent a night in his house once on my way home from Scotland and I could see happiness written over his face.'

These last remarks led the conversation round to the Slasher and they lead me to say a few words about him in passing. The Slasher lived by himself on the roadside in the lonely moor, midway between Dunlewy and Meenadreen, on what was then the road from the Rosses to Letterkenny. At the time of our story, he was about fifty years. He made his living by raising sheep, of which he always kept a big flock. Very often, in winter, Rosses men walking from Letterkenny, on the last leg of the journey home from Scotland, found themselves exhausted when they reached the Slasher's. They always found the door unbolted and when they went in, the Slasher got up and gave every man a glass of poteen. Then he provided a meal of potatoes and buttermilk, after which he put more turf on the fire. And his guests stretched themselves on the floor and slept soundly till morning.

The Slasher had no tariff list. On leaving, you paid what you could. If you had no money left, you gave no explanations, you made no apology. And, to the credit of the Rosses men, be it said that very few, if any, of them ever took a mean advantage of their host's generosity. Thus the Slasher was the last link with the days when the Friars of Donegal kept a light all night in the tower window and the traveller got food and shelter in the monastery without being asked whether he could pay or not.

The Slasher loved his sheep. He knew them all. If one of them strayed, he would, like the shepherd in the Gospel story, leave the ninety-nine in the desert and go off in search of the lost one and keep searching until he found it. Only once did he allow himself to be distracted when out in search of a lost sheep. This time the strayed sheep had been set upon by dogs and killed, which would not have happened if its owner had continued to search without a break as was his wont on such occasions. But, to his credit, he never afterwards regretted having suspended the search.

IV

The day came when fair-haired Mary left home. At that time, the intending emigrant and the accompanying neighbours walked to Gweedore. There the emigrant could get the mail-car to Letterkenny. For about five miles beyond Gweedore, the road lay along a steep slope which meant that the horse had to go at a walking pace to the top of the height and that the 'convoy' could keep up with it as far as the Sandy Lake. It was there that the final farewells took place. For over a century many a bitter tear had been shed on the same spot. For the parting at Sandy Lake was regarded by many as being the same as the parting at the brink of the grave.

Fair-haired Mary had a big convoy. A huge concourse of people accompanied her to the parting-place. Charlie Daney was one of the convoy but he kept about two yards behind the main body. They plodded along up past Dunlewy and on to the level road at the Sandy Lake. There the parting had to be. The last farewells were taking place. Mary's mother set up a heart-rending scream. Her father was weeping silently. One by one her friends and relations and neighbours were coming forward to bid her goodbye and to wish her God-speed on her long voyage. Charlie Daney was outside the fringe of the crowd, leaning his back against a rock. He was making no move to come forward. Mary had her eye on him all the time. At last she went across to him and held out her hand.

'Goodbye, Charlie,' she said in a subdued voice.

'Goodbye and God bless you, Mary,' Charlie managed to stammer.

The convoy party turned back – all except Charlie Daney. He remained with his back to the boulder, looking after the old car going along the dreary road towards Meenadreen until, at last, it disappeared round a bend.

The members of the convoy would not, of course, return home immediately. Some of them were sad. All of them were tired. They would halt at the Cúirt – as the Gweedore Hotel was then called – to refresh their minds and bodies.

Charlie came along for about two miles. Then he left the road and turned right, up the slope of Errigal. At last, he sat down in a clump of heather between two rocks. He thought he was in a sheltered spot. No one could see him from the road. No one could hear him. Here he could sit undisturbed and wail out his woes to the mountain. Here he could sing (or keen), over and over again, a song that was most appropriate to the occasion. The name of the song was 'Máire Bhán' or 'Fair-Haired Mary.' It had been composed over a century before by some unknown poet who, having been lured towards the stars by his own Máire Bhán, went up in a parabolic curve and came down in a perpendicular.

However, if Charlie Daney had known that it could be dangerous for him to remain too long where he was in a certain kind of weather, the instinct of self-preservation might have caused him to take notice of his whereabouts. There was a deep ravine on each side of him, and only by following a narrow path had he reached the spot where he was. He did not notice the thick fog rolling down the Poison Glen on the one side and on the slope of Errigal on the other. He did not know that it could settle there for as long as two days and nights on end. He was oblivious to everything as he sat there lamenting the loss of his fair-haired Mary.

The Slasher too was in trouble. He had lost one of his sheep. For a whole day he searched the moors to the east and south-east of Errigal but did not find his quest. He had a clue, however. He had been told that a sheep answering to the description of the missing one had been seen straying in the direction of the other side of the mountain.

The second day he set out again accompanied by one of his faithful dogs. He carried a stout cudgel in his hand and wore heavy, hob-nailed boots specially made for climbing. In the hip pocket of his trousers he carried a small flask of spirits. This was a precaution against the *féar gortach*, a kind of weakening hunger that is supposed to attack people if they tread on a certain kind of grass.

The Slasher came down Dunlewy. He noticed the fog rolling through the Poison Glen and down the shoulders of Errigal. But he knew his way. He would have plenty of time to look around the lower part of the mountain before the fog closed in.

All of a sudden, a mournful wail reached his ears. He could see nobody. But he could hear the words of the song clearly. I give the last verse (in translation):

> My fair-haired Mary, when first you promised
> Your love for me would be loyal and true,
> The song-birds chanted in joyful chorus,
> The sunset glistened on flower and dew.
> But you have left me to pine in sorrow,
> Bereft of reason, bereft of grace.
> For me 'twere better to have no eyesight
> Than that I should ever have seen your face.

'Find him, Bran!' shouted the Slasher to his dog. Bran was off like a shot. In a few minutes, he returned and guided his master to where Charlie Daney was. 'In the name of God,' said the Slasher, 'what are you doing there and the fog falling fast? Get up quick!' he added, taking Charlie's arm.

'She is gone forever,' said Charlie, speaking to himself, as he struggled to his feet.

'I am afraid she is,' agreed the Slasher. 'The Glentornan dogs will get at her and slaughter her before I have time to get here tomorrow.'

They made their way down to the road. The Slasher asked Charlie where he had come from. Charlie replied that he was from the Rosses and that he was one of a convoy that had accompanied an emigrant as far as the Sandy Lake.

'Saw the mail-car passing,' commented the Slasher. 'Knew by the way the passenger was dressed she was bound for America. I wish her luck. She is a sensible girl. She has done the right thing.'

Charlie was wobbly on his feet and still clung to his companion's arm. 'I know what is wrong with you,' said the Slasher. 'You have the *féar gortach*. You have walked on hungry grass. But I have your cure. Take a sup of this,' said he, taking the flask out of his pocket. 'Take a good slug ... Are you feeling better now?'

Charlie Daney told his tale of woe. The Slasher looked at him in blank amazement. He could not understand how any man could get into such a state over a woman. 'Cheer up, man,' said he. 'Look at me. I've lost a fine sheep. The best sheep in my flock. I know she is doomed. As I have said, the Glentornan dogs will get at her before I get round this far tomorrow.'

But while he grieved for the loss of his sheep, the Slasher was not indifferent to the state that Charlie Daney was in, physically and mentally. 'I'll leave you down as far as the Cúirt,' he volunteered. 'Your neighbours will be there. The Rosses folk never go home before night when returning from a convoy.'

When they came as far as the hotel, they could hear the noise inside. Condy Nanny was singing a song. They could hear the words distinctly:

> There's a girl called Kate Malone
> Who I thought would be my own
> For to see my little cabin floor adorning;
> But my heart is sad and weary
> How can she be Mrs Leary
> Since she's off to Philadelphia in the morning.

'I won't go in,' said Charlie. 'I think they are all drunk. God knows when they'll leave. I think I will go home while it is still daylight,' he said. And he managed to thank the Slasher for his help and kindness.

In due course, the news reached the Rosses of Charlie's lamentation on the slope of Errigal the day of the convoy. The neighbours were commenting on it and, of course, Shoogey Brennan was there. Shoogey had a niece in Bayonne, New Jersey, who, she alleged, sent her nothing but genuine news. Whether Shoogey received information or manufactured it on occasion, we do not know for certain. All we know is that she had a plentiful supply of it any time she thought it expedient to retail it.

'Well, has he any sense at all or where did he come out of?' asked Shamey More. 'One would forgive a man for making a bit of a lamentation over his dead wife. But about a girl who went to America! That is surely something new in the Rosses.'

'He is a born idiot if there ever was one,' said Owen Roe. 'Better for him to be without eyes than ever to have seen her. God between us and harm, but if he were to lose his eyesight, he'd know the differ.'

'It's the Slasher I pity,' said Black Hughdie Boyle. 'Lost his fine sheep in the game.'

'I wonder why she left him?' said another. 'For nearly a year they were together night, noon and morning.'

'I think I know why she left him,' said Shoogey. 'The cousin in America is making a match for her with Shoney Forker. She had her eye on Shoney before he went to the States. Poor Charlie Daney was only a pawn in the game. But he'll get over it. And, as I have said before, it's all for his luck.'

V

Three years passed and then one fine summer day fair-haired Mary lands back home in the Rosses. She was more attractive in appearance than ever, partly because she was well-dressed. Charlie was away on one of the islands burning kelp when she arrived. Shoogey welcomed her back, congratulated her on her dazzling beauty and later on explained the sudden return to another old woman from the neighbourhood. 'The Shoney Forker affair is blown skyhigh,' she said. 'Shoney is getting married next fall to a girl from Fanad. And my brave, fair-haired Mary is back to cast her net once again in the Rosses.'

When Charlie came home he enquired about Mary, as casually as he could. 'She is gone up to Moorloch to spend a few weeks with her grandmother and her uncle,' he was told.

Charlie was debating with himself whether or not he should call to see Mary when she came back from her visit. But the decision became unnecessary. They met when neither of them expected it. One day Charlie went to the forge in Derrybawn to get a boat-hook made. The forge was on the edge of the road. As Charlie came out the door, whom should he see coming sailing towards him in all her finery and dazzling beauty but fair-haired Mary carrying a basket on her arm. She smiled at Charlie – one of the most heavenly smiles that ever beamed on a man – and she held out her hand to him.

Charlie did not know what to say. 'Is your basket heavy?' he asked. 'I will carry it for a spell.'

'Heavy enough over a long distance,' she replied, handing him the basket. 'I came to Dungloe by the mail-car and had to walk the rest of it ... Be careful and don't shake the basket. A clutch of hatching eggs Granny sent down to my mother. A bit late in the season, I thought. But they made me take them. Granny is a marvellous old woman. Skips along like a young girl. And she's gone eighty-six.'

They walked along for a time without exchanging further remarks. At last, Mary broke the silence. 'Spent a fortnight up in Moorloch. A very friendly people. But I would not live there for a mint of money. Do you know what I am going to tell you, Charlie? I am never happy except when I am beside the sea. And I think there is no sea in the world like the sea around the coast of our own Rosses.'

Was there a fair ray of hope piercing through a sky that had been dark for three years?

'Are you going to the regatta on the fifteenth?' Mary asked after a pause.

'I might,' replied Charlie. He was feeling his way. He had fully intended going to Magheragallon on the fifteenth. Every man in the parish would be there. At that time, men enjoyed very much those annual contests of skill and strength and stamina, whether with oar or helm or paddle. A later generation of Rosses men abandoned these contests and, for Ireland's sake, took to kicking a leather ball. But, in the days of our story, our patriotism had not been so finely developed.

'It will be a great day, I'm told,' said Mary. 'I'd like to go myself but I can't find any girl to go along with me. Girls who have never left home have a primitive outlook. They look on sport as an interest for men and for men only. That is the way it is. And I can't go by myself.'

If a man was a man at all he would take a chance here. 'Would you come with me?' he ventured.

'Oh, you are very good, Charlie,' she replied. And she smiled another of her heavenly smiles.

That part of the affair was settled.

'It will be a day of days,' said Charlie Daney's father a week or so before the regatta. 'In the first-class rowing race it will be a great contest between the Magheralosk crew and the O'Donnells of Ballymanus. And in the sailing race between Eamon Bawn of Gola and the Buckies of Inishmacdurn. Sorry I can't see it. What a time to get my cursed rheumatism back.'

The fifteenth of August came round. Charlie Daney and fair-haired Mary went to Magheragallon. They walked away from the crowd and they sat on a grassy knoll behind the old graveyard ... The contests began, one after the other. From time to time, cheers long and loud came from the crowds on the beaches. But neither Charlie nor Mary had the slightest interest in the contests. They had far more important things to occupy their thoughts. Mary, by virtue of some magic known only to women, induced the young man to renew his declaration. He was accepted. There still remained what a poor, innocent man would consider a difficult hurdle to get over: why did she go back on her promise of four years ago? That was dead easy, and the explanation was given even before the question was asked. Marriage was a serious affair. The most serious affair in life. And men were such fickle things. It was not their fault, just their nature. They had to be tested. Fair-haired Mary had tested Charlie Daney and Charlie stood the test, she said.

That evening, at sunset, Charlie accompanied the loved one to the end of the lane leading to her home. 'We've had a great day,' said Mary. 'The greatest day in all my life.'

Charlie went on towards his own home. He was like a prisoner that had been condemned to death and then pardoned and set free on the morning of the day fixed for his execution.

His father was sitting by the fireside, eagerly awaiting news of the day's contests. 'Who won the first rowing race?' he asked as the son came in the door. 'The O'Donnells of the Rosses or the Dohertys of Gweedore?'

'The Dohertys of Gweedore,' said Charlie. He was not really answering the question. He was merely repeating the last words his father had spoken.

'So the O'Donnells are conquered at last,' said the old man. 'Did they put up a good show? Were they many lengths behind at the winning post?'

'The winning post,' echoed Charlie. 'I think the two boats were together at the winning post.'

The old man asked no more questions. Clearly there was something wrong with his son. What was it? He appeared to be sober. What magic spell had been cast on him?

The news soon got abroad that Charlie Daney and fair-haired Mary were getting married and the neighbours were as merciless in their comments as ever.

'Let us hope,' said Owen Roe, 'she won't go off to America and leave him in the lurch a second time.'

'He had better watch his steps this time,' said Shoogey. 'Three years ago he could easily have fallen down a ravine on the slopes of Errigal and broken his neck. And he was rescued. But there are things that don't happen twice. The Slasher may never again lose another sheep.'

VI

Charlie Daney and fair-haired Mary got married. I will leave them to find their bearings in their new state and, while they are doing so, I will say a few words about a woman I once knew. She was a Dublin landlady and I went to live in her house as a boarder when I came to the capital as a young man. She owned a large, ramshackle house on the North Quays. The house was set in flats. The part that the landlady had reserved for herself had a small, spare bedroom, and she always kept a boarder.

She was recommended to me and I called to her house. She showed me the bedroom and said I could share with herself the use of the small living-room in which there were shelves for my books. She gave me the approximate times at which meals would be served. She stated her charge which, she said, it was her custom to receive weekly and in advance.

In due course, I moved in. Mrs Byrne (for such was her name) was placid and polite. She had certain accomplishments, especially a well-developed taste for music. She was very patriotic too, down to a certain date in the history of our country. At this, she became discreetly quiet.

In many ways, she was an ideal landlady. But, in several respects, her establishment left a lot to be desired. I never got enough bread at a meal. The meat was often tough, the tea weak, the butter rancid. The bedclothes were light and scanty. And, on chilly evenings, she never lit a fire in the living-room except she was staying in herself, which she seldom did.

I felt that I was being imposed upon and I often intended to ask, not for this or that concession, but for my just rights. But Mrs Byrne appeared to divine my thoughts beforehand and she would embark on a topic with such enthusiasm and eloquence that any mention of my grievances or just claims on my part could only be regarded as an unmannerly interruption. One day, however, I made up my mind to have it out with her that evening. I had the words prepared. After all, I was a man, not a mouse.

When I came in in the evening, my landlady was in the living-room. 'I called in with Mrs Cassidy today,' she began. 'You know the house three blocks down. She has given her boarder his week's notice. She just couldn't stand him. A big, horsy lout from Kildare without a scrap of refinement in his whole being. The first time I saw him I knew he would be an awful bore in any house. She was, I believe, induced to take him because he could pay a few shillings extra. But, as I told her at the time, money is not everything. And today I repeated it to her. I told her I had a boarder of culture and refinement, a young man who was a credit to himself and to the part of the country he came from.'

She went on singing my praises for over five minutes. Then she went out to the kitchen to get the tea. As for me, I put forward no claim. I voiced no grievance. I was beaten flat. My landlady had placed a crown of laurels on my head. I could not tarnish it by making the slightest allusion to such vulgar wants as bread, butter or bedclothes.

What did I do next? It does not matter. What I did has no bearing on my story. I merely relate the incident to show that some women are gifted with a power to rule that mere man can never hope to resist.

Fair-haired Mary was one of those women. From the first day of her married life she took over. She never allowed herself to get angry or even irritated. She never shouted. Another woman would shout to her husband to come home at meal-time if he happened to be working some distance from the house. But Mary never shouted. She had a small whistle on which she blew a blast. When she had attracted her husband's attention in this manner, she beckoned him home with a wave of her hand.

The poor man was as meek as a lamb. There was nothing he could do. If Mary were a boisterous virago who got into fits of temper, he could hold his own, at least some of the time. He could tell her to go to the devil for that she was not going to make a doormat of him and that that was that. But, getting into a temper or anything even faintly approaching it, was not the code of the 'holy terrors'. It was not their strategy. Their genius lay in another direction.

Five years passed. The fifteenth of August was approaching. This year's regatta would be a memorable event. A crew from Cloghaneely had got a new boat with Hopkins of Portrush. She was light in construction, low in the works, narrow in bows and flooring, which would leave her of little value in a heavy sea. She was built for speed. Still, she could not be classed as anything but an ordinary yawl. And so she was declared eligible to run in the first rowing-race in the coming regatta.

Charlie Daney wanted to go to the regatta. He had made up his mind to ask Mary's permission and put his request in words that no woman with a heart could refuse. He would not have to ask for pocket-money: he had a few shillings hidden away that he had accumulated by selling an odd dozen of mackerel on the quiet.

The fifteenth of August dawned bright and glorious with the promise of a very fine day. Charlie Daney and fair-haired Mary went to Mass. When they came back home Mary put on the potatoes for the dinner. Charlie went out and looked in all directions. What a superb day! ... After dinner, he would present Mary with his request. He had the very words of it thought out.

Mary was tidying the kitchen while waiting for the potatoes to boil. She took up a small, three-legged stool that she used to sit on by the fireside when knitting. 'Do you know, Charlie,' she began, 'I was lost without that stool. You've made a great job of the mending of it. As good and as neat a job as any tradesman could do. Biddy Andy was looking at it yesterday. "Mary," says she, "it's great to have a man who is both able and willing to do things like that." Poor Biddy, she knows to her cost what it is to be without such a man. Of course, I said nothing. I think a woman should count her blessings and say nothing about her less fortunate neighbours.'

After dinner Mary spoke again. 'You had better put the fish out in the sun. Just one more day and we can dry-pack them.'

Charlie took the creel of fish and proceeded to lay them out in rows on a flagstone beside the house. Mary came out after him. 'That was a very fine catch of fish you made last week,' she said. 'Over four dozen rockfish in one single night. I am sure it has broken all records.'

'I think the calf needs fresh bedding,' suggested Mary when Charlie had finished spreading out the fish. 'It is thriving very well. I think it should fetch a good penny at the November fair.'

Later on, Mary gave another order. 'Take the cow and tether her on the grass down at the shore. In a spot that has not yet been grazed. And, since you are going down, take a bucket and bring me a bucket of water from the spring well. When you've come back, I think it would be a wise thing to shake out the handcocks you made last week. We can make them up in the evening before the dew begins to fall. I'll give you a hand myself. I'll be with you as soon as I get the dishes washed and things tidied up.'

The timetable for the day was complete. Charlie took up the bucket. He then went to the byre. He attached the tether to the cow's halter, turned her out and proceeded to drive her down towards the pasture. When he was half-way down, he came to where Billy Jack sat on a rock with a stick at each side of him.

'Charlie,' said Billy, 'it is a terrible thing to be old and crippled. What would I not give to be in Magheragallon today. It will be a day of days. Boats from four parishes competing. From what I hear, the Rosses O'Donnells haven't much chance this time. They have, of course, the practice. They have an excellent skipper. They have the pride of past victories, from Lough Swilly to Killybegs. But I am told their boat is no match in speed for the Cloghaneely boat. But it will be only for this year, though. This time twelve months the O'Donnells are sure to have a new boat of the same class.'

Then the old man began to describe the great rowing contests he had witnessed in his young days. At last, he noticed that Charlie seemed to be getting impatient. 'But I am holding you up,' he said, 'and you haven't too much time. Considering the stage the tide is at, the best thing for you to do now is to cross to Gweedore by the Blackrock ford. You'll have, of course, about five miles to walk to Magheragallon but you have plenty of time. Have a good day. If a man doesn't enjoy life when he is young, he won't enjoy it when he gets old. We only pass once on this journey.'

Charlie drove the cows down to the grazing plot. He drove the stake of the tether into the ground. He looked in all directions. The last boat was going out from Weaver's Cove. A few stragglers were going down the White Strand on their way to the ferry. The coast around Charlie was deserted and lonely. No one to be seen anywhere except two little lads who were building a sandcastle in a creek below the ledge where the well was situated.

Oh, to be a little boy and to be building a sandcastle!

He was wakened from his reverie by a shrill blast of a whistle. He looked up in the direction of the house. Fair-haired Mary was beckoning him home.

Yes, he understood. She wanted to have the water at hand to make the evening tea at nightfall. In the meantime, the two of them would shake out the handcocks.

Charlie went across to the well. He filled his bucket with water and set it down on the brink of the well. He looked towards the North. The last boat from Corfin was crossing the inlet to Bunbeg.

Charlie wasn't inclined to move. He stood there like a man in a dream.

Another blast on the whistle.

He looked up towards the house a second time. Mary was beckoning him home, with more eagerness this time.

He answered her. But she did not hear him. They were too far away from one another. Nobody heard him but the two little lads who were building the sandcastle. They looked up in wonder and, in their own childish way, they realised that the words came straight from Charlie Daney's heart as he quoted:

> For me 'twere better to have no eyesight
> Than that I should ever have seen your face.

The Woman Spy

She was a stranger in Crawbawn and, as she was red-haired and her name not familiar to the people, they called her Biddy Roe. She was born in Glenveagh and was over seven years of age when the family, along with scores of others, were evicted from their little holding. She remembered the day all her life. She could see her grandfather limping out with the aid of two sticks. Then followed the mother with the baby in her arms. The other children followed. The little bits of furniture thrown out. She could see her father standing looking on with a look of madness in his eyes. The battering-ram was brought into action. A slice of masonry fell down. Her father rushed at the bailiff and struck him. The police rushed in. The next time Biddy Roe saw her father, he was standing some yards away, handcuffed, and his face covered with blood.

In due course, he was tried and sentenced to twelve months imprisonment for a violent assault on the officers of the crown in discharge of their lawful duties.

Biddy came to Crawbawn via America. There she met a young Rosses man. They were married and, in due course, they came back and settled on a poor, little holding in the Lower Hills, as they were called.

They had three children. First, two girls with only a year and a half between them. And, five years afterwards, a boy. The boy was only a year old when the father died. And so we leave the poor widow to bring up her children as best she could while we make the acquaintance of other characters in our story.

II

Tommy McGee was a young man. He lived in the townland of Glenkeel, about two miles from Crawbawn in the direction of the coast. Before he died, Tommy had amassed considerable wealth although, like many another, he began in a small way. At the time he began, bull-calves were valueless in the Rosses. No man reared a bull-calf. He slaughtered it and tried to get a few shillings for the hide. But to dispose of the hide was not always easy. Sometimes the merchants of the town bought them, sometimes they didn't.

Tommy McGee saw an opening in the hides business. He learned about some way of dressing them so as they would keep for a few weeks. Then, when he had a boxful collected, he railed it to Derry.

'I suppose you are making a nice penny out of the hides,' said an old man from the neighbourhood to him one day.

'Indeed I am not, Mickey,' replied Tommy. 'If I were working in Scotland, I would earn three times as much. But I don't like to leave Ireland. I think that is the curse of this country – the best of her young men and young women emigrating. I think it is the duty of all the young men to stay at home, especially now.'

'Well,' said the old man, 'I don't know anything. I was never a day at school in my life. But I'm just curious to know why you say they should stay at home, especially now, any more than when I was young.'

'The times are totally different now,' said Tommy. 'Before this day twelve months, Home Rule will become law.'

'In that case, we are all right.'

'You don't understand,' said Tommy. 'You can't read the papers. If you could, you would know that Carson is organising and arming the Ulster Volunteers to fight against Home Rule. You see, a victory in the British House of Commons is only half a victory. England will grant us Home Rule, but we must fight to enforce it. That is why I say it is the duty of every young man to stay at home. That is why I am staying at home trying to earn a few shillings a week on the lousy job I am at.'

'I didn't understand,' said the old man. 'However, it does not concern me. I am an old man and I have no sons.'

'But you have a native land,' replied Tommy, hotly. 'Ireland is your country. If you are too old to fight for her, you should at least love her. Think of the countless men who have died for her down the ages. Think of the men who spent anything up to twenty years in British dungeons. Think of all that and you won't say again that Ireland is nothing to you.'

'You have set me thinking. I haven't been fair to myself.'

'Of course you haven't,' said Tommy, glad that he rekindled in this old man's heart a dying spark of patriotism.

'No, I haven't, now that I think of it. Every time I meet Big Billy Coll from Gweedore at Jack's Fair, I shake his hand. Billy led the attack against scores of armed police the day they came to arrest Fr McFadden. A police inspector was killed in the fight. Billy was tried on a murder charge. They couldn't hang him on the evidence but he spent ten years in jail. Yes, I was wrong. I always admire a man who does a brave act.'

Tommy said nothing but walked away.

Frank O'Donnell was a Rosses man and a Rosses man he remained all his life. A few summers ago, he came back from America after a stay of forty years in that country. He was as much a Rosses man the day he came back as the day he went away. He hadn't the slightest tinge of an American accent. He never talked about America. His conversation was always about his native Rosses, about the old men and women (all dead years ago) he knew when he was young, of the things they did, the stories they told, the songs they sang over sixty years. Frank would walk to Crohy Head to watch the flood of golden light pouring from the setting sun through the gap between Aran and the mainland. He would get up before dawn to see the morning star poised on the peak of Errigal. He would visit some old ruin and sit on stone, musing sadly. Then he would give a burst of musical laughter and tell a story about the old man or woman who lived there when he was young. That was Frank O'Donnell.

III

Tommy McGee was worried when, one year, at the beginning of winter, an IRA Flying Column came from Derry to the Donegal Highlands. By that time Tommy had given up dealing in calf hides and had opened a small shop down at the crossroad.

A member of the Column called on him one day. Tommy felt a lump in his throat, but he recovered.

'What I want to know,' said the Volunteer, 'and, by all accounts, I can rely on the information you give me – what I want to know is the safe houses in this townland. There will come times when we'll have to break up in twos and threes and lie low for a spell. I want to know the people we could trust.'

'In this townland of Glenbeg,' said Tommy, 'you can trust everybody. Every man and woman is loyal to the cause of Irish freedom. But, as you see yourself, the Glen is anything but safe. We are low down here and we would not see the enemy until they were on top of us. That rules Glenkeel out. But, as for the other districts, I will give you all the help I can. I believe it is the duty of every man now to do his bit for Ireland.'

'What about the districts out near the hills? Crawbawn, for instance?'

'I have a lot of useful information about Crawbawn,' said Tommy, 'and I'll supply you with a list. Most of the houses are safe. A few of them would talk without meaning any harm and that is very dangerous. Talk could get round until it reaches the ears of the spy.'

'Do you mean to say there are spies in Crawbawn?'

'There is one person that we all suspect. Of course, so far her treason has not been proved. If it were, she would not be allowed to remain in the county. But she is under strong suspicion.'

'A woman spy?'

'A woman. They call her Biddy Roe. Her only son was in the British army during the war. He is working in England now. Has a good job. The reward of his loyal service to his country's oppressor. Biddy Roe lives by herself. Her two daughters are married away beyond the hills. Hardly any of the neighbours go into her house.'

'But is there anything against her except that her son was in the British army?'

'There is enough to make her suspect. She cursed the men of Easter week all roads. Said they had brought destruction on the country.'

'I see. We'll be careful. I'll be round again soon and I hope you will have detailed information about Crawbawn and the surrounding districts.'

'I'll do my best. As I have said, it is every man's duty to do his bit for his country now. The real struggle is on. But you must be very careful. Don't mention my name to a living soul. If the police heard anything, they would come and arrest me. And, as you know yourself, one free man outside is better than a thousand men in prison.'

Frank O'Donnell went away after this interview. He had formed his own opinion of Tommy McGee. He would remember all he had heard about Biddy Roe. She might be a spy. She might not. He would not mention her name to anybody. But he would warn his comrades to keep away from the townland of Crawbawn until he got definite information one way or the other.

IV

Biddy Roe had a hard struggle rearing her three children. The men of the neighbourhood often helped her. They cut her turf for her. They helped her to put in her little bit of crops in the spring. For all this charitable help, Biddy was very grateful. But if it were not forthcoming, she would never ask for it. The women sent her milk for her tea when her cow was dry. But, if they forgot on occasion, Biddy would drink her tea black sooner than ask for it. She had another characteristic that differed from the women of the neighbourhood. She did not gossip or talk about the neighbours. The day came when all this operated against her. A woman that would not gossip and talk about her neighbours was unnatural. She was a creature with dark secrets hidden in her heart. She was a person that one would need to be on one's guard against.

In due course, Biddy's eldest daughter got married. The second daughter married the following year – both of them to men from beyond the hills. Biddy was left with nobody but her son.

For a few years she knew hard times. But things became even worse in 1914. The son was then nineteen and a half years old. He decided to go to Scotland to earn some money. His mother was very sorry to see the last of her children crossing out over her threshold. But it had to be. She prayed that he would be lucky enough to get work. He would be back at the beginning of winter with a good handful of money. He would go every year and she would get used to it. In due course, he would get married and he would bring in his young wife to live with them. And, in the course of time, she would see children once again playing on the floor of her little cabin.

About the middle of July, the young man left home and crossed to Scotland. He went to a part of the country that he had often heard old men talking about. For over a fortnight he tramped the Lothians up and down looking for work, and no work was to be found. He slept in hayricks by the roadside. He begged a bit of bread at farmhouses as he went along. Sometimes he took off his boots and bathed his blistered feet in a running stream. He would soon have no boots to take off. The soles were falling off. His toes were showing through the uppers of one of them. His clothes were worn. He was in a bad way if ever a man was.

One Saturday afternoon he walked into Edinburgh. Why, he did not know. Just because a man must go somewhere. He cannot stand in one place until he lies down to die.

As he wended his weary way up Princes Street, he met one Charlie McCole from Dunlewy, a distant relation of his father. Charlie looked at him. There was no need to ask questions. However, the young man told of his experiences for the past fortnight.

'I haven't much money,' said Charlie, without waiting to be asked for help. 'But I am working. I got work with a farm out Middletown way, a man I used to work with years ago across in Fifeshire. This is going to be a very bad season. No hope for youngsters across for the first time. As I have said, I haven't much money but the little I have, I'll give it to you,' said he, handing the young man a pound note.

'Go up to the model in the Grass Market. You will get a bed there for sixpence and a mug of tea and some bread for fourpence in the morning. On Monday morning, take the train for Glasgow and the boat for Derry that night. It's all I can do for you. By the way,' he concluded, 'England declared war on Germany yesterday.'

The young man took the money, thanked his friend and walked away. 'It was very good of him,' he said to himself, 'and he hardly knows me. But he advises me to go home. Go home to my mother penniless, to lie down and die along with her. I can't do that. I won't. I'll try another part of the country. Across to Perthshire. But my boots. I'll take them off and walk in my bare feet and put them on only when I go up to the door of a farmhouse. However, I will go up to the Grass Market and get a bed in the model for the night. But why did Charlie McCole tell me that England had declared war on Germany? What is that to me? He might as well have told me there had been an earthquake in Japan.'

Later on, he went to the model in the Grass Market and bought a ticket for sixpence with the number of his bunk on it. He was told the dormitories would not open until ten o'clock and he was shown into a bare hall where he could sit down. There was a big crowd of men in the hall. Some of them were old, some young, some neither old nor young. And their one and only topic of conversation was the war.

A man with a strong, Scotch accent said it was the duty of every true Briton to join up and he was going straight to the nearest recruiting office on Monday morning. Germany was out to conquer the world. Her aggressiveness must be checked, as checked it would be. With all her fiery speeches she would soon reel and stagger and fall back before the British army. 'We'll be in Berlin before Christmas,' he concluded.

An Irishman said he also was going up on Monday morning. This war was different from past wars. In the past, it used to be said that England's difficulty was Ireland's opportunity. It was this time too, but in a different sense. England's difficulty was Ireland's opportunity of securing Home Rule. The measure was on the Statute Book. If England should be conquered by Germany, it was goodbye Home Rule. Therefore, the Irishman that fought on the side of England in this war was fighting for the freedom of his country.

The third man that Biddy Roe's son listened to was an Irishman also, and it was obvious by his accent that he was a Donegalman. He did not mind, he said, whether England was defeating Germany or not. Furthermore, he didn't give three straws for Home Rule in comparison to other things. He had tramped the roads of Scotland for five weeks looking for work, without getting any. He had a wife and three children away in the hills of Donegal. They would be facing starvation in the winter if no money came into the house. It was his first duty to keep his wife and the children that God gave them to rear and mind from dying of hunger as long as he could prevent it.

Another man gave figures of the scale of allowances. So much for a wife, so much for every child, so much for a widowed mother.

Our young man went to his bunk after ten o'clock. Although he was tired, he lay awake for a long time deliberating. He looked at things from every angle. What the Donegalman had said made a deep impression on him. There was no other course open to him. Either let his mother die of starvation at home or join the British army.

On Monday morning he was at the recruiting office as soon as its doors opened.

V

Biddy Roe got a letter from her son enclosing his photograph and a certificate authorising her separation allowance. Biddy thought the boy looked nice in his uniform. Still, she was sad. Her child was going off to the wars. Men were killed in wars.

However, when she read the letter she had a ray of hope. The war would be over in a few months. They would be no more than trained by that time. He would never be sent out to fight.

She had her boy's photo framed and hung over the kitchen mantelpiece. From time to time, curious women from the neighbourhood came in. They looked slyly at the photograph, but none of them ever pretended to notice it. This was hard on the poor mother. For, after all, she was the boy's mother. And people would call him a traitor. Who?

In due course, Biddy Roe's son was along with thousands of others sent to France. The poor mother was heart-broken when she got the news. Many a winter night she lay awake, sometimes sobbing, sometimes trying to pray as the storm howled outside and the hailstones lashed the windows. Where is he now, my poor child? Up to his knees in mud. Dying on a lonely hillside with his heart's blood ebbing fast and no one to whisper an Act of Contrition in his ears.

However, the time was passing, one month after another, and the widow's son was still alive. Biddy began to have a ray of hope. Maybe her prayers had been heard. She would continue to pray. Particularly, she would pray to the Virgin Mary. Mary would take pity on her.

Then, one day at Eastertide, a piece of news reached the Rosses that shook the poor woman's heart and soul. There was a rebellion in Dublin. The city was in flames. Thousands of soldiers were arriving from England with every boat.

This was cruel. The poor widow reasoned in her own way, thousands of British soldiers coming to Ireland. If it weren't for the rebellion, these men would go to France. Their absence would mean that the war would last longer. And so the demented mother saw only one aspect of things – the prolongation of the war and the consequent danger to her child. She took another view of the Easter rebellion. It was grand and glorious to see the tricolour flying from the turrets of the GPO. Grand

and glorious to hear the opening sentences of the proclamation: 'In the name of God and the dead generations of Irishmen', etc. But Biddy Roe saw things from a different angle and it is understandable that she was not in sympathy with the heroes of Easter Week. Everything she said about the event was exaggerated and twisted, with the result that the poor woman was becoming more and more an object of suspicion every day that passed.

One day she saw Tommy McGee coming along the road. Tommy, she thought, was a knowledgeable man. He might have an idea of how long the war was going to last. She would ask him for his opinion.

'The war will last for years,' said Tommy. 'It will last until the British empire – the empire of Hell, as John Mitchel called it – is beaten to its knees. It must come this time. It is only God's justice to put an end to the rule of the hypocrites who are pretending they are fighting for the rights of small nations.' And then, as if it had occurred to him that he had been a little bit too harsh, he added: 'I hope your boy will come safe through it all. If he had come to me before he joined the British army, I would have given him a bit of good advice that would save him.'

'You would have given him good advice,' replied Biddy. 'Another thing you would have given him, good example. And between your example and your advice, there would be no fear that my boy would ever go anywhere where there was the slightest danger.'

This blow struck home. It hurt Tommy to the quick. It could never be forgotten. From this it is easy to understand why, a few years afterwards, the IRA Column were warned against Biddy Roe.

VI

It was in the winter. The Column attacked the police barracks in Invermore and burned it to the ground. Their plan after that was to hide their arms in safe places, break up into twos or threes, and lie low until the invasion was over. In two days time the Donegal Highlands were swarming with British military. They converged on the districts from three points. A contingent came from Derry, another from Finner and a third landed from a troop-ship on the coast of the Rosses.

When the men of the Column had decided on where they would meet again, they dispersed. One man decided to go off by himself. He had decided to go out beyond the Lower Hills and hide in a certain house he knew. About an hour before sunset, as he was passing through the townland of Crawbawn, a woman came out of nowhere, as it were, and stood before him.

'Is it any harm to ask you where you are going?' she asked him.

'Out to Knocksharragh to look for a lost sheep.'

'Out to Knocksharragh to look for a lost sheep at this hour of the night? Listen, I know a thing or two about you. I know you are one of the Column. If you go out beyond the Lower Hills, you are in danger of running into them coming from Letterkenny through Glendowan. And there will be no escape open to you. Come with me and you will be safe with me until the danger is over.'

'I am very thankful to you. But I hope you don't mind my saying it, I don't know you. Who are you?'

'They call me Biddy Roe and I live in that little house up there on the brae face.'

The Volunteer looked her straight in the face. He had heard of Biddy Roe, certainly. They had been warned against her, especially by Tommy McGee. But the Volunteer forgot all the warnings. He looked the woman straight in the face and some instinct told him she could be trusted.

He went into her little cabin along with her. There was a nice fire on the hearth and the kettle singing on the pothooks. The young man sat beside the fire and spread out his hands to the flame. 'This is great,' said he.

'It is as good as we have,' replied the woman. 'The best thing about it is that it is given with a heart and a half.'

Then she prepared a meal for him and sat beside him while he was taking it. Was his tea strong enough? Was his egg all right? Would he like some more home-made bread?'

Later on she showed him his bedroom.

'But, my dear woman, what about yourself?' asked the Volunteer. 'Where will you sleep?'

'Where I always sleep when my son is at home,' she replied. 'On the settle bed in the kitchen.'

The following evening, sitting one on each side of the fire, Biddy Roe began to talk. 'Some of the patriots around here would be afraid to give one of you boys a night's shelter,' she said. 'Afraid of reprisals. The great fire-eaters. The things they would do. The Erne at its highest flood they'd dash across unseen. Quite easy when the Erne at its highest flood is fifty miles away from you. But Biddy Roe is a spy. Biddy Roe is a traitor. And all because her son served in the British army during the war.'

'Would that be a photograph of him?' asked the Volunteer, looking up at the mantelpiece.

'That's him all right.'

'A fine man, God bless him.'

'He is working in England at present. In a year or two he will be getting married to a girl from Lettereach. A grand girl. I am looking forward to it. Looking forward to hearing the prattle of children again on my hearth.'

'Listen, Biddy,' said the Volunteer, 'one request. If I am alive when your son is getting married, will you promise to invite me to his wedding?'

'I will,' said Biddy, and her eyes lit up.

This promise was fulfilled. It was not difficult to fulfil. The Volunteer was alive and could easily be communicated with, for Biddy's son got married during the Truce.

Five nights the Volunteer spent in Biddy Roe's house. During that time he noticed that his landlady had a strange habit. She always made an early dinner. After the dinner, she disappeared and did not appear again until nightfall. Where did she go at all, the Volunteer used to ask himself. But he was only curious to know. That was all. No matter what odd ways Biddy had, the young man knew she was as true as steel.

On the fifth morning, the Volunteer woke early. He had decided to leave. He had a long road to travel. He got up and began to dress. When he was dressing, he said to himself that if the old woman were asleep, he would not disturb her. He would call some other time and say what he had to say to her.

He came into the kitchen noiselessly. The fire was raked. The settle bed was folded. Evidently, it had not been slept in. He opened the door and went outside. It was a cold morning in early spring and the sun sending its first pale rays from behind the peak of Errigal. The Volunteer looked in all directions. Not a wisp of smoke could be seen from any of the houses around. The people were asleep in their beds. Where, under Heaven, had the old woman gone?

The young man went to the top of the house, about 200 yards away. And there, sitting behind a rock, was Biddy Roe. She had a heavy, woollen muffler on her head and neck, and a blanket covering her from the shoulders down. Under her were a few old boards to keep the damp ground from her.

'In God's name,' exclaimed the Volunteer, 'what are you doing there? Do you want to get your death of cold?'

'I wasn't cold. I was well protected, as you see. And, as I invited you to my house and you put your faith in me, I wanted to make sure that no one could come unknown to us. There are only the two roads that cars or lorries could come and I could see their lights three miles away.'

'But what danger was I in last night more than any other night? In fact, far less as the chase is over.'

It was then that the Volunteer learned that Biddy had been out on sentry for five nights.

'But when did you sleep?' he asked her.

'I had a good, long sleep in the barn every afternoon,' she replied.

'Come on,' said the young man as he took the old woman's hand and lifted her onto her feet.

Later on, when he was leaving, he took her withered hand in his and raised it to his lips.

'Goodbye, Biddy Roe,' he said. 'I hope we will meet again at your son's wedding, if not before it. I have got to know many people since this struggle began and I suppose I'll get to know many more. I suppose, if I live, I'll forget a lot of them. But I will never forget Biddy Roe.'

VII

When the Civil War broke out, Frank O'Donnell took the wrong side. I mean the wrong side from the point of view of those who cashed in on past records, whether real or pretended. When the Civil War was over and all was lost, Frank emigrated to America.

After forty years in the States, he decided to come back and pay a last visit to his native Rosses. He knew that all the old people and middle-aged people, and even many of his own generation, would be gone. But he would see the hills and the sea and the islands once more. He would visit the ruins of the old shack and Croveigh where he and the rest of the Column used to stay. He would visit a certain house in Dunlewy where he and his greatest friend Charlie Daly used to get a night's shelter when they were being hunted through the mountains during the Civil War. Above all places, he would visit the old graveyard in Cruit and kneel and pray on the grave of Plunkett O'Boyle. And there was another grave too he would visit.

When he was a few days back at home, he came to me. 'I am promised a car for Saturday,' he said, 'to go and visit some old spots. I want you to come with me.'

'But Frank, I can hardly walk. The old ticker, you know.'

'I can't walk much myself. Besides, there will be no walking to do in the places I am going.'

There was no refusing him.

He visited several places. He stood in certain spots, silent as if lost in thought. Then he told a story of what some old man or woman had said or done.

Late in the afternoon, we arrived at the old graveyard in Cruit. We went to Plunkett O'Boyle's grave. A few yards beyond that there was a very imposing marble headstone. We went across to it and read the inscription:

Pray for the repose of Thomas McGee, died, such a date and so many years. To God and Ireland true.

Frank wandered around the graveyard for over half an hour reading the inscriptions on the different tombstones. Then he came down to where I was sitting. 'I thought there would be a tombstone to mark the place I am looking for,' he said. 'There isn't any, as far as I can see. I must ask in this house opposite the gate. Maybe they don't know. If not, I'll have to make further enquiries and come back another day.'

Then he looked up towards the far corner of the gate. 'There's somebody up there. Looks as if he were cutting the grass. We'll go up and ask him. He might be able to direct me.'

We went up to the corner and there was an old man, a very old man, on his knees cutting nettles and wild grass. Frank spoke to him.

'There is nobody to do this but myself,' said he. 'I couldn't do it last year. I was laid up with my rheumatism.'

'A relation of your own?' asked Frank.

'The man was,' replied the old man. 'I am the only relation left. Their family have all gone to Scotland.'

'Show me your reaping-hook,' said Frank. The old man handed it to him. Frank ran his finger along the edge.

'Not too sharp,' he said.

'Indeed I know it's not. It's only pulling instead of cutting. But there's no judgement left in my old fingers. And, what is worse, my hearing. I remember the time when I'd know from the music of a scythe or hook when the right edge was on it. But that is what old age does.'

Frank sharpened the reaping-hook. Then he took a handful of grass and knelt on it with one knee. And, in a short time, he cleared away all the nettles and wild grass.

'May God spare you your health,' said the old man. 'It would take me hours to do that. Before I die I must find someone who will promise to cut the grass on these graves every summer. As I have told you, I am the only one left of the man's people.'

'And what about the woman? Has she no relations in this parish?'

'She was an outsider. Came from Glenveagh. A strange woman she was, was the same Biddy Roe. They said she was a spy in the days of the Troubles. And those who started the story – but the dead are dead and it is not for us to judge them. However, Biddy Roe came out of it all right. If one man blackened her character, another man cleared it. God be good to him. He went to America ages ago ... I'll tell you what happened. One of the boys who was on his way to the Upper Hills and the English soldiers scouring the country was passing by Biddy Roe's house.

Nobody would give him shelter. The people were afraid. Well, Biddy came out before him and invited him to her own house. He stayed in that house for five days and five nights. But, that is not the best part of the story. Every night, after the young man had gone to bed, Biddy went up to the height with a blanket wrapped round her, and spent the night there on sentry. Would you believe it?'

'I can believe it,' said Frank, 'because I know it's true. I was the Volunteer who slept comfortably in Biddy Roe's house while the grand, old woman was out on sentry. Of course, that part of it was all over before I knew it.'

Frank knelt down and prayed. Then he stood up and looked down at the mound from which he had shorn the grass and weeds. 'God rest your soul, Biddy Roe,' he said. 'It has taken a lot of the sting out of my life to have known you.'

The Fruits of Education

Cormac Roe O'Donnell and Shamey McGinty were born on the same day. The one water baptised them – as we say in Irish – and their parents were neighbours. It was to be expected that the boys would grow up to be great pals or, possibly, great rivals.

Shamey McGinty's mother thought her baby had started off with a bit of a handicap: she was not too pleased with the name. Someone has been put on record as asking 'what's in a name?' and by replying that a rose by any other name smells as sweet. But there is a false analogy here. A name is principally a matter of sound, not of perfume. Then names have certain associations which can affect them favourably or adversely. The first of little Shamey's ancestors known to the Rosses people was one Hughie McGinty from the townland of Srathnabratogy on the banks of the Finn. The name of the townland itself was associated with *bratóg*, a rag – in all probability, a dirty clout cast off by a verminous beggarman. Years afterwards, an attempt was made by a scholar to save the reputation of this townland. He came forward with the theory that *bratóg* also meant flag. It was on this very spot, he contended, that the Irish flag went down when the remnants of our retreating army made its last desperate stand after the disaster of Scariffholis. But this point of history, whether it could be verified or not, had no weight with the people of the Rosses. *Bratóg* meant an old, lousy rag, and only lousy people could come from a townland called after it.

Next came the Christian name Shamey. There is something about the sound of it that we Rosses people do not like. But why did Mrs McGinty call her baby Shamey? Well, custom is custom, and the Rosses custom of naming the first boy after his paternal grandfather is, and has been, as immutable as the laws of the Medes and the Persians.

And now we come to the surname McGinty. The sound of it is very poor in the ears of people accustomed to rich Gaelic sounds. But it was not exclusively a matter of phonetics. The impression made by Hughie McGinty, the first of the clan to come to the Rosses, was anything but favourable. Hughie went about with his boots half-laced. He had a constant drop at the end of his nose which he used to wipe with his thumb and forefinger. And he had a white patch on one of the legs of his trousers.

And his profession? He made his living partly by hawking domestic articles such as flail thongs, fine combs and tin mugs. In addition, he had other means of supplementing his income. He would castrate a male lamb for twopence, and a bull-calf for threepence. He could give the womenfolk advice on how to cure fowl suffering from the pip and advice on how to feed hens so as to keep them laying till the end of the season. All round, there was a marked contrast between himself and the rugged, sturdy men among whom he came to live and settle down for the rest of his days. As marked a contrast as there was between the wild, foamwashed Rosses and one of the flat, lifeless holms of the Finn valley.

All these factors combined to give poor, wee Shamey McGinty a name which his mother did not like. It was a terrible tag to attach to any child. But, you will ask, why had she herself married a McGinty? There I leave you. I just don't know the answer to the question.

And then the neighbours' baby – Cormac Roe O'Donnell. Cormac was a mouthful of a word. And the name had great associations. According to Gaelic folklore, it was the name of an ancient, high king of Erin who, before his death, had a vision of the true faith and asked to be buried at Rosnaree and not at Brugh of Boyne beside his grandsire of the Hundred Battles. The name O'Donnell was, and still is, looked up to in all parts of Tír Chonaill. It had derived its greatness from a long line of chieftains and, particularly, from Manus of whose brilliant verses and witty sayings several had still survived in the folklore. Lastly came the epithet Roe (red). Roe in a woman implies rashness, hasty temper, liability to change allegiance. In a man, it is supposed to denote strength, courage, manliness. Hence, from the point of view of names and everything associated with them, Cormac Roe O'Donnell started off in life with a decided advantage over Shamey McGinty.

II

When Shamey began to lisp his first words, his mother had a ray of hope that he would have mental qualities that might go a long way towards offsetting patronymical defects. She had spent a few years working in Derry as a domestic servant before she married. She knew some English, as did her husband who had worked several seasons in Scotland. Hence they decided to speak English and English only to their child. Their contention was that some understanding of the medium of instruction would be of immense help to him when he went to school. In this connection, it could be said of them that they were wiser in their generation than the self-styled experts that appeared on the scene later on.

The two boys went to school on the same day – exactly at the age of five years. From the very beginning, Shamey understood almost everything. It was Greek to Cormac Roe.

As the years passed, Cormac's position in the school was getting worse. He was being hammered for not understanding what was being taught to him in a language he did not understand. For some time he had been thinking of refusing to go to school any more. Then he would be up against the wishes of his parents. He was afraid his father and mother – especially his mother – would not consent to let him have finished with school. In the end, he decided there was only one thing to do, that was to present his parents with a *fait accompli*. He would mitch from school and keep it up until the delinquency was discovered, which would happen sooner or later.

He had a great fortnight hiding in a cave which, one would imagine, had been created for the purpose. But, in the end, he was discovered.

The father was rather cool about the affair. The mother was very upset. 'What will we do with him at all, at all?' she exclaimed. 'Taking things into his own hands already without as much as "by your leave". You must be firm with him, Manus. Tell him he must go to school and that you'll take no nonsense from him.'

'I don't think you'll get anywhere by trying to teach a child against his will,' replied the father. 'It is the same as if you forced him to eat when he has a sick stomach.'

'But what will he do when he grows up and has to go to Scotland or to America to earn his living?'

'What the people of this townland had to do when there was no school. What I had to do. I went to Scotland when I was seventeen years. Tarlach More McGrenra got my ticket for me in Derry. The following morning I held on to his coat-tails on the way from the Broomilaw to the Glasgow Central. That evening we arrived at a farm in Ayrshire. Tarlach got work for me in the farm beside where he was. Then I started to learn English in the only way that a language – first or second – can be learned, that is, by hearing it spoken and having to speak it yourself.'

'I know all that, Manus. But I thought things would be better now. And, in any case, why can't he learn English at school like other children?'

'We don't know. Maybe he was made approach it in the wrong way.'

'What do you mean? Isn't the way as right for him as for the other children? Why must he fail where the other children succeed?'

'It could be that the other children's minds are less active, less original.'

'Well, I'm blest! That is the best I've heard yet. Our boy can't learn English because he is more brainy than the other children. For Heaven's sake, don't let anyone outside the four walls of this house hear you say that. If you do, you will become the talk of the parish.'

'And I wouldn't be the first man to become the talk of an ignorant parish. I am always sure that our Cormac would soon learn English if it could be taught to him the right way – I mean, what happens to be the right way for him. I don't blame the poor master. Like many more of his kind, there is nothing in him only what the spoon put in him – as my poor grandmother used to say ... Cormac is anything but stupid. There isn't a seabird around the coast that he doesn't know his name and habits. Or let him once see a boat anywhere between the Foreland and the Stags and he is sure to recognise it the next time it appears – aye, away on the rim of the ocean. And think of all he knows about wild flowers. Now, if a master could talk to him in English about any or all of those things, Cormac would soon begin to understand the language.'

'But you don't expect the master to have a special system for your boy?'

'I know the master would not be allowed. What is more, I know the poor fellow couldn't if he had all the freedom. So, it is pure waste of time for you and me to be talking. But don't worry about the boy. When he grows up, he will go to Scotland or to America, as thousands have done before him, and he will get on all right. Of that I am certain.'

That concluded the debate. The mother had to become reconciled to the decrees of Destiny. And, before long, when she got time to reflect, she began to see some wisdom in her husband's argument.

III

His father used to take Cormac out in the boat to fish. 'Now, when you get the bite,' said he to his son the first day, 'don't give a violent pull. Just a little tug to flesh your hook. Then pull for all you are worth.' It was not necessary to repeat the instruction.

The boy was becoming anxious to take a turn at the helm out beyond the bar. Fourteen years old he was when the father gave him his opportunity. And when he arrived home that evening, Manus O'Donnell told his wife, with a light of pride in his eye, how the boy had steered the boat from away beyond the islands, right across Gola sound and all the way home.

'I often gave him the helm in here on the calm of the inlet,' he began, 'so that he learned how to sail close to the wind. Today I thought I would teach him another lesson. The sea was choppy. No heavy swell but that nasty little breaker you get when wind and tide run in opposite directions. I was sure he would get a drenching from the splashes and I was prepared to take a drenching myself along with him – just to give him a lesson. I was afraid he thought he knew more than he really did. So, when I had the sails set, I left him the helm. "Now," I said, "she is in your hands. And remember, you are to keep her dry."

'Well, we set out. The first thing I noticed was that he wasn't sailing close enough to the wind to clear the Yellow Rock on one tack. But I said nothing. When we were about 150 yards from the Rock, he shouted the command to me: "Stand by your jib-sheet," he called, like an old pilot. He put her about and cut a short tack towards Doonbeg. Then he put about again, cleared the Rock with over 50 yards to spare, across the sound and in over the bar. And all the time he didn't let her ship a single wavelet.'

'He is a great lad,' said the mother.

'But wait till I tell you the best part of the story,' continued the father. 'When we were in on the calm of the inlet, I began talking to him. "I noticed," says I, "you didn't try to clear the Yellow Rock on one course."

'"But you warned me to keep her dry," said he, "and you haven't enough control over a boat when she is sailing too close-hauled."

'"But would you have tried it had there been no choppy sea?" I asked him.

'"I would not," he replied. "At best," said he, "I'd have only about a dozen yards to spare. That's not enough," said he, "if any hitch were to occur. A man should never take a risk at sea. He may succeed, but if he fails with the Yellow Rock in his lea, he won't get a second chance."

'Those were his very words to me. Now, isn't he a great lad?'

'He is, indeed,' agreed the mother.

IV

We must now leave Cormac Roe to carve out his career in his own way and turn to Shamey McGinty. Shamey was getting on better and better at school, year after year. The master lent him books from time to time. His mother became a subscriber to a weekly newspaper *The Derry Searchlight* which the boy used to read for a few of the neighbours who dropped in of an evening.

Soon Shamey, in the eyes of some people, became the oracle of the townland. He had items of news that would never have reached them otherwise. England was civilising some savage tribe in dark Africa. The Anchor Line had launched a vessel that could cross the Atlantic in 20 days. There had been an outburst of rioting in Belfast. Heavy catches of salmon had been landed at Killybegs. A most enjoyable concert had taken place in Letterkenny. And fat cattle were in brisk demand at the Milford fair.

'Isn't he great?' said Mrs McGinty to her husband one night when the visitors had left and the boy had gone to bed. 'And when I think of that poor clown over there – Cormac Roe O'Donnell – and that in a few years he'll have to leave home without a word of English in his head. But that is the way they reared him. Instead of taking down his trousers and giving him a spanking he would remember till his dying day, they allowed him to stay at home and to grow up wild. And the best of it all is his father saying that the reason he could learn nothing at school was that he is too brainy. What is the next thing we'll hear?'

'You are uncharitable in all you say,' protested the husband. 'And you are unfair in one of your remarks. The boy is not growing up wild. Far from it. In fact, he is as sensible a boy for his years as you could find in the whole parish.'

Mrs McGinty, sad to relate, was not pleased with this attitude on the part of her husband. Where was the use of having a bright light shining in a room if one were not allowed to snuff out every smoky candle that made its appearance?

Shamey was going from success to success at school. One day an inspector called and examined the senior classes. He gave Shamey great praise and in the presence of the whole school. But that was nothing compared to what was to come. One day the parish priest paid a routine visit to the school. Shamey was in the sixth class at the time and the priest took a notion to hear the class at their reading. The lesson they had just begun that morning was a poem by Byron. It was difficult for children whose vernacular was Irish and all the more so because they had not had time to study and rehearse it. But Shamey would never be caught unawares. He always made it a point to keep a lesson or two ahead of the class and to memorise the relevant notes and explanations at the back of the book.

The pupils' attempts at reading were very poor. And when they were tested on the meanings of words and phrases, they were a complete failure.

At last came Shamey's turn. He read two or three verses clearly and accurately.

'Very good,' commented the priest. 'By the way, what is your name?'

'Shamey McGinty, Father.'

Then the priest began to ask the boy the meaning of certain words and phrases. The answer came back every time. At last the examiner asked a question that even a good pupil would be pardoned for failing to answer: 'Now, could you tell me what episode in the history of Greece was the poet alluding to when he asked for three of the three hundred?'

The answer came like a shot: 'When 300 Spartans defeated the flower of the Persian armies at the Pass of Thermopylae.'

'Very good, Shamey, very good indeed. Excellent. You are, I believe, the brightest boy in my parish.'

The priest continued talking for a spell. He asked the boy what he intended doing when he left school. He said it looked as if there was a bright future before the lad.

That is all we can truthfully record. The final version of the story came from Shamey's mother. It meant that the priest said that the boy would be sent to college in due course. 'Isn't he great?' said she to her husband that evening. But there she stopped. She was afraid that she would incur her old man's displeasure if she were to make any derogatory remarks about a neighbour's child. All the same, if you could have listened attentively to her from time to time and put her hints together in a coherent statement, it would read something like this: 'Now let him name all the seabirds along the coast and all the wild flowers in the fields, let him sail a boat dry across Gola sound, let him tack at the right moment to clear the Yellow Rock on his next course, but what is all that compared to what my boy can do?'

V

Shamey McGinty left school at the age of fifteen years after passing out of the Sixth Class Second Stage. It was all the far a boy or girl could go at a primary school. A year passed and nothing happened. A second year passed and nothing happened. Nobody was talking about sending the boy to college. For all her ambitions, poor Mrs McGinty had nothing left but the image of a vision that had perished. Shamey was seventeen years old when it had to be admitted that he must go to Scotland to work as an ordinary labourer. And to make the poor lad's lot sadder and lonelier, he had to go by himself as the father was crippled with rheumatism that same season.

Cormac Roe O'Donnell, accompanied by his father, left home for the same destination the same day. A ship from Sligo bound for Glasgow put in in Rosses Bay to collect passengers from that part of the country. She steamed round Owey Head, an ugly, black hulk, belching black smoke. She came across to Gola Road where she stopped for a while to take aboard the passengers that had been waiting there in groups of small boats. After some time, she picked up steam again and continued on her course.

Poor Mrs McGinty had a heavy heart that afternoon as she stood on a height above the shore looking after the ship until the last wisps of black smoke broke up and vanished behind the beak of the Foreland.

Cormac Roe stood for a while watching a school of porpoises as they tossed and tumbled in the bay. He noticed Shamey McGinty sitting on a seat outside the galley with his head in his hands. Cormac went off to where his father was and had a long talk with him as to the best way of helping and encouraging the poor lad that was facing the 'land of the stranger' on his own. After a while, he returned to the galley side.

'I am sorry for you, Shamey,' he began, 'but this won't last. The wheel will turn. It always does. And you are not as much alone as you may think. My father and I have a promise of a season's work on a farm a few miles from Peebles. He is sure there will be work for a third man on the farm beside it and he will get the place for you. He knows lots of farmers in that part of the country.'

'You and your father are very good,' stammered Shamey, in a choking voice. 'But I was thinking of trying to find work in one of the towns so that I could attend night-school and learn a lot of things I didn't learn at school.'

'You will do that when the time comes,' encouraged Cormac. 'But I am told you will find no night-school at this time of the year. Besides, you will want to earn a bit of money.'

'It is very hard to think that this is going to be the end,' sobbed Shamey.

'The end!' said Cormac. 'This is not the end. Your star never rose over the Hills of Donegal to set in a turnip field on the banks of the Tweed.'

Shamey consented to avail himself of his neighbour's offer.

'Well, did you succeed?' asked his father of Cormac afterwards.

'He has consented to come along with us.'

'How did you manage him?'

'I said all the things you told me about work in the towns, night-school, etc. He wasn't moving. Then I poured a ladle of flattery on him. It got him.'

'What exactly did you say to him by way of flattery?' asked the father.

The son told him.

'Where did you get that?'

'It was in one of the Bacach Fada's stories. Just changed names of places to make it fit. I knew that he never listened to the Bacach's stories. His mother wouldn't let him. Afraid they might interfere with his school work.'

Shamey worked the season with the farmers. But, instead of coming home along with the rest of the Rosses men at the approach of winter, he went to the Lothians and started to work in the oilworks a few miles from Edinburgh. This he thought a wise move. He could find out all about night-schools in the capital and attend one or two evenings a week. But, before long, something else attracted his attention – something with a stronger personal appeal than school studies. And that something was politics.

VI

There was at that time in Edinburgh a society known as the United Irish League. The League was composed of Irishmen or men of Irish descent. And its object was to assist, financially and otherwise, the Irish Parliamentary Party, then supposed to be advancing on all fronts towards Home Rule.

Shamey joined this society and made himself a very active and efficient member. After some months, he was appointed Branch Secretary. He communicated the news to his mother and sent her such information as he thought she could understand. How much exactly the mother understood from reading her son's letters, we do not know. But we do know some of the things she told the women of the neighbourhood. 'He does all the writing for them,' she would say. 'Gets dozens of letters every day. He will be making a speech in Glasgow next week. Some of the big men are coming down from London. Shamey says Home Rule is a certainty. It must come this time. In a few years' time, of course,' she said to old Shoogey Brennan one day when the two met at the well. 'Won't it be great?'

'What will be great?'

'Home Rule, of course.'

'Maybe I'd say it will, if I knew what it meant,' replied Shoogey.

This was a nasty thrust but Mrs McGinty recovered from it, at least in a kind of way. 'It would take me too long to explain,' she parried, got to her feet and approached the well to fill her bucket. 'I haven't time. I left a bannock of oaten bread baking in front of the fire before I left.'

'This is indeed a nasty habit of Shoogey's,' she said to herself as she moved away from the well. 'In future, I must be careful to say nothing to her that I cannot explain if she asks me.' It was indeed a nasty habit. Why couldn't the people accept Home Rule and enjoy its blessings without looking for definitions?

At Easter-tide Shamey came home for a short holiday. He was well-dressed. He was beginning to have a professional look. He used to read the articles in *The Derry Journal* and explain points of policy and strategy. 'Ireland has a leader this time that will succeed where others have failed. Where O'Connell made the mistake was not to press for Repeal first and Emancipation afterwards. Where Parnell made the mistake was not to resign for a short time as Gladstone had requested him. He could then come back stronger than ever. But Redmond will make no mistake. He knows he holds the balance of power and he will open up when the time comes.'

Mrs McGinty had a lot of stuff now that she could explain to Shoogey if challenged to do so. She could make a shot at explaining it all except one thing: she did not know what kind of a balance was the balance of power. But she would not play that card, she had enough without it.

She and Shoogey met again at the well. 'Where Parnell made the mistake,' began Mrs McGinty. But she was suddenly interrupted by Shoogey.

'Do you see where my clutch hen and her chickens have wandered to?'

'Where Parnell made the mistake,' resumed Mrs McGinty.

Shoogey was on her feet like a flash. 'Go away! Go away!' she shouted, waving her hands frantically ... 'Look at him! The hawk I mean.'

The mother hen saw the hawk as it stalled in the sky without moving a wing. She emitted a series of noises for which I cannot find a name in any language. At last, there was a slight flutter seen on the tips of the hawk's wings and down he came like a shot. But the attack was beaten off and, after four or five more swoops, the hawk abandoned the pursuit.

Shoogey drove the hen and the chickens in front of her towards the house. Mrs McGinty cleared her throat to continue what she had begun to say when the hawk appeared, but Shoogey got away before her.

'It's terrible,' she said. 'There's Nelly Wanais over there in Rinamona had three of her chickens carried off one day last week. Three fine pullets that would be laying next autumn.' She continued this theme until she had driven the hen and her brood into the barn, examined the window and locked the door.

'Now,' she said, 'they are out of danger until I get a safe place ready for them. I don't know where Parnell made the mistake but I know where my old man made his. He made it when he neglected to cover the wee garden with wire netting. But I'll see to it that he puts up the netting before the sun goes down this evening.'

'And these are the people that my poor boy is trying to get Home Rule for,' said Mrs McGinty to herself as she went across towards her own house.

VII

Five years passed. Shamey McGinty was spending all his time in Scotland with the exception of an occasional run home for a week or two. He was still very active in the United Irish League. From time to time, his name appeared in the newspapers. The cuttings were sent home to his mother who had them carefully put away in a box specially procured for the purpose of keeping such relics.

As the years passed, Shamey was becoming more ambitious. He wanted to get into politics in a big way. Already he began to imagine himself an MP. He often imagined his maiden speech in the British House of Commons ... And then that greater speech, and on a far greater occasion – the opening session of the Irish Parliament in the Old House in College Green.

To prepare himself for his future career he decided he must read a lot. He must read not alone books on history and on politics, but he must become acquainted with the literary masterpieces of the English language. Just to be able to make appropriate comparisons between momentous events, to clench an argument with an immortal quotation!

To equip himself still better, he took up the study of Psychology. Psychology was a great subject – a study of the human mind and its workings. It would be of immense importance to him. To be able to read the mind of a political opponent, to see through his plans and motives and to be able to forestall his arguments.

One day, in a bookshop in Edinburgh, he came upon a book that was to have a great influence on his future career. The title of the book was *Tales of Mystery and Imagination*; its author, Edgar Allen Poe.

There was one story in this collection that made a very deep impression on Shamey – 'The History of the Purloined Letter'. A letter, compromising a member of the Royal Family of France, had been stolen and given to a man who would be sure to use it with deadly effect. The problem facing the man was how to keep the letter concealed. Could he carry it on his person day and night? No, he could not conceal it that way. He would be followed, waylaid, beaten, murdered, perhaps. Could he hide it somewhere in the house where the police could not get at it? ... After having done some thinking, he hid the letter. Then came the police. They tore up the floors. They ripped the mattresses. They sounded every inch of walls and ceilings, looking for secret recesses. They bored the furniture with gimlet holes. But they failed to find the letter.

And how did the man hide it? He just threw it on the mantelpiece of the principal salon along with five or six other letters. That was the great psychological factor in the failure of the police. The hiding-place was too simple, too obvious for a police force trained and experienced in making the most complicated and difficult searches. Shamey spent weeks and weeks pondering over the story.

One year, at the beginning of winter, he got word to present himself at the manager's office at a specified hour on a specified day. After his shift was finished, Shamey washed, changed into his good clothes and went to the office. The manager came to the point immediately. Their head clerk was due to retire at Easter, he said. Changes would be made. A new appointment would be made. It was their policy, continued the manager, to recruit the clerical staff from among the workers. But this was not always possible as so few of the workers had the necessary educational qualifications. He then stated the salary that a clerk began with. 'From what I gather from reliable sources,' he concluded, 'you have got a good school education and you have continued to improve it still further since you have come to work here. I am offering you the post now because it occurred to me you might like to spend a winter at home with your people before you take up your new duty.'

Shamey snapped at the offer. It was the very thing he wanted. After a week he would put off the miner's blackened, greasy duds, never to put them on again. He would be wearing good clothes, and a collar and tie every day. He would be earning his living sitting at a desk. And, of course, he would continue to read and study in preparation for the great days that lay ahead.

VIII

In the meantime, let us come back to the Rosses to see how Cormac Roe is getting along. For one thing, he has fallen in love and intends to get married the following Easter. The girl is a native of the district. She is good-looking, lively and somewhat impish. Her name is Nora Villy but she is called Dolly Varden. The teacher called her by that name one day at school, and it stuck.

Falling in love and planning to get married are commonplace events in men's lives. But we have to record another turn in Cormac Roe's career. He had taken to poteen-making and had become an expert at baffling the police. For three years they had been on his track and he had always outwitted them. Time and again he humiliated them by working some ruse they had not expected. They had become so eager to get him that the man who would lead to his capture or hit on a plan that would lead to his capture would be sure of getting his stripes immediately.

'I heard you were getting married,' said Shamey to Cormac the first time they met after Shamey came home.

'I have heard so myself.'

'And to Dolly Varden.'

'They have put that label on her. The master called her by that name one day at school. I don't know where he got it.'

'It is a character in *Barnaby Rudge*.'

'Who is Barney Ridge?'

'Barnaby. And Rudge, not Ridge. A novel by Dickens ... However, she is a grand girl. I saw her yesterday. A grand girl, that is what she is.'

'I've heard quite a lot about your exploits in the poteen line,' said Shamey a few weeks afterwards.

'A dangerous game,' replied Cormac.

'You must have a lot of useful experience.'

'Experience would not be much use to me. I have always to hit on a new plan.'

'They say Napoleon was like that. That he never learned from previous experience. Always found his inspiration in some circumstance as the battle went on ... Do you know what I have been thinking about? That you and I should join and make a go of poteen together. I have a plan that cannot fail,' he concluded, and he told the story of the Paris police and the purloined letter.

Cormac refused at once. But Shamey was so confident in himself and in his ruse that he meant to go ahead. He unfolded his plan to Johnny Andy Hughdie and told the story of the purloined letter. 'Over there on the tip of Illanbwee,' he said, 'about a mile from the barracks and right opposite their windows. They'd never for a moment dream that anyone would come there to make poteen, and there's where the safety lies.'

'But the smoke?' objected Johnny.

'There is a lime-kiln burning there once, sometimes twice a week. You are protected every way.'

Still Johnny hesitated to join him.

'Do you think I would risk my new job by breaking the law if there was the slightest danger?' asked Shamey.

Johnny consented to co-operate.

After a few more weeks, it became known and proven beyond the shadow of a doubt that Cormac Roe, working with a new partner, had made a fresh go of poteen and that the police had been once more outwitted and when they were dead certain they had their man in the net.

Then came Shamey's turn. The first step was to get the lime-kiln going on Illanbwee. Then Shamey and his partner filled three barrels with wash and set them to ferment. They next proceeded to build a grate for the still and to place a vat for the worm. They would be ready to start the 'singlings' by noon the following day.

About an hour before sunset, the tide was out and a person could walk across the strand from Murlach to Illanbwee. Johnny Andy was still a bit nervous and he was keeping his eye on the barracks. At last, three policemen came out and proceeded to walk across the strand in their direction. Johnny drew his companion's attention to the matter. 'Never fear,' replied Shamey. 'Just what they call a routine march. That's all. They won't climb up the rocks to inspect a lime-kiln as if it were a battery of artillery.'

Nearer and nearer came the police. At last they came to the rocks and proceeded to climb up. Johnny Andy hesitated no longer. He took to his heels and hid in a cave. But he was discovered afterwards, arrested and fined £6 the next court day.

Shamey stood his ground for a while longer. He could not believe that the plan based on the psychology of the 'purloined letter' would fail him. For a short space he thought that the uniformed men who were advancing on him were only shadows. But, at last, he woke up to the reality of the situation and he made a dash for freedom with a policeman hot in pursuit, only a few yards behind the culprit. Shamey stumbled and fell. The policeman tripped and fell across him. In the twinkling of an eye, a second policeman rushed up with drawn baton and he gave Shamey a wallop on the head that made him see stars.

When the trial came, Shamey was fined £6 for illicit distilling. But that was not all. The scuffle was interpreted and sworn to as a violent assault on an officer of the law in the discharge of his lawful duty. For that second offence Shamey McGinty was sentenced to six months in prison.

IX

One evening shortly after Shamey's trial and conviction, a group of men from the neighbourhood were gathered in Cormac Roe O'Donnell's. It had been proved that Cormac had made a go of poteen with all the police in the Rosses hot on his trail. The neighbours wanted to know from Cormac himself how he had accomplished such a feat. For his part, Cormac was not in the least reluctant to relate the adventure, knowing that when he made the next attempt, he should have to make new plans, and, therefore, that any revelations on the past would not endanger him.

'Well, to begin with,' he opened, 'Dolly Varden had a hand in the game. She played her part and played it very well. For some time I had been convinced that I must make the next attempt in another police district. That would be easy enough. I had my man in Gweedore – Pádraig Airt across there in Magheralosk. I knew Pádraig would join in with me any day. I also knew that he was a man of sound common sense as well as being a first-class boatman. So I would make a go of poteen in Gweedore. But that wasn't enough. I had to lead the police to believe that I was operating at home – on one of the islands off the Rosses.

'That was the stage my deliberations were at when a young policeman in Moorloch took a notion of Dolly Varden. Dolly, after their first talk, came to me for instructions. "Lead him to believe that you've taken a fancy to him," says I, "but in such a way … "

'"Listen," says she, "leave the love-making part to me."

'And I did. Well, you all know Constable Mulligan is a fine man, tall and handsome, looks smashing in his uniform and his flaxen curls showing under the rim of his cap. He told her he came from Mullaghmore in the County Sligo. Was an only child. His parents had a big farm there. He only joined the police to see what the force was like. He had found out that its chief function was to keep Ireland in slavery.

'Later on, his proposals became clearer. And here Dolly Varden excelled herself. (She went through the whole act for me afterwards.) Her voice became sad. Without saying it in so many words, she gave him to understand that, first of all, she was fond of him and, secondly, that it would be great to have a rich, comfortable home in Mullaghmore and get away from the drudgery and the poverty of the Rosses. She had not actually promised Cormac O'Donnell to marry him. But she liked him (and here she became sad). He was to pardon her for being sad on such an occasion. But Cormac Roe O'Donnell had been so good to her "and he is in danger now," she said. "He is going to run a risk and he is sure to get caught. That on top of this shock."

'"But," said the policeman, "I can save him, at least this time. Just tell me where he is going to operate and I'll lead the chase in another direction."

'When I heard this, I knew I was well away. Dolly would give Constable Mulligan the information. He would pass it on. Then what would the police say? They would say that Dolly would be taken in by Constable Mulligan and had given the right information or that she had suspected a plot and had given information calculated to mislead the police. So they would decide on raiding all the islands, one after the other. But why would they believe I had gone to the islands at all? They would have every reason for it. My boat would be missing from the creek where it is usually moored.

'So I sent word to Pádraig Airt. He came across that night. We put the stuff on board my boat and brought it over to Magheralosk under cover of darkness. And Pádraig and I began operations. For three days the police kept searching the islands to find out at the end that I had been operating on the mainland all the time.

'Of course, Pádraig Airt is as closely watched as myself now. The Middletown police are keeping their eye on him day and night. When our next venture will be, I don't know. Even if I did, I would not tell anyone, needless to say.'

Donal More McRory, an old man, sat and listened very attentively to Cormac's story. 'Well, Cormac Roe O'Donnell,' said he when the narrator had finished, 'you have a great head on you and nobody can deny it. Listening to you telling your story, I said to myself several times that it was a pity you did not stay at school when you were a boy. Where would you be now if you had got a good education?'

Cormac Roe looked up at the old wall clock that was ticking on the chimney-breast. 'Where would I be now if I had got a good education?' said he. 'I would be lying on a plank-bed in a cell in Derry jail.'

Edward Devanny

Edward Devanny was a Rosses man. He was locally known as Neddy Chonaill a' Ghleanna which, translated, means Neddy, son of Conall who lived in, or came from, the Glen. We first meet Neddy when he was a boy at school. Unlike the vast majority of his classmates, he was very good at English. This was partly due to the fact that he had a gift for languages. But the main reason for it was the home training he got. Night, noon and morning, it was being drummed into his ears that to make his way in the world, he must know English. He would be a dummy, they told him, when he left the Rosses. Stories were told to illustrate this fact. There was the story of the Rosses men going to Glasgow for the first time. A man who was out before would go in front. The man next him would hold onto his coat-tails and so on, and the procession would set out on their journey to the station. There was the story of the young man who went to America. He met with an accident. Had to come home. Pinned a label on his coat. These stories made a deep impression on Neddy. In addition, he had a gift for languages. He became fond of English. In his last years at school he read many books in addition to his class books – books lent to him by the teacher and by the local priest.

Neddy had the gift of imagination. In addition, he had the ambition to shine when he grew up. In the course of his reading he got to know of certain characters and he would like to imitate them. He often did – in his imagination, I mean. There was nothing to hinder him, nothing to distract him. He had the whole of the White Strand to himself with the solitude of the ocean. Here he could realise his ambitions undisturbed.

We could mention a few of the things he did. One day, he had information that a small English garrison was besieged in Portmore and that Marshal Bagnal was on his way from the South with a huge army to relieve them. Neddy went out to intercept them at a place called the Yellow Ford and inflicted a signal defeat on them. Later on, he selected a place known as Benburb for his field of operations. George Munroe and his brother Henry were marching from two different points to attack. Neddy sent a detachment of his army to keep Henry from advancing.

Then he manoeuvred George into the tongue of land between the Oona and the Blackwater. When he got them hemmed in there, with the evening sun in their face, he attacked and annihilated them.

After a few less spectacular operations, he took on the defence of his country in another field. The scene was in Cork in the middle of winter. Three men had been tried and convicted and sentenced to death on the charge of a conspiracy that had never existed. The same fate awaited twelve more. The Attorney General was building up a case which the defence lawyers were powerless to break. Then Neddy walks into the court, took up the cross-examination of Clourfer Daly, the principal witness for the Crown, and tore it to ribbons. All the prisoners were set free.

II

Neddy was about sixteen years old when a visitor came to the Rosses that kept some of the people talking for a few days. It was on a Sunday in winter. After Mass, the priest announced that an organiser from the Gaelic League would like to address the congregation outside the chapel gates. He followed this announcement with a piece of sensible advice: 'If you don't want to stay and listen to what he has got to say, you needn't; you can go home. But, if you do stay, listen to him without interrupting him, whether you agree with his views or not.'

The congregation's curiosity was aroused. They did not know what an organiser was. They had never heard of the Gaelic League. They gathered round the gate opposite the high ground inside the chapel wall. The organiser appeared. He was a fine cut of a man, immaculately dressed, and he wore a massive signet-ring on the little finger of his left hand. He spoke for over half-an-hour in fluent Irish. It was the usual stuff. The Irish language was the priceless heritage of the Irish nation. If the language died, the nation died. And the language would surely die if those whose vernacular it was stopped speaking it. Then he made some scathing remarks about some of the Rosses people who were turning to English.

Of course, he was talked about. 'It is all very fine for him but, if he had to go to work in Scotland, he'd have to play a different tune.'

'Did you all understand him?' asked one.

'Of course we did. Not a bit of bother. Of course, he said some things that would make you laugh: *crainnteacha* for *crainn*, *adharcacha* for *adharca*, *thúrfadh sinn* for *bhéarfaimis*, *a theach seisean* for *a theachsan*.'

'He's from Aran, they say.'

'Indeed he's not. I know they say funny things in Aran, but they are not that bad.'

'I mean, the Aran off the coast of Connaught.'
'And is there another Aran in Connaught?'
'There is, of course.'
'Ah, that explains it.'

'To a certain extent he could be right,' said an oldish man who had spent over twenty years abroad. 'It often occurred to me in the States and in Canada you'd meet French, Germans, Italians, all speaking their own language. Why should we not have ours?'

Then a youth spoke. 'The cases are totally different,' said he. 'The countries you mention have a language of their own. We haven't. French is the language of France, German of Germany, Italian of Italy. English is the language of Ireland. Irish is dead for centuries. And, to say that if the language dies, Ireland dies, is just moonshine. The freedom of Ireland never was, never will be, nor ever can be dependent on any particular language.'

Everyone became silent. It was as if an oracle had spoken. And Edward Devanny's parents were proud of their son that evening.

'Where did he get all the knowledge?' said one elderly man to another on their way home.

'Well, you know he has a great head on him. And he was very smart at school. The master often said it. The priest said it. More than one inspector said it. Besides, he is always reading.'

'I think he has got a lot of his knowledge from the Bacach Liath.'

'But sure the Bacach Liath is mad.'

'I know he is most of the time. But he says some wise things.'

At this stage, it becomes necessary to say a few words about the Bacach Liath. He was over sixty years at the time of our story. He was a stranger in the Rosses. Some said he was not a native of the county although he spoke Irish fluently. They said he came from Tyrone. His hair was snow-white which earned for him the sobriquet of Bacach Liath. He has been in the Rosses for over twenty years and, except in very inclement spells in the winter, never slept under a roof. Instead, he made his habitation in caves along the coast. And, of course, he was never allowed to go hungry. In certain ways, he was mad. He often got up from his bed of bracken to hear the birds salute the dawn. He knew a lot of herbs and of old-world cures. And, although he very often said things that, judged by normal human standards, were the utterance of a madman, he sometimes said many things that were full of wisdom and that stuck in the people's mind.

III

In 1913 Edward Devanny went to America. He was then twenty-one years old. Periodically, he wrote to his father and mother, letters full of filial affections such as a devoted son would be expected to write. He also kept up a correspondence with his old teacher, of which the teacher was proud. To a degree, he looked on Edward Devanny as his own child. It was the teacher who guided the pupil's footsteps. It was the teacher who had moulded the pupil's mind. And the teacher was proud.

In due course, Edward made the acquaintance of an Irish-American organisation known as *Clann na nGael*. He wrote a long letter to his teacher giving him his impression of the party and its chances of success. He said he was particularly impressed by John Devoy. He had heard Devoy one night addressing a public meeting in New York. Devoy, he concluded, was a great man.

In 1919 the old teacher had a long letter from his old pupil. The old pupil had great hopes for the coming Peace Conference. Ireland's case was being ably presented. The war had been fought for the rights of small nations. The president of the great republic of the west had laid down the foundation stone of the principles by which human society would be ruled in the future – government by the consent of the governed.

It was a most interesting letter. It clearly showed the development of this interest which the boy had shown in his young days. But it contained one little thing that made the teacher wonder, and the neighbours as well. The writer had signed his name Éamann Devanny. Éamann Devanny! This was a union of name and surname hitherto unknown in the Rosses. Your name was either in Irish or in English. A man was either Séamas Ó Dónaill or James O'Donnell, a woman either Máire Ní Ghallchóir or Mary Gallagher. But it had never been known that a concoction had been made up of two separate ingredients. The people could not understand it.

'Would Devoy by any chance have called himself Eoin Devoy?' asked the Bacach Liath.

'No, he hasn't,' replied a young man, only a few months back from America. 'Only last Saturday I was mailed my usual copy of *The Irish World*. Devoy is still John Devoy, as he has always been.'

It was strange. The people could not understand.

An explanation came some months afterwards. In a long letter to his old teacher, the emigrant went on to say that the most important consideration for Ireland was the revival of her language. If the language died, he maintained, the nation would die. At the moment, if he got his choice and if only one of the objectives could be achieved, he would rather have the language without freedom, than freedom without the language. Freedom could be lost and won and lost again. But, if the language were allowed to die, it could never be revived. He thought the best possible beginning could be made by everyone adopting the Gaelic form of his or her Christian name. It was only a small beginning. But the rest would follow, bit by bit. That was why he had decided to change from Edward to Éamann.

'I wonder what he would say if he were to meet the Gaelic-spouter from Aran that made the speech long ago outside the gate of the chapel?' said one old man. 'Would he apologise for what he said on the evening of the same day?'

'Not at all,' replied the Bacach Liath. 'You can apologise for a mistake when you are thinking for yourself, never while you are copying someone else.'

This, like many other things the Bacach Liath said, was lost on his audience. However, it did not matter. The audience were made up of sane persons. The Bacach Liath was mad.

In due course, there was a further development in our emigrant's name and a long letter to the teacher explaining it. The correct form of his name, said Éamann, was De Vanni. He had proof positive of it in an article written by an Irishman who had access to the Spanish archives. Captain De Vanni commanded one of the ships of the ill-fated Spanish Armada. His ship was wrecked on the coast of the Rosses of Donegal. The captain managed to come ashore and to remain in hiding until better times arrived. County Donegal was one of the few places where the survivors of the Armada had landed and were neither executed nor handed over to the English. Eventually, Captain De Vanni married one Mary O'Donnell and settled in Carnamadoo in the Upper Rosses.

Had we read history, we would have known that Devanny was an old and respected name, well known in Tír Chonaill centuries before the Armada was wrecked on our shores. But what could we poor Rosses people know about the *Annals of the Four Masters*?

IV

Another bulletin from the emigrant in 1921. He was, he said, an ordinary individual not capable of passing judgement on questions that needed supreme qualities of statesmanship. But he was afraid of the destiny of Ireland. Her hopes for the intervention of other nations were dashed at the Peace Conference or, rather, outside its closed doors. England had emerged victorious from the bloodiest battle in her history. She had already set up a separate government in the north. She would not grant an all-Ireland Republic. In his last letter to the Irish leaders, the prime minister stated that if they took their stand on the rock of an Irish Republic, they were to send no delegate to a Peace Conference. 'In the face of that,' continued the letter, 'the delegates were either going or gone. That is, accepting compromise beforehand. To my mind, the best thing would be to cease all resistance. Any country can be brought to that pass. Would be no better off than after Kinsale or after Cromwell or after '98. And we would have a unit to rise again when the opportunity offered ... Of course, as I have said, I am not competent to judge and I have great confidence in the wisdom of our leaders.'

'There is some wisdom in what he says,' remarked the Bacach Liath. 'There is also a little bit of inconsistency.'

When the Civil War came, Éamann wrote that he was sorry it had to be. But the protest had to be made. It would be a guide for future generations. And, once more, he repeated his faith in the wisdom and patriotism of the leaders.

'That seems to be his weakness, faith in leaders,' commented the Bacach Liath. 'He has carried it so far that he tries to copy their diction. I have never bothered with Ireland. Why should I? What good would it be? A poor madman, mad from the moment he was born. But, if I were not mad and if I were interested in Ireland, I would put my faith in a principle, in a truth, and not in a leader. You never know what men will do under temptation. Very often men who would face death over and over again, they can be lured away from their path in other ways. Sometimes by the attraction of a beautiful woman, sometimes by the prospect of wealth and power.

V

After some years, Éamann de Vanni (as he now called himself) returned from the States to his home in the Rosses. He got married to a local girl and settled down on his father's holding.

When he came home, people noticed several changes in him. He had stopped smoking. He was wearing large, horn-rimmed glasses and would not take a drink under any circumstances. The people could not understand these changes.

'Can't understand it at all myself. He was smoking before he left school and his parents allowed it. His mother used to say he needed a smoke to rest his tired brain. Before he went to America, he had seven pipes. Now he has stopped it completely. Who will explain that mystery?'

'Maybe John Devoy doesn't smoke,' said an elderly man who wasn't noted for an excess of Christian charity.

'Or maybe somebody else,' said the Bacach Liath.

'And, as for taking a drink, sure a wedding or a christening wouldn't be complete without it. What does America do with people at all?'

'What I wonder most at is the glasses. I never saw such eyesight as that young man had before he went away. Let but a boat appear at the Stags, when she'd be only a speck to me – and I have fairly good eyesight – and he'd say, "That's so and so's boat. I know her by the white patch on the corner of her main sail." And, right enough, an hour and a half afterwards, when she'd come sailing up the bay, I'd recognise her.'

'Maybe it's John Devoy he's copying,' someone said.

'No,' said the young man recently returned from the States. 'If he were copying Devoy, it's a hearing aid he would have.'

'He is mad,' said someone.

'No, he is not,' said the Bacach Liath. 'None of you understand what it is to be mad like I do. But a madman gets an odd ray of light from time to time and, while it lasts, he sees right down to the bottom of things. This Éamann de Vanni, as he calls himself, is not mad. But he never gets a ray of light that will enable him to see beneath the surface of things. At bottom, he is a good-natured fellow. And some day he may see the light. Who knows?'

VI

At that time, two political parties had made their appearance in the Rosses. One of them supported those who had accepted the Treaty (the vast majority) and the other, those who supported the policy of the men who had opposed it in arms and continued their armed opposition until they were defeated.

Rival clubs sprang up in the Rosses. A club was called a *cumann*. Other words like *dáilcheantar* and *mórchuid* sprang up, and they were used freely by Rosses men. Such was their loyalty for their respective leaders that they would use such atrocious concoctions without batting an eyelid.

Éamann de Vanni joined the party in which he believed. He was a fluent speaker and, for that reason, he was soon made president of his club. Every day he was becoming more and more enthusiastic about the revival of the Irish language. In this, none of the members of his own party agreed with him in their hearts. On both sides the parents of school-going children felt they had a grievance. Too much of their children's time was taken up with Irish at school with the result that they knew little or no English when they left school. And then, when they grew up, they should have to emigrate to English-speaking countries to earn their living. The situation was all the more galling by the fact that the men who had decreed such a school system could, and did, send their children to private schools where no Irish was taught. But nobody could say that. Loyalty to your party took precedence over all other considerations. And the slogan of Irish parties was 'not merely free but Gaelic as well'.

After a time, a movement for withholding the payment of land annuities was started. It was founded and organised by a Rosses man, a man of dynamic energy and a man with a very fine record of national service. It took well in the Rosses. It was a movement of non-payment for which there is always a strong human appeal.

Éamonn de Vanni was very enthusiastic in support of it. He ignored, he said, the demands he had got himself. Everyone else should do the same. They couldn't put the whole county in jail.

Some of the neighbours were brought to court for non-payment. Decrees were obtained against them. When the amount was not paid, seizures were made.

Éamann de Vanni was not interfered with. I don't know why and, since I don't, I won't give any opinion. He said himself they were afraid of the damage that could be made to them by the propaganda of his own party. Some believed him, others did not. And, as usual, some bitter, possibly unjust things were said against him.

'Egging the rest of us on to refuse payments and then paying it behind our backs.'

'Did he really pay?'

'Of course he did.'

'Yes, I heard that. I heard he went to Letterkenny and paid. But he denied it afterwards. He says he hasn't set foot in Letterkenny for the past two years.'

'Which is true, I am sure. The man never says anything that hasn't two meanings. Afterwards, he takes the meaning that suits his purpose. He did not go to Letterkenny. He paid it nearer home. He paid it in Dungloe. The man is paving the way for himself to Leinster House. And he'll be well-qualified when the day comes.'

VII

In due course, the party supported by Éamann de Vanni became the government. 'What will they do now?' asked Black Hughie Boyle, a next-door neighbour. 'I never took an active part in politics. I believed, and do still, that those who accept the Treaty did what they thought was best for Ireland. Your crowd opposed it in arms. They can't accept it now. To be consistent, they must repudiate it and declare a Republic.'

'Which you may be sure is the very thing they will do,' said Éamann de Vanni.

'I don't know,' said Black Hughie. 'Last Saturday night I saw a lot of bonfires out, most of them by men who were in the Free State army in their day. Men who would be only too glad to pump your leaders full of lead if they got hold of them during the Civil War.'

'That is what we want,' said de Vanni. 'We want converts. You can't run a country with a minority. We want to convert those who were against us in the past. The poor devils were misled. And now they see their mistake. You may rest assured that the first thing the government will do is to repudiate the Treaty and declare a Republic for all Ireland.'

'The poor idiot!' was all the comment the mad Bacach made when this conversation was relayed in his presence.

A few years passed. Éamann was as active as ever in his *cumann*. Not alone that, but his activities brought him outside the Rosses. He addressed meetings from time to time in different parts of the constituency. It was taken for granted that he would be a candidate in the coming general election. And I believe myself he had ambitions in that direction. He was dissatisfied with certain things. And, with all his faith in the leaders, he was confident that they would listen to him and modify their policy to agree with his viewpoint if he had the opportunity of meeting them every day.

Then, one day, the postman brought him the paper and a letter. The letter was from the general secretary for five clubs (sorry, *cumainn*) in the Rosses. The letter went on to say that there would be a meeting of delegates from the various clubs in Dungloe on a given date. A general election was not due for two years. But then one never knew when it would be sprung on them. It was felt that the Rosses was being neglected as far as parliamentary representation was concerned. The object of the meeting was to appoint delegates for the coming convention due to be held in Letterkenny. They must do their best to have a Rosses man selected at that convention to be the party's standard-bearer in the coming election. There were some very mean intrigues going on in different parts of the constituency. Fanad wanted their own man elected. Glenties wanted their man, etc. One district wanted a man whose sole qualification was that he was a county footballer and they expected the GAA to be solidly behind him. But they, the letter repeated, wanted a Rosses man and they hoped he would attend the coming meeting.

Éamann read the letter. He read it over and over again. Then he put it down and began to think. They don't say who is the candidate whose case they want to press at the convention in Letterkenny. It can hardly be myself or they would have mentioned it in the letter. Still, my loyalty to the party and my faith in the leaders demand that I should attend. And, no matter whom they select, it will be my duty to support him. I will campaign for him to the best of my ability.

Having decided on this course of action, he put away the letter. He then took up his newspaper and slit open the wrapper. He spread out the paper and began to read. Suddenly he turned pale. He looked again at the heading to make sure he was not mistaken. Then he exclaimed, 'My God, this is shocking.'

'What is wrong?' asked his wife anxiously.

'Republican prisoner dies on hunger strike,' he said, looking again at the heading.

He sat for a while silently and sullenly looked into the fire. Then he went out and down to the shore and walked for hours along the strand. His wife was getting more and more anxious. At last, when the dinner was ready, she went out and called to him. She beckoned to him to come home, which he did.

When he came in, she noticed the wild, demented look had gone from his face. The terrible torture was over. He had made up his mind.

Before he sat down to his dinner, he took off his glasses, put them into a case and put the case away in a drawer.

'Why are you leaving off your glasses?' his wife asked him, still somewhat anxious about his sanity.

'For some time I notice I see better without them.'

'They no longer suit you, I suppose. You ought to run down to Derry and have your eyes tested.'

'No, I am all right. I see better without them.'

Later on, his wife said to him: 'The baby is asleep now. I think he'll sleep for hours. He hasn't slept all day. I want you to stay in if you have nowhere to go. I have to go to the shop.'

'Are you going to the shop now?'

'I'd like to. I want tea and sugar and I'm told they have very good salt mackerel. A boat from Tory sold them yesterday evening.'

'Very good. I'll mind the house and the baby. And now I want you to bring me something.'

'Certainly. What is it you want?'

'Two ounces of plug tobacco. *Yachtsman*, if they have it. If not, whatever they have.'

His wife set out to the shop, wondering and worrying. What had happened her man at all? Of course, he was terribly upset at what he had read in the paper. Yes, she could understand that. But the things he did. He left off his glasses and put them away and says he sees better without them. And now he wants tobacco. Of course, I don't begrudge him his smoke. I hope and pray that it will soothe him and settle his mind!

When the wife returned from the shop, she handed him the tobacco. He took down one of his pipes from the shelf. Then he cut a pipeful of tobacco and teased it in the palm of his hand with all the art and skill of bygone days. He lit it and smoked until there was nothing left but a grain of ashes in the bottom of it. He filled it a second time, and a third time. When he had the third pipe smoked, the house was one cloud of smoke.

He got drowsy and was inclined to doze off to sleep. 'Lie down here on the kitchen bed,' suggested the wife. 'You are sleepy. Maybe you have smoked too much and you not used to it.'

He lay down on the kitchen bed fully dressed. The wife put a quilt over him and fixed the pillows under his head. In a few minutes he was asleep.

It was nightfall when he woke.

'Do you feel all right now?' asked his wife, still anxious.

'I feel grand,' he replied. 'Quite settled. Don't worry, girl.'

Then he added: 'My God, it's a terrible thing to try to come to a decision in a crisis. It is no wonder that the old people at the end of the rosary used to pray for God to guide them when they were between two minds, as they put it.'

That night he slept soundly and got up in the morning quite tranquil and refreshed. After breakfast, his wife suggested that the early potatoes were ready for moulding.

'I know,' he said. 'I was looking at them on my way up from the shore. I'll mould them this very day. But, before I do anything, I must write a letter. One of us can leave it in the shop in the evening so that the postman will collect it tomorrow.'

He got his writing material and sat down at the end of the kitchen table. He was going to reply to the letter he had got the day before asking him to attend a meeting to select delegates for the convention to be held soon in Letterkenny.

He wrote down his address and began his letter. 'Dear Sir,' he wrote. Then he looked at what he had written. Dear Sir! It looked strange to a man who, for years, began every letter with 'A *Chara*'. He continued:

Dear Sir,
I have to say – and this is my final word on the subject – that I will not attend the meeting to which you have invited me. I don't care who are selected to attend the convention in Letterkenny. I don't care who is selected to be the party's standard-bearer in the next election. I am finished with politics. I see no hope for Ireland until a generation of Irish men and women come who will have no allegiance to any of the political parties of the present day.

I remain, dear sir,
Sincerely yours,
Edward Devanny.

The manuscripts of the stories contained in this collection are lodged in the Séamus Ó Grianna collection in James Hardiman Library, National University of Ireland, Galway. The following notes give details of the original stories, where applicable. No attempt is made here to conduct any analysis of the English stories or any detailed comparison between the Irish and English versions.

GOD REST MICKEY

This story is a close translation of 'Grásta Ó Dhia ar Mhicí' which first appeared in *Cioth is Dealán* (Preas Dhún Dealgan, 1926). It is probably the author's best-known story and, in theme, treatment and style, one of his best.

This is the only story of the author's to be translated by someone else. It was translated by Séamus Ó Néill and was published in *Irish Writing* (1955) pp. 19-32 and again in Devin Garrity, *The Irish Genius* (New York, 1959) pp. 74 ff.

DENIS THE DREAMER

This story is based on 'Mánus Ó Súileachán' which was published in Séamus Ó Grianna's earliest and best-known collection of short stories *Cioth is Dealán* (Preas Dhún Dealgan, 1926). The first few pages of the story differ considerably from the original.

MANUS MAC AWARD, SMOKER AND STORYTELLER

This story is based on 'Peadar na bPíopaí' which was published in the collection *Scéal Úr agus Sean-Scéal* (Oifig an tSoláthair, 1945). The *dénouement* of the story is changed considerably in the English version. In the original, Manus starts smoking again as a reaction to his wife's prattling on about a trivial matter while he is recounting his serious news. Also in the English version, the author tends to expand more learnedly and at length on the philosophy of short story writing.

HOME RULE

This is an English version of the story 'Gréasán Aimhréidh' which was published in *Tráigh is Tuile* (Oifig an tSoláthair, 1955) pp. 102-9.

THE SEA'S REVENGE

This story is based on 'Díoghaltas na Fairrge' which was published in the collection *Fallaing Shíoda* (Oifig an tSoláthair, 1956). The English version is quite faithful to the original in this case.

BLAGADÁN
This story is a translation of 'Blagadán' which was published in *Fallaing Shíoda* (Oifig an tSoláthair, 1956).

SINGLE COMBAT
This story is a translation of 'Fear a Chomhraic' which was published in *An Bhratach* (Oifig an tSoláthair, 1959).

AT SUNSET
This story is based on 'Luighe na Gréine' which was published in *An Bhratach* (Oifig an tSoláthair, 1959).

MAYDAY MAGIC
This story is based on 'Cúl le Muir' which was published in *Cúl le Muir agus Scéalta Eile* (Oifig an tSoláthair, 1961).

A DOG'S LIFE
This story is based on 'Urchar a' Daill' which was published in the collection *Úna Bhán agus Scéalta Eile* (Oifig an tSoláthair, 1962).
    There is a substantial, new element introduced into the English story. The matter of the mooted legacy and the greed it instils in the son and his mother is a new dimension to the story. The practical, worldly aspect of unions between men and women is a favourite theme of the author.

THE BEST LAID SCHEMES
This story is based on 'Aisling Shiubhán Fheargail' which was published in *Úna Bhán agus Scéalta Eile* (Oifig an tSoláthair, 1962).

FAIR-HAIRED MARY
This story is based on 'Úna Bhán' which was published in *Úna Bhán agus Scéalta Eile* (Oifig an tSoláthair, 1962). The English version has expanded and developed the original story considerably, introducing new elements.

THE WOMAN SPY
This story is based on 'Fealltóir Mná' which was published in the collection *Oíche Shamhraidh agus Scéalta Eile* (Oifig an tSoláthair, 1968). The last pages of the English version where Frank returns from America to visit the graveyard where his old acquaintances are buried is new material. It provides the author with an opportunity to say some things about the Civil War and some of the parties directly involved with it.

THE FRUITS OF EDUCATION
This story is based on an amalgam of the two stories 'Cor i n-Aghaidh a' Chaim' in *Oíche Shamhraidh agus Scéalta Eile* (Oifig an tSoláthair, 1968) and 'Fear Feasach' in *An Clár is an Fhoireann* (Oifig an tSoláthair, 1955).

EDWARD DEVANNY
There is no original Irish version of this story.

This is the most overtly political of the author's stories. Earlier in his life, Séamus Ó Grianna sided with the Republicans during the Civil War because he did not believe in the partition of Ireland. When the Republicans came to power, he fully expected that the original ideal of a Republic would be actively pursued. Disillusioned with the course of Irish history in the twentieth century, he denounced all the main political parties.

APPENDIX 1
AUTOBIOGRAPHICAL NOTE

This is my own translation of a letter sent by Séamus Ó Grianna to Muiris Ó Droighneáin who was then researching the history of Gaelic literature from 1882 onwards and the results of which research appeared in his *Taighde i gComhair Stair Litridheachta na Nua-Ghaedhilge ó 1882 Anuas* (An Gúm, 1936). The letter was published in *The Irish News* (13 December 1969) shortly after the death of Séamus Ó Grianna.

25 Parnell Square,
Dublin,
20.12.27

Dear Sir,
I received your letter today. I never imagined that anyone would be interested in the time or place of my birth or in any aspect of my life. But, anyway, I'll send you some snippets if they are of any use to you.

I was born in the Rosses of Tirchonaill on the seventeenth of November, 1889. I am told the weather was cold and snowy. (I don't know. I don't remember it.)

I went to school in my native townland when I was four years old and I didn't know a word of English then (Chapter 1 of *Caisleáin Óir*).

My father or mother never spoke any English. My grandmother lived with us and her repertoire of stories was amazing – stories and lays about the Fianna, fairy tales, songs, stories about the Red Branch, etc.

I attended school until I was fourteen and, by that stage, I was well able to read English but I had no experience of speaking it.

The first book I became interested in was Burns' poetry. I got the loan of it from a man who had spent a while in Scotland.

I left school when I was fourteen years old and I spent a few years fishing – that is how I got to know all about fishing, boats, etc.

Then I went to Scotland and England and I spent four years there (*Caisleáin Óir*).

1910 – I went to the Irish college in Cloghaneely. I spent a while teaching Irish for the Gaelic League.

1912 – I went to St Patrick's in Drumcondra. I finished there in 1914 and I taught between 1914–1920. I worked for the Ministry of Education in the First Dáil (and the Dáil was not as fashionable then as it is now) until 1922 when the last war began. Between then and 1924, I was in prison. I am Secretary of the *Fáinne* ever since except for one winter which I spent in the south of France.

I had no intention of writing anything when I was young. I was of the opinion then (and still am) that I wasn't capable of writing fine literature. But when I saw the type of Irish that was being written, sometimes by people who had barely digested their first book, I resolved to demonstrate the difference between native Irish and learned Irish. In 1919 I wrote an article (the first one under the pseudonym of 'Máire') and sent it to *Fáinne an Lae* for publication. 'The Irish of the people and book-Irish' was the title of the article. For three months afterwards, there was a lot of controversy and the upshot of it all was the consensus that I was an acrimonious person.

In 1920 I wrote *Mo Dhá Róisín*. I believed that it was high time for us to try to write stories which would be read as stories and not always to be thinking about grammar, idioms and poems which consisted only of sounds. Ten thousand copies of *Mo Dhá Róisín* were sold.

In 1924 I wrote *Caisleáin Óir* and I was happy enough with it. (I wasn't happy with *Mo Dhá Róisín* and still amn't. I have let it go out of print.)

In 1925 I wrote *Micheál Ruadh*. It is a story that my father used to tell four times each year when I was small. I published it just to please him.

A while after that I began to get interested in French literature and in the short stories in particular. And I felt that I would be better at writing short stories than longer ones. And so I wrote *Cioth is Dealán*. (Dundalgan Press published them all.)

I am not writing anything at the moment. To be quite honest, I despair of the people of Ireland. Many of those who would appreciate a story cannot read Irish or buy a book. And those who can read Irish are only interested in the language element. If they were dealing with Shakespeare's works, they would only be interested in his grammar.

I hope I have supplied you with the information you need – and I probably gave you a lot more than you needed. But, if it is of any assistance to you, I'll be happy.

Your friend,
Máire.

APPENDIX 2
FROM THE GAELIC OF MÁIRE[1]

The significance of this article is that it is by the leading Gaelic writer of today and was originally written in Gaelic for his readers. Its bitterness reflects a disillusionment that must sound ominous to sincere workers in the language movement.

It comes on you with age. You are sitting alone by the fireside and you doze off to sleep. You think you are wide awake while you are in reality dreaming ...

I came home tired. And, in addition to being tired, I was angry. My soul was in rebellion against puffery and quackery, against 'genteel dastards and bellowing slaves,' and yahoos with the reputation of writers. Suddenly a youth appeared standing before me, a curly-headed youth, with a boy's face, but with manly determination in his eyes.

He spoke softly to me. 'I would like to do something for Ireland,' he said.

'For Ireland!' I replied. 'I am greatly afraid that Ireland is suffering from an incurable disease. But that does not mean that she is not useful to those who want to get on in the world.'

'I want to be a writer,' he repeated, 'and to write in Irish.'

'Very good,' said I. 'I can give you sound advice, culled from experience of thirty years. You want to write in Irish. Well, now is the time. A Gaelic writer has a fine opportunity at the present moment. Ireland is lying in the mud. If you attempt to raise her with your pen, you will suffer for it ... You will get blows and stripes and kicks a hundred-fold. Some will say you have deserved it all and more. Others will pretend to feel pity for you. These will try to write you down as a lunatic ... But if you want to do something in Gaelic letters that will advance your own personal interests, steer clear of the truth. And, since you are on the subject of steering, keep your eye riveted on your sails. Trim them to every breeze that blows. If you do that, you will eventually sail into the harbour of peace and happiness.'

'I want to be a writer,' he repeated for the third time, as if he had failed to understand me.

'I *don't*,' said I ... and then Jean shook me by the shoulder ...

I am awake now; my curly-headed youth is gone. But it makes no difference. I am going to speak to him. For this curly-headed youth exists. I know he does, although he visits me only in my dreams.

He would come to me in the light of day, only he is afraid. He is afraid because I have a bad name. He has been told that I am a sour, bitter, old crank; not of course a criminal lunatic, but at the same time suffering from incurable delusions on the subject of Gaelic writing. He has been told that I would wither him with vituperation the moment he crossed my doorstep, my eyes blazing with wicked madness. That is what the man with the white waistcoat told him, for the man of the white waistcoat has been posing as a writer all his life. And there is such a thing as the Law of Self-Preservation ...

And now I will continue my advice. The youth wants to be a writer. Very good. He needs only one qualification – sincerity ...

But he is afraid that he hasn't enough Irish ...

He has, and enough seven times over.

But he only spent three weeks in the Gaeltacht ...

I don't care a damn if he never spent an hour in the Gaeltacht. He doesn't need such a wonderful amount of idiom. Anywhere he sees a big, bloated, ignorant, white-waistcoated lie masquerading as truth, let him attack it with all the strength of his soul, and he will be surprised at his eloquence. When the battle is at its hottest, the Holy Ghost will descend upon his few dozen phrases, and he will speak like an angel, trumpet-tongued, and people will understand. If he is sure that he has a message he can be a great writer.

'But you yourself did not tell the whole truth in your writings,' he says.

I certainly did not. I was afraid. That is why I am only a clever writer. I never was *great*. I told only a thin slice of the truth. If I had told it all, I'd have been *great*. And, in addition to my being great, I'd have been hanged in the autumn of 19—.[2] But if my young, curly head is the stuff that writers are made of, this is his hour ...

A ravenous pack will gather round him, to be sure. For they will fear him. He will not have written much when he will hear them snarling. And soon he will feel their fangs in his flesh ...

But he is a youth of courage. Very good. So let me continue. If he become a great Gaelic writer, let him not expect any reward other than to be crucified. He won't believe me? And yet, look at Seosamh Mac Grianna.[3] Read the terrible, despairing cry in the last line of *Mo Bhealach Féin*.[4] Think of Pádraic Ó Conaire.[5] Look at his body, wasted by want, laid out in the pauper ward of a public hospital, with his worldly possessions on a table by his bedside – an apple, a pipe and an ounce of tobacco. And when he was dead, they made a Pádraic of limestone and put it sitting on a rock in Galway. Then the pack gathered round, with much jostling and pushing, everyone doing his very best to bring his own snout inside the scope of the camera ... Like the poor wretch whose only claim was that Burns in his day had lampooned him, and who sought to cash in on it after the poet's death. 'Gie's a bawbee,' he would say to the visitors to the ould clay biggin, 'gie's a bawbee, I'm Burns' bletherin' bitch ... '

'But I will awaken the people. I will put new life into them. They will arise and carry me aloft on their shoulders,' the youth declares.

What did you say, young man?

The people! The poor, bewildered people, robbed of poets, fed on lies, prodded by fears, ach, the poor people. The men of lies will raise them against you and they will rend you ...

'I don't mind,' he shouts at me, my youth.

Very good. Get a pen and paper and a pipe and plenty of tobacco. If you feel cold, wrap a blanket round you. And when the ground is asleep, begin your book. Don't be afraid of any man or of any mortal consequences ...

You will write a book. It will not be great. But men will recognise the beginnings of greatness in you. At first an attempt will be made to ignore you; then to damn you or explain away your 'disease' by saying that your Gaelic brain never developed because you had not studied the *Aisling* of the eighteenth century. Don't let that dishearten you. You will write another book, and yet another. Then, you will get the first instalment of your punishment. You will lose whatever means of livelihood you had. But you won't worry. You will turn your back on house and home, and go out into the wilderness ... You will write your *great* book ...

You have finished it. It is your great masterpiece. It has killed you. But you are dead and immortal at the same time. Your dead body will be found under a tree. On the morning after it will be reported in the daily papers. And a professor of Celtic Studies will read it, before going to lecture in English on the infixed pronouns in the Milan Glosses ...

> The body of a middle-aged man of the tramp class was found dead at Dromonachta yesterday evening. It was removed to the town hall where an inquest will be held. In the inside pocket of a tattered overcoat was found a manuscript of considerable size. It is believed to have been stolen by the deceased and, as it is written in the Pollawaddy dialect, it may serve as a clue to the identification of the body.

At the same time the language movement will, according to all reports, be making great progress. On the very day of your funeral, perhaps, *Comhdháil Náisiúnta na Gaeilge*[6] will be weaving webs of resolutions and amendments, and, upon my soul, talking about literature – not in the least afraid that you will burst forth from your grave and squeeze out their most unliterary souls.

But courage, lad, courage! Your day will come. Folklorists will become interested in the peculiarities of the Pollawaddy dialect. There are a few good jobs still to be manufactured. Gradually recognition of your great work will come. In due course a monument will be erected to your memory. That will be a great day for your native village. Thousands upon thousands will be there assembled to do you honour, and you must feel elated if honour's voice can provoke the silent dust, or flattery soothe the dull, cold ear of death. Politicians and professors, 'writers' and scholars will be there, stampeding to get inside the range of the camera, the poor beggarmen, the children of Burns' bletherin' bitch ...

SÉAMUS Ó GRIANNA

1 This article appeared in the literary magazine *The Bell*, February 1947, pp. 16-20. It is a translation of an original article which appeared in *An Iris*, February 1946, pp. 28-34.
2 He is probably referring here to atrocities committed during the Civil War.
3 Seosamh Mac Grianna, a very distinguished writer in his own right, was the author's younger brother. After a short but very productive literary career, he suffered from a mental disorder which lasted for most of his life.
4 This autobiographical novel appeared in the same volume as an unfinished novel *Dá mBíodh Ruball ar an Éan* in 1940. The latter work comes to an abrupt end with the following note from the author: 'The well dried up in the summer of 1935. I will not write any more. I have done my best and I do not care.'
5 Pádraic Ó Conaire from Galway was one of the most influential and innovative Gaelic writers of the early twentieth century.
6 This national organisation was founded in 1943 to promote the Gaelic cause. It is still in existence.

Notes

Séamus Ó Grianna: the Voice of the Gaeltacht
1 This article, with some alterations, was originally published in *Éire-Ireland*, Fall 1993, pp. 103-13. I am grateful to the editors of that journal for granting permission to reproduce it here.
2 A translation by A. J. Hughes of the first part of Séamus Ó Grianna's autobiography *When I Was Young* (A & A Farmar, 2001) has recently been published.
3 'Of course I got the best education available in Ireland at home. And I didn't get it from school teachers but from the old inhabitants of Rannafast. Most of my learning I got from them. From them I learned about the literature of the Red Branch and the Fianna, about Carolan, the blind Mac Cuarta and Cathal Buí. But I was still afraid that learning was no good. I was afraid that lack of intelligence kept me from understanding *Lycidas* when I was a boy. Milton hovered over me like a black cloud until Burns shone forth as a bright, radiant, summer sun to disperse the cloud in all directions ... Perhaps I would still meet learned people. Perhaps I would go to college, for who knows what fate has in store. But no matter where I go henceforth, no matter who I'll meet, I'll be bold and assured, and I'll have courage and hope. I was at Frank McGarvey's school and I'll never again be deceived by big, exaggerated words which have no basis except ignorance and stupidity,' Máire, *Nuair a Bhí Mé Óg* (Baile Átha Claith: Clólucht an Talbóidigh, 1942) pp. 246-7. All the translations are my own unless otherwise stated.
4 Séamus Ó Grianna, 'Úirsgeal na Bliadhna', *The Irish Weekly* and *Ulster Examiner*, 24 July 1915, p. 12.
5 I have edited and published this novel recently in *Scríbhinní Mháire 1: Castar na Daoine ar a Chéile* (Coiscéim, 2002).
6 'I soon stopped writing in English. I had an apparition which opened my eyes. I heard a voice as if coming out of the clouds ... Ireland as we would surely have her.' Not free merely, but Gaelic as well. 'And then I imagined I saw a flame of fire rising from the Hill of Tara and that I was rebaptised in the creed of the Fianna. That is what made me start writing in Irish,' 'Comhairle do Scríbhneoirí Óga', *Comhar*, Nollaig 1946, p. 1.
7 'Speech all the time is what this college is about. Songs, storytelling, telling stories about the Fianna, debating, proverbs, idioms, and everything that is to be heard coming from the native speaker's mouth. No time is wasted fingering the hard palate or the uvula. The teachers and students are interested only in Irish. And contemporary Irish for that matter – alive and vibrant as spoken by native speakers. They pretend that declensions and suchlike don't exist at all,' 'Iolscoil Uladh', *Misneach*, 7 August 1920, p. 2.
8 'It was my opinion that it was time for us to attempt to write stories which would be read as stories and not be forever thinking about grammar, idioms and poems which consisted only of sounds,' 'Ag Féachaint Soir agus Siar', *The Irish News*, 13 December 1969, p. 6.
9 'When I saw the sort of Irish that was being written, sometimes by people who had barely learned their first book, I thought to myself that I would demonstrate the difference between Irish and Irish,' *ibid*.

10 '[Máire] who is addicted to harsh truths, and there is usually contradiction and bitter contention wherever he is declaiming.' An Reachtaire, 'An Fáinne – Gasra Átha Cliath', *Fáinne an Lae*, 17 May 1924, p. 4.
11 'That Government is in power for seven years now and what have they done for Irish? Let us see. The Gaeltacht Commission? That evaded the question for a few years. It provided those in power the opportunity to make promises while they sought votes. Irish in the schools? Anyone with eyes in his head can see that what is being done in the majority of schools is worthless. Irish in Civil Service matters? 'A chara' at the beginning of every letter and 'mise le meas' at the end – something which could be done with a few thousand rubber stamps. To make a long story short, the promises which were made were never fulfilled,' 'An Ghaedhealtacht', *Fáinne an Lae*, Feabhra 1929, p. 4.
12 Máire, 'Plight of Irish Artists', *An Phoblacht*, 6 June 1932, p. 7.
13 *See* Nollaig Mac Congáil, 'Máire agus an L.F.M.' in *Féasta*, M. Fómhair 2001, pp. 11-13.

INTRODUCTION
1 *See* Nollaig Mac Congáil, *Máire – Clár Saothair* (Coiscéim, 1990) pp. 42-52, 59-74.
2 'Destiny' in *The Derry Journal*, 28 January 1916, p. 2; and 'Two Days a Teacher' in *The Derry Journal*, 3 March 1916, p. 2; 10 March 1916, p. 2; 17 March 1916, p. 2. I have edited and published this story recently in *Scríbhinní Mháire 1: Castar na Daoine ar a Chéile* (Coiscéim, 2002).
3 The present collection represents a selection of those stories.
4 *The Derry Journal*, 3 March 1922, p. 6.
5 'Comhairle do Scríbhneoirí Óga', *Comhar*, Nollaig 1946, p. 1. Séamus Deane gives a good appreciation of MacGill in *London Review of Books* Vol. 7, No. 2, 7 February 1985, p. 12, p. 14.
6 *The Derry Journal*, 28 January, 1916, p. 2. I have edited and published this story recently in *Scríbhinní Mháire 1: Castar na Daoine ar a Chéile* (Coiscéim, 2002).
7 *The Derry Journal*, 3 March 1916, p. 2; 10 March 1916, p. 2; 17 March 1916, p. 2. I have edited and published this story recently in *Scríbhinní Mháire 1: Castar na Daoine ar a Chéile* (Coiscéim, 2002).
8 'Comhairle do Scríbhneoirí Óga', *Comhar*, Nollaig 1946, p. 1.
9 Séamus Ó Néill translated one story by Máire and it was published in *Irish Writing*, 1955, pp. 19-32.
10 'Plight of Irish Artists', *An Phoblacht*, 6 August 1932, p. 7.
11 My own translation of 'Mé Féin is Baile Átha Cliath', *The Irish Press*, 14 February 1951, p. 2.
12 'Irish Artists', *An Phoblacht*, 2 July 1932, p. 6.
13 'Compulsory Irish', *The Irish Times*, 10 June 1966.
14 'The flame is quenched and the fire has gone out' in 'Comhairle do Scríbhneoirí Óga', *Comhar*, Nollaig 1946, p. 1.
15 Nollaig Mac Congáil, 'Máire agus an L.F.M.', *Feasta*, M. Fómhair 2001, pp. 11-13.
16 Séamus Mac Grianna, 'Compulsory Irish', *The Irish Times*, 10 June 1966, p. 6.
17 I have published a more detailed account of Máire's English stories in an article 'Scéalta Béarla Mháire' in *Féasta*, Meith. 2002, pp. 21-23; Iúil, pp. 21-24.

Glossary

airneál	visiting houses at night. Before the advent of electricity, motorised transport and formal, organised entertainment in rural Ireland, people would visit in different houses to converse or be entertained with story, song or dance
bacach	a beggar, a person of no fixed abode
bán	white, fair-haired
Bealtaine	May
blagadán	a bald-headed person
bratóg	a rag, piece of cloth
brocky	freckled, pock-marked (Ir. *brocach*)
bully	grand, fine, splendid
clout	a blow
convoy	group of friends, family and neighbours accompanying person emigrating for part of journey
dáil	match-making gathering
differ	difference
fada	long, tall, thin
féar gortach	an unnatural, sudden and debilitating hunger
feis	Irish language and cultural festival
Gaeltacht	a rural community where the Irish language is the predominant language of communication
gansey	a jersey
geas	a taboo
keen	lament over a corpse (Ir. *caoin*)
liath	grey
louser	mean, scheming person
marteen	footless stocking (Ir. *máirtín*)
ochone	exclamation expressing sorrow; vb. lament
out with	no longer friendly with (Ir. *amuigh le*)
pet	a fine day during bad weather (Ir. *peata*)
piece	a slice of bread and butter
pinkeen	a small fish, minnow, runt used derogatively to describe undersized person
pishrogue	superstition (Ir. *pisreog*)
poteen	illegally distilled whiskey (Ir. *poitín*)
red polly	a red, hornless cow
Roe/ruadh	red (of hair) (Ir. *rua*)
scraw	a sod, scraw (Ir. *scraith*)
screabán	stony land

seanchaí	a storyteller
singlings	part of distillation process
streachlán	straggling, tattered thing
wind-dog	a light on the horizon portending a storm (Ir. *madadh gaoithe*)

Names

In traditional, Gaelic-speaking communities in Ireland, surnames were a rarity as so many families shared the same one. People were identified and particularised by placing after their Christian name that of their fathers or mothers e.g., John Chondy, (Ir. *Seán Chondaí*; lit. John son of Condy), Jimmy Elimy (Ir. *Séamas Fheilimí*; lit. James son of Felimy), Bidí Vickey (Ir. *Bríd Mhicí*; lit. Bridget daughter of Mickey), etc.

Sometimes people were particularised by placing an adjective after their Christian names to denote particular features, e.g., colour of hair John Roe (Ir. *rua*; lit. red of hair), Mary Wawn (Ir. *bán*; lit. fair hair), height John More (Ir. *mór*; lit. big), place of residence, etc.

Most of the names in these stories have been Anglicised but some have been retained.

All the place-names mentioned in these stories have been Anglicised.